FASHIONABLY
LATE

Previously published Worldwide Mystery title by
LISA Q. MATHEWS

PERMANENTLY BOOKED

FASHIONABLY LATE

LISA Q. MATHEWS

W🌐RLDWIDE®

TORONTO • NEW YORK • LONDON
AMSTERDAM • PARIS • SYDNEY • HAMBURG
STOCKHOLM • ATHENS • TOKYO • MILAN
MADRID • WARSAW • BUDAPEST • AUCKLAND

Recycling programs
for this product may
not exist in your area.

Fashionably Late

A Worldwide Mystery/December 2018

First published by Carina Press

ISBN-13: 978-1-335-50687-0

Copyright © 2017 by Lisa Q. Mathews

Printed in U.S.A.

To Kerri B., who never gave up hope.

ONE

"YOU ARE GOING to *love* this, Dorothy," Summer Smythe said, as she pulled open the heavy glass door of Waterman's on the Bay. "Because I have a special surprise for you."

"How…nice." Dorothy Westin hesitated for just a moment in the doorway. Her young friend and sleuthing partner was always full of surprises, some of them slightly questionable.

"Don't worry, it's much better than that crazy place I took us to last week, I swear."

"That wasn't your fault, dear." Dorothy straightened her sunhat and stepped into the bright, high-ceilinged foyer of Milano's newest dining establishment. Summer, a relative newcomer to their Southwest Florida town, hadn't realized that Dorothy would be the most senior patron at Senoritas.

By, say, half a century.

Dorothy liked to think of herself as young at heart—but the pounding music, taco bar and noontime margaritas were a bit much. She might have steered them elsewhere, of course, if she paid better attention to the local social scene.

"Are you here for our holiday fashion show?" A deeply tanned woman in a sleeveless black tunic and long black skirt patterned with enormous pink poinsettias looked up from the hostess stand.

"I didn't know about the fashion show," Dorothy said. "But my friend and I do have a reservation for lunch. It's under 'Sloan,' I believe."

Summer always used her film producer father's name for reservations, she knew. Apparently that strategy for obtaining an overbooked seating or a more coveted table worked as well in Milano as Los Angeles.

"I'm sorry, but all the members of your party need to be present for me to seat you," the hostess said.

"Hey, I'm here.'" Summer reappeared from the alcove she'd ducked into to check her lipstick in the convenient, gold-trimmed mirror. "So that's the surprise, Dorothy. We're getting a fashion show with our lunch."

"What a lovely idea," Dorothy said. She wasn't a clotheshorse, in truth, but it was the thought that counted.

A whisper of a wrinkle threatened the hostess's forehead. "You're late," she said.

"The reservation was for noon," Dorothy said. "It's only five-past."

"No, *this* one is late." The woman jerked her highly coiffed head toward Summer. "All the models were supposed to be here at ten for last-minute fittings, young lady. At least your hair and makeup are done. We'll have to see if Jeanette can still use you."

"Oh, I'm not a model. Trust me on that." Summer flashed her usual sunny grin, and tucked a strand of chin-length blonde hair behind her ear, revealing a perfect-diamond post. "My friend Esmé is working here today, and she gave me tickets. We're getting one of those last tables by the window, right?"

The hostess's lips pursed into a tight, red stop sign. "Those seats are reserved."

"Good thing we have reservations, then," Summer

said, cheerfully. "Look, there's Esmé, and she's headed this way right now."

Esmé—Dorothy wasn't sure of her last name, although she'd met her several times—hit the foyer like a wave crashing Benton Beach. The dark-haired girl wore slim black jeans, beaded gold sandals and a black T-shirt with "GET MIF-D: Milano Institute of Fashion and Design" printed across the front in bold white letters. "Am I glad to see you," she said to Summer, as she smiled and waggled her fingers at Dorothy in greeting. "We just had a major issue backstage and I could really use your help."

"I was about to seat these ladies in the dining room. By the window." The hostess looked considerably put out now.

"No problem, go ahead," Esmé said, with a wave. "It's Nadine, right? I'll follow you guys in. But I can only stay for a minute or two, because I have to get back to work."

Dorothy made an extra effort to keep up with Nadine, who snapped two leather-bound menus from a wicker basket and swished through the arched doorway into the crowded main dining room.

It seemed like a long hike toward the floor-to-ceiling windows, which streamed dazzling sunshine and offered a gorgeous view of Milano Bay. A flotilla of boats—including several impressively sized yachts—lazily crisscrossed the waves, and a long promenade crowded with early-afternoon strollers snaked toward a cheerfully striped pavilion that advertised a holiday art show.

Florida: the land of eternal sunshine. Most of the time, anyway.

Sometimes it was easy to forget it was December. That was why Dorothy kept the Year of Seasons calendar in the kitchen of her condo.

"This is perfect, thank you," she said, as Nadine deposited the menus on their table with overly exaggerated care.

Summer jumped to pull out a blue leather chair for her, as the hostess was oddly hovering.

"Are you by chance a resident of one of our local senior living communities?" Nadine said to Dorothy.

"Hibiscus Pointe," Dorothy said, unfolding her cloth napkin.

"How lovely. We have quite a contingent here from the Pointe today. Are you sure you don't want a table across the room, closer to those ladies?"

Dear heavens, no, Dorothy thought. The last thing she needed was to be anywhere near that busybody, loudmouth Gladys Rumway and her friends. She saw enough of all of them back at the complex, thank you very much.

"No thanks." Summer dropped into her chair and positioned the strap of her large designer tote firmly over the back. "My friend is a serious birdwatcher. See?" She motioned toward a highly overweight pelican, strutting the boardwalk in search of stray croissant crumbs. "And those crazy gulls dive-bombing everyone out there? She just loves them."

Dorothy raised an eyebrow. She rather preferred the graceful snowy egrets and tiny, chipper sandpipers.

"Jeez, she sure didn't want us sitting here," Summer said, when the hostess finally left. "Who else was she going to seat here, the Queen of Milano? There's another empty table right behind us."

"I may be able to answer that," Esmé said. She leaned closer to Dorothy and Summer. "Zoe Z is in the house."

"You're kidding." Summer craned her neck. "Where?"

Esmé ran a hand over her loose French braid and sighed. "Remember that backstage issue I mentioned? All about her. The brat should be showing up in the dining room any second. Hopefully Aleesha, her agent, can keep a better eye on her this time."

"Who on earth is Zoe Z?" Dorothy asked.

"A celebrity train wreck," Summer said. "She was ZeeZee's daughter on that reality show *Life with ZeeZee*."

"Never heard of it," Dorothy murmured. It was hard to believe that a young TV star would be interested in a luncheon and fashion show with an audience of older ladies.

"And after she got out of rehab Zoe Z made the worst pop album ever," Summer went on. "So when her big music career didn't work out, she decided she wanted to be a serious actress. She actually bugged my dad to cast her in his next movie, but he said no way. Huge insurance liability."

"Well, I can't trust Aleesha—she's totally useless— so I need you to watch Zoe for me," Esmé said. "She happens to be my cousin."

Summer stared at her friend. "You never told me that. Are you serious?"

"Unfortunately, yes. I'll explain later," Esmé said. "But I promised Aunt ZeeZee I'd look out for Zoe while she's here in Milano. And I think, actually, she's in town to see *you*."

"Me?" Summer said. "I've never even met her. Besides, she's like nineteen. I'm ten years older than her.

I mean…seven. And how come you never even mentioned you're related to ZeeZee?"

Esmé shrugged. "Never came up, girl. And being linked to Zoe in any way isn't exactly something I'm proud of. All I know is, she's asked me about you a zillion times."

"Perhaps Zoe is hoping you'll put in a good word for her with your father." Dorothy took a sip from the glass of ice water a harried waitress had just placed in front of her.

"Ha," Summer said. "Like Syd ever listens to me."

Dorothy was quite sure he did listen—possibly more, it seemed, than he heeded the concerns of Summer's overly sensible sister, Joy, or his many former wives.

"Esmé, what are you doing out here?" A sharp-chinned, red-haired woman in a long, green linen wrap skirt rustled up beside Summer's friend. "I've been looking for you everywhere. Backstage. Now. The other interns are completely disorganized."

"Sorry, Monique," Esmé said. "There was a mix-up with these guests' reservations."

"All under control. She fixed everything." Summer threw the woman a mega-watt smile. "What exactly is it we need to do, if there are any more, uh, Zoe issues?" she asked Esmé.

"Just keep an eye out, okay?" Esmé said over her shoulder, as her employer pulled her away. "We'll talk later."

"I have a really bad feeling about this," Summer said to Dorothy, when the two women were far enough away from the table. "I'm the worst babysitter, remember?"

"That's not true," Dorothy said. "You do a wonderful job with Juliette-Margot."

"Yeah, but she's only six," Summer said. "And she's

a good kid. If this Zoe Z girl is anything like she was on TV—or off—she's impossible to deal with."

Dorothy glanced toward the entrance. Summer had hardly finished her sentence before a slender, raven-haired teen began to cross the dining room. The girl wore a skintight, daffodil-lace dress and she navigated the slippery floor without the slightest wobble of her canary yellow, sky-high heels. "Well, dear, I believe we're about to find out."

SUMMER WAS CAREFUL not to turn around or even look up from her menu as Zoe Z and her thirty-something manager—Aleesha Berman, who was famous in the industry for being way too chummy with her difficult clients—seated themselves directly behind her and Dorothy. Apparently those two hadn't wanted the uncool hostess to escort them and wreck Zoe's big entrance.

They'd probably stuffed Nadine in that giant vase in the foyer. But none of the luncheon guests were paying much attention to Zoe, anyway. Probably not a lot of *Life with ZeeZee* or celebrity gossip fans in this place.

Why would Zoe wreck whatever low-level celebrity cred she had by showing up here?

Unfortunately, there was zero time to eavesdrop on their new neighbors, because a helmet-haired woman draped head-to-toe in silver lamé appeared at the front of the room.

Major overkill on the tinsel, Summer thought. *For lunch, anyway. And maybe anyone that old.*

"Good afternoon, ladies," the woman greeted the crowd through her wireless headset. "I'm Martha Kirk, president of the Milano Women's League, and I'd like to welcome you all here to Waterman's on the Bay for

our first annual Christmas on the Catwalk Lunch and
Fashion Show."

The attendees all clapped loudly. Was Martha that
same lady she'd seen in practically every society section pic in *Milan-O!* Magazine?

Yep. Summer recognized the bling.

"And I am thrilled to introduce you to our celebrity
designer and brand-new sensation Roland Cho, who created the fabulously unique pieces of jewelry our models are wearing this afternoon. Roland, can you step
out here, please?"

The crowd burst into even more enthusiastic applause
as a very short, spiky-haired man in his early thirties—
white jeans, white turtleneck, purple jacket—emerged
through the velvet curtain that had been set up to create a backstage area.

Roland smiled and waved, bowing a few times to
his fans. Across the room, Gladys Rumway split the
air with a screeching wolf whistle. "Really?" Summer
whispered to Dorothy. Her friend just shook her head.

Summer was glad she'd worn something fairly con-
servative. With this crowd, you couldn't go wrong
with a flowered sundress, strappy sandals and pale
pink pearls. Dorothy looked great as usual, in a coral-
knit twinset and pleated white skirt. Summer had almost suggested that she lose the thick-heeled AeroLite
pumps, maybe, but she didn't want to hurt her feelings.
Besides, her friend should be comfortable.

At least she and Dorothy weren't wearing red and
green, like everyone else in the room. Except for Zoe
and Aleesha, anyway. Zoe probably didn't have one
green thing in her closet.

Martha Kirk droned on, introducing a bunch of local

boutique owners. Summer hadn't heard of any of them. She'd been in Milano for a while now—*months*—and she was pretty sure she knew all the retail options. The decent ones, anyway.

This fashion show was sure to be a snooze, but that was okay. She wasn't here for herself, anyway. She'd brought Dorothy here to get them out of Hibiscus Pointe for a fun afternoon.

Things had been a little boring there lately. She and Dorothy had been so busy earlier, investigating two different murders, that it seemed really quiet now, back at the complex. Not that she wasn't working hard—well, sort of, since it had been raining for weeks—at her volunteer job as Hibiscus Pointe Aquatics Director. It kept the Residents Board off her case for living in her late Grandma Sloan's condo, at least.

Why anyone cared that she was technically under the required age to live there, she had no clue. What a stupid rule, the over-fifty-five deal. Her dad owned the place now, and she paid her rent to him on time each month, didn't she? Well, so far, her sister Joy had. But that was going to change soon, when she got a decent, paying job.

"So let's give a big round of applause for our gorgeous, hardworking models," the silver-bullet MC said, as Summer tuned back in. "They'll be stopping by your tables before the show begins, handing out goodies from our sponsors."

Goodies? Summer hoped Martha K. meant cookies or something. She hadn't had breakfast yet since she'd had to get up way earlier than usual, and she was starving.

She was about to ask Dorothy if she wanted her to

go get their waitress, when she felt a sharp, pointed tap on her shoulder. "Hey, you know me, right?" a nasally voice said behind her.

Summer turned. "Um, no. Sorry."

"Of course you do," Zoe Z said, flipping her shiny dark hair. "*Life with ZeeZee?* Hello?"

"Nope," Summer said. Dorothy raised an eyebrow at her over her menu.

Okay, so maybe she was being a little harsh. The kid was related to Esmé, after all, and she'd promised to keep an eye on her. "Oh, yeah, right," she said, pretending to knock herself on the head. "Great show."

"Well, your dad definitely knows me," Zoe said. "He offered me a major role in *The Girl on the Ledge*. I haven't decided whether I'll take it yet."

Aleesha, Zoe's manager, gave her client a not-now look. "Congratulations," Summer said, forcing a smile.

"Good afternoon, ladies." An attractive older woman, tall and graceful in a long silk dress that matched the colors of the bay through the window, stopped at their table. She carried a shallow white basket filled with cards, perfume samples and those smelly little closet sachets. "Won't you please take a card with these lovely gifts, courtesy of Monique's Boutique?"

Ugh. Monique could have come up with a better name for her store.

"Why thank you, I believe I will," Dorothy said, reaching into the basket.

The model glanced over her shoulder. "I see you have a Hibiscus Pointe tag on your purse," she said, in a low voice. "My name is Angelica Downs, and I just moved my ninety-year-old mother into Hibiscus Glen."

Hibiscus Glen was the memory care unit on the other

side of the complex from her and Dorothy, Summer was pretty sure. She'd never been over there.

"Oh, that's a very nice facility," Dorothy said. "I have several friends who…"

"Her name is Frankie, and I'm quite worried about her," Angelica said, without waiting for Dorothy to finish. Why was she talking so fast? Summer wondered. The woman sounded really nervous.

"Can I trust you ladies?" Angelica asked.

Summer frowned. Trust them? Why?

"Let's move along, please, Angelica. The other tables are waiting, and we need to get the show on the road."

Ugh. Esmé's pointy-chinned boss again. Didn't she have anything better to do than chase underlings back to work? What was her problem?

"I'm sorry, Monique," Angelica said, and Summer frowned. Was Angelica's hand actually shaking on that basket handle? She was a nervous wreck. And why had she asked them if they could be trusted?

"No, *I* apologize," Dorothy spoke up. "I'm afraid I delayed Angelica on her rounds. I couldn't help but notice the beautiful bracelet she's wearing. Is that a Roland Cho piece?"

"Why yes, it is," Monique said, stepping in front of Angelica before the model could answer. "We carry several of his styles at Monique's Boutique. They'd make wonderful holiday gifts. Angelica gave you my card, didn't she?"

"I don't think so," Angelica said quickly. "Sorry, I forgot. And if I didn't, here, take another one." She glanced down, fumbling in her basket, and handed a second card to Dorothy.

"Enjoy the show, ladies," Monique said, as she hustled Angelica to the next table. Zoe Z and Aleesha were gone, Summer noticed. Jeez, had they left already? Not that either of them would be interested in a bunch of old-lady clothes, but didn't they at least want some lunch?

She sure did.

"Oh my," Dorothy said, looking around the poinsettia-filled room. "Where did Angelica go? Do you see her anywhere?"

"Nope," Summer said. "But she couldn't have gone far. Monique's probably giving her a lecture backstage, or something."

"I don't think so. Look at this." Dorothy pushed the pale pink boutique card across the tablecloth.

Summer leaned forward to peer at it closer. "Whoa."

Below the lines of raised-gold, swirly letters, a single word had been scrawled in shaky red pencil. *HELP*.

TWO

"WAIT, DEAR," DOROTHY said, as Summer immediately reached for her cell phone.

"What do you mean?" Summer's perfectly shaped brows drew together in a frown. "Angelica needs our help, or someone does, anyway. That's what the card says."

"We can't be sure. This might be some sort of prank."

"Well, yeah, maybe," Summer said. "But better safe than sorry, right?"

Her friend did have a point. Still… "Let's try to talk to Angelica first, just in case," Dorothy said. "She must be backstage by now. And it's very possible she had no idea there was anything written on the back of that card."

"Okay." Summer didn't sound convinced. "But *some-one* wrote it. Don't you think we should call 911?"

"We don't want to overreact, and get them involved for a twisted joke," Dorothy said. Heaven knew, there were plenty of real emergencies in Southwest Florida taking up the first responders' valuable time. Why would anyone ask for help in a note?

"I guess, but let's find Angelica quick. She seemed super nervous when she was talking to us."

"Agreed." Dorothy rose from the table.

"You go ahead, I'll catch up in a sec." Summer was struggling to unhook her bag strap, which had caught a snag in the woven back of her chair. "This is why I hate wicker."

"Try not to pull, dear, you'll damage the chair." Dorothy began threading her way through the tables of festively dressed ladies toward the door. It looked as if most of the models had already returned backstage.

From the corner of her eye, she spotted Gladys Rumway eagerly trying to flag her down, but Dorothy pretended not to notice. No time to chat with Hibiscus Pointe's most prolific conversationalist right now.

Or anytime, really.

"Hey, Dorothy, where ya going?" Gladys practically yelled across the room. "You guys can't leave now. The fashion show's gonna start any minute."

"Ladies room, Mrs. Rumway," Summer called back at Dorothy's heels, just as loudly. Dorothy resisted the urge to cover her ears. "We may be a while."

Dorothy cringed, but kept moving, her eyes on the door.

"Keep a lookout for Zoe and Aleesha, too," Summer said in a low voice as they stepped out of the dining room. "Bet it wasn't a coincidence those two left right after Monique grabbed Angelica. Zoe's probably up to something."

"May I help you, ladies?" Nadine popped in front of them like a black-and-pink spider from her post at the hostess stand. "The powder room is in the other direction."

"Wonderful, thank you." Dorothy continued down the hall, quickening her pace. Hopefully that first unmarked door on the left led to the backstage area. Choosing the wrong door and bursting through the curtains into the dining room like the Keystone Kops was the last thing they needed.

If Angelica—or anyone else—was actually in danger, they needed to proceed with caution. The note writer must have had a good reason for staying low.

The backstage area was abuzz with activity, as cheerful holiday music played through speakers set up on a folding table. Bored-looking models stood, in various stages of dress, as interns in MIF-D T-shirts buzzed around them, adding jewelry and taping hems. Hairdressers frantically sprayed stubborn cowlicks and tamed stray curls as makeup artists applied finishing touches with blush-dusted brushes on the models' foundation-caked faces.

There was no sign of Angelica.

"She could be practically anywhere back here," Summer said. "I'll talk to some of those ladies in the chairs over there, with all the makeup mirrors."

"It seemed to me as if Angelica was ready to go out onstage," Dorothy said. "I'll try the dressing area by the windows. Maybe she was scheduled for a wardrobe change after she finished handing out her gifts in the dining room."

"Oh, wait, there's Esmé. Perfect." Summer pulled Dorothy toward a group of tables piled with clear plastic boxes and open bins of color-coded accessories. Her friend was kneeling on the black-and-white tiled floor, a set of pins held firmly between her teeth as she expertly brought in the waistband of a petite senior model's starfish-print skirt.

"Hey, Esmé, hate to bother you, but do you know a model named Angelica?" Summer asked. "Tall, older, really pretty, seafoam chiffon? Dorothy and I need to find her quick."

Esmé shook her head. "Hold on," she mumbled, around the pins. She swiftly removed them, one by one, and stuck them in the fabric of her T-shirt. "Sorry. There are a whole bunch of women here who fit that description. Seafoam's really 'in' this year."

Well, that was true, Dorothy thought. On the other hand, seafoam was *always* "in" in Florida. "Angelica may need our help," she said. "The last time we saw her, she was headed back here with Monique."

"She was one of those basket ladies," Summer added.

"Oh." Esmé cocked her head, thinking. "Right, I remember her now. She was acting a little strange, if you ask me. But I haven't seen her since she picked up her basket from that table over there by the door."

"Weird how?" Summer asked. "Sorry, this is kind of an emergency."

Esmé's perfectly arched brows shot up. "Emergency? Oh, jeez, Zoe again? I swear, I'm going to kill that girl."

"No, no," Dorothy assured her, quickly. "Nothing to do with your cousin, dear. Well, we don't believe so, anyway. But if we could just locate Angelica…"

"Wait, Esmé, back up, okay?" Summer broke in. "How exactly was she being strange? You never told us."

"I don't know." Esmé shrugged. "She was just jumpy, I guess. Seemed really worried. Kept looking at the door."

"Did you notice anyone else around here doing anything weird?" Summer pressed. Once she was focused on something, especially for a case, she rarely gave up. A cheery, determined blonde pit bull.

"Not any more than usual." Esmé jumped up, brushing off her jeans. "Oops, no offense, Bryana," she added to a twenty-something model still standing in front of her. "I didn't mean *you*. You're totally normal. I think we're done here."

The model gave her a tired smile and moved away.

"Just don't eat anything before you go out there," Esmé called after her. "We need those pins to hold, okay?"

"Esmé, dear," Dorothy said. "We need your help. Tell us whatever details you can remember about Angelica, no matter how unimportant they seem."

"Ouch." Esmé extracted a stray pin from the knee of her jeans. "Well, when Angelica first got here, she was real sweet and friendly, but then she got all jittery, like I said. Kept asking me whether there was another way out of here. Which there isn't. Just back through that door you guys came in, or through the dining room."

"Did each of the models who visited the tables have her own particular basket?" Dorothy asked.

"Yes. They were different colors, to go with their outfits."

"Was anyone minding the baskets beforehand?" Dorothy asked.

"Monique, I guess," Esmé said. "She's been pretty much directing everything, though. She handed the models the baskets on their way to the dining room because she didn't want anyone to pick up the wrong color. That'd be a serious fashion faux pas, in her book. She loves things all matchy-matchy. Totally old school."

"Maybe we should just find Monique, then," Summer said to Dorothy. "If anyone's going to know where every single person is, it's her."

"She's a beady-eyed witch, all right," Esmé said.

"I haven't seen her back here for at least ten minutes, though, thank the lord."

Summer sighed. "Well, this is fabulous. No Angelica, no Zoe, no Monique." She reached into her pastel-pink shoulder bag, which had a slight scuff on the handle from her battle with the dining room chair. "Maybe we should just call the cops now, Dorothy."

"You're absolutely right," Dorothy said.

They should have done that in the first place and avoided wasting valuable time on this wild goose chase. Why had she been so concerned about a possible false alarm? At this point, Angelica might be in terrible danger.

And if she is, it's my fault, Dorothy told herself.

Summer was pawing frantically through her bag now. "Where is my stupid cell phone? It's not in here."

"You had it right beside you on the table," Dorothy said.

"Yeah, but I'm a zillion percent sure I didn't leave it there. It's practically brand-new, and I've been sooo careful with it."

Dorothy tried not to think about what had happened to Summer's old phone. Her friend had dropped it in the mangroves near an escaped giant python on their last case.

"Esmé, lend me yours, would you?" Summer sounded exasperated now.

"Sorry. Monique made us all put our phones in a cubby she locked up when we got here."

Summer muttered something under her breath, which Dorothy was happy she didn't hear clearly. "Well, *someone* had to have kept theirs," Summer said. "I would have."

"Don't worry, we'll find one." Dorothy glanced

around the bustling room, where models were being herded swiftly through the dining room entrance by a frazzled-looking intern.

Then she felt a set of long, thin fingers close on her arm, and an extra burst of frost from the more than sufficient a/c.

"This area is absolutely off-limits, ladies," a familiar voice said.

"LET GO OF my friend." Summer wasn't about to budge for the angry-looking woman who had to have a hot curling iron up her butt.

"Monique, we're looking for Angelica Downs," Dorothy said, brushing the woman's hand off her arm. "It's quite urgent, I assure you. And we are *not* leaving here until we've spoken with her."

"Way to go, Dorothy," Summer said in a low voice, impressed. No one messed with her friend when she put her foot down.

"Well, if you find that useless woman, you can inform her she's fired." Monique's tone was crisp. "I'm replacing her in the lineup." She looked hard at Summer. "You'll do. We need someone tall to pull off our holiday ornament hat."

"What? No way." Summer took a step back. Why did people always think she could be a model? Strutting down a runway, even in a restaurant, was harder than it looked. Especially without tripping. "Sorry, but that's really not my thing. I'm a detective."

"Detective?" Monique's dark brows shot toward the ceiling fan. "You're joking."

"Angelica is missing, and she may be in trouble,"

Dorothy broke in. "As we said, it's extremely important that we find her."

"Join the club," Monique said, with a haughty sniff. "She was wearing an extremely expensive gown carried exclusively by Monique's Boutique, not to mention a one-of-a-kind Roland Cho bracelet." She turned, and almost caught Esmé rolling her eyes behind her back. "What are *you* standing here for? Go over and help that other intern girl make sure the models stay in line."

"You mean, literally, stay in line?" Esmé asked. "Or you just want me to make them follow your stupid rules?"

Monique bristled like a boar's-hair brush. "That's it. I've had enough of your ungrateful, disrespectful attitude—what is your name again? Whoever you are, you're fired. Very soon. I'll let you know when you can leave."

Esmé's eyes flashed like a crazy laser show. "Guess what, Monique? This job isn't worth it, especially when I'm doing it for free. I quit. And I'm leaving right now."

Uh-oh. There went her friend's big internship. Summer knew that feeling. She'd lost a zillion internships herself, over the last couple of years. In her case, just a streak of really bad luck. Well, mostly.

"Summer, we have to go," Dorothy murmured. "We're wasting time here. We need to make that call."

"We'll catch you later, Esmé." Summer waved and bounded after Dorothy, who was walking briskly toward the wall lined with brightly lit, portable cosmetic mirrors. The super-bright light those bulbs gave off was never flattering, in her opinion, but cosmetic artists swore by them.

One of her former stepmothers—Bianca, maybe?—

had the lighting completely redone in every room of the house, before Syd wised up and divorced her. There were still a bunch of those mirrors left in some of the guest wings.

Now that she thought of it, Bianca and Monique looked sort of alike, except Bianca was Rodeo Drive–blonde.

"Goodness, how did everyone in here clear out so quickly?" A dozen worried-looking Dorothys stood still now in front of Summer, staring out from the long line of mirrors. "And not a single phone in sight."

"We'll find one," Summer said, searching through the jumble of combs and foils and hair accessories on a nearby rolling cart. "I hate to say this, Dorothy, but maybe Angelica just took off with the fancy dress and bracelet. I know she seemed nice and everything, but she's probably halfway to Miami or somewhere now."

"I truly doubt that," Dorothy said. "She seemed so lovely, and she seemed genuinely upset about something. Why don't you go back into the dining room, and see if you can borrow one of the guest's phones? Or better yet, there's probably a landline at the hostess stand."

"Okay." Summer pointed herself toward the foyer.

"Whatever you do, don't alert Gladys, or we'll have to deal with her, too," Dorothy said. "Just call the police. I'll keep looking for Angelica."

The hostess stand was empty, as Summer headed toward it. From a distance, it looked like there was a landline phone there, all right…the kind with the zillion confusing buttons that had gotten her fired from a temp job once.

Loud, crackly music suddenly sounded from behind the closed French doors to the dining room, replacing the holiday tunes. The big fashion show had officially started.

What was that weird song they were playing for the models to twirl around to? Super retro, and way cutesy, probably from the sixties or something. The guy who was singing kept asking a cat what was up. Over and over. *Oh-oh-oh-oh-whoa...*

Yikes. She'd never get that cat song out of her head now. This was the most bizarre-o fashion show she'd ever been to.

Nadine was watching the show through the dining room doors. Purr-fect. Summer leaned over the hostess stand and extracted the other, much simpler phone she knew she'd find, under the reservations book. Bingo.

"911. What is the nature of your emergency?"

"We have a missing person," Summer told the operator. "And we think she may be in trouble."

"What is your name, please?"

"Summer Smythe. I mean, Sloan." Oops. Which would be better to use this time? It didn't matter, actually, because the police already knew her under both names. Detective Donovan always called her Ms. Smythe-Sloan, her full name, just to annoy her.

"And how long has the person been missing?"

"About half an hour. Maybe a little longer," Summer said. "Her name is Angelica Downs. I'm not sure exactly how old she is, maybe in her sixties, but she's really tall and has..."

"Give me that." She felt a hard tug on her arm as a furious Nadine snatched the phone from her grasp. "This is my private phone. How dare you?"

"It's an emergency," Summer began.

"Disregard that call," Nadine told the operator. "And she's not calling you back."

"That was 911," Summer informed her, as the hostess jammed her cell into an artfully hidden pocket in her overly blooming skirt.

"You called the *police*?" Nadine's jaw dropped halfway down her long, tanned neck. "*Here? What on earth for*?"

"One of the models is missing," Summer said. "Angelica Downs. My friend Dorothy and I are really worried about her."

Nadine's face didn't look so tanned anymore. "Oh, this is terrible," she said, bringing a hand to her cheek. "Waterman's can't afford one more shred of bad publicity. Especially right now."

Was this woman for real? Who cared about the stupid restaurant?

"When someone calls 911 and hangs up on them, they can trace it, you know," Summer said. "The cops will be here any second, whether you like it or not."

"No one mentioned anything to *me* about a problem," the hostess said. "And I assure you, I'd be the first person to hear. Besides, I just saw Angelica with Monique about half an hour ago in the dining room, and she was perfectly fine. She's probably onstage right now, in fact."

Summer was already scanning the room over the woman's shoulder. Nope, no sign of Angelica. Bryana, the pale, younger model whose dress Esmé had pinned, was walking quickly down the wide aisle that had been set up between the tables. When she reached the middle of the room, she stopped, swung out her bony hip, and

started back again, without a glance at any of the clapping women in the audience.

She seemed very professional. The ugly purple,
angel-wing sleeves of her dress were a little distracting, though, as she moved.

Now everyone in the crowd was focused on a whole
string of models starting down the aisle. They were carrying those dumb baskets again, and every few seconds
they tossed little prizes out to the audience, enclosed
in filmy, black gift bags. But none of the models was
Angelica.

"Gotta go," Summer told Nadine. "Send the cops
backstage when they get here, okay?"

The hostess glared back at her.

Summer snuck another peek back into the dining
room as she turned away. Were they actually playing another song with a cat in it? Yep. Who'd thought up *that*
crazy theme for a holiday fashion show? You couldn't
make this stuff up.

Gladys Rumway grabbed for a gift bag that had
fallen on the floor, and almost tripped the poor model.

Jeez. People were so greedy, Summer thought, as
she headed down the hall. It was obvious no one was
paying attention to anything but the free swag. They
could care less about the ugly clothes.

Would they even notice if someone was kidnapped
and carted out of the restaurant, screaming? Probably
not.

"Where have you been?" Dorothy asked, when Summer found her surrounded by racks of garment bags in
the far corner of the now-deserted backstage area. "No
sign of Angelica. It seems she simply vanished. Did you
reach 911, I hope?"

"Yep," Summer said. Her friend looked really upset and frustrated. That wasn't like Dorothy at all. She hardly ever lost her cool. "Here, let me do some looking around for clues. You sit down and chill."

"I'm fine." Dorothy's lips were set in a thin line. "But you could check those shelves over there. Some of the models left their street clothes and bags on them, and I didn't do a very thorough job of going through them. Maybe, if we can find anything at all that might belong to Angelica, it will give us a start."

"Got it." Summer crossed the black-and-white checkered floor. She hated to agree with Monique, but what if Angelica *was* just a thief who'd lifted a dress and a few pieces of pricey jewelry?

But how could she have snuck out of the restaurant wearing that long, seafoam chiffon dress? Wouldn't someone have noticed? If Angelica had had enough time to change—pretty doubtful—she might have been carrying a garment bag or something, but the hostess would have spotted her for sure.

Well, maybe not. Nadine hadn't been paying attention a couple of minutes ago. She'd had her back turned as she watched the fashion show, long enough to have her cell phone nabbed at the hostess stand. *Borrowed*, Summer corrected herself, as she started sifting through the models' bags and scarves and tees.

What a mess. Some people would have to do a *lot* of clothes steaming before they left. No one went around looking like a slob in Milano. If they did, they'd probably be beaten with wire hangers and run out of town by the Fashion Police. Even the very oldest ladies at Hibiscus Pointe never missed a hair appointment at the community's salon.

Eww. She drew back in disgust. There on the shelf, underneath the T-shirt she'd just lifted, someone had left a pair of strappy, size-twelve sandals. The soles were covered with gobs of black, sticky stuff that was now all over her hands. Probably tar from the Bay Village Pier outside Waterman's window. Or the restaurant's half-melted parking lot.

How could the person not have noticed? "Thanks, whoever-you-are," she muttered, moving the models' things aside with her elbow. "You're super thoughtful."

As she was trying to scrape the gross tar off her hands onto the edge of the shelf, she noticed another door half-hidden in the wall behind the mountains of piled-up clothes.

Huh. Where did that lead to? Was it just a closet— or a closed-off exit? Maybe that's how Angelica had made her getaway.

Summer grabbed the left-hand bars of the rolling shelves and pushed the whole thing down a few feet, very carefully. She didn't need the ginormous shelf to collapse on her. It looked like one of those assemble-yourself deals, and she'd never had much luck with them.

At least she could get to the door now. But Dorothy came up and beat her to it. "I'll get it, dear, your hands are filthy," her friend said, reaching across her to twist the fake-brass knob.

The door opened easily, and an oversized, pink-and-green hanging storage bag fell out on the floor in front of them.

Summer tugged on the bag and dragged it all the way from the closet. It was super bulky. *Heavy, too,* she told herself.

She definitely had a bad feeling about this.

Dorothy sprang forward and pulled on the zipper. It moved just a few inches before it stopped short, with a crunch of metal and a nasty, ripping sound.

"Oh, no." Dorothy stared at the broken zipper. "I pulled it too hard."

"Don't worry," Summer said. "It's just off track. There's a trick to fix that. I think I saw a pencil around here somewhere."

She glanced around the room, then rushed over to the table that had held Monique's color-coded gift baskets and dropped to her hands and knees. After a second or two of feeling around on the dusty floor, she popped back up in triumph. "Found it!"

It only took a few seconds of rubbing the pencil point across the metal track to put the zipper back on track. There was a small hole in the fabric of the garment bag, but that was okay. They just had to get the stupid thing open.

As soon as she did, Summer wished that pencil trick she'd seen in a YouTube video once hadn't worked.

Angelica Downs lay crumpled inside, still wearing her seafoam dress—and a clear plastic dry cleaner's bag over her head.

THREE

"No, no, no!" Dorothy clawed desperately at the clammy plastic wound tightly across Angelica's face. The poor woman was probably half suffocated.

"Dorothy, stop." A pair of gentle, but very strong, hands descended firmly on her shaking shoulders. "I checked her pulse," Summer said. "There isn't one. I'm really sorry."

Dorothy didn't want to look more closely at the model's face. Because now she'd realized it was an ominous, purplish red, with chilling blue lips.

If she didn't glance again, it might not be real.

"Come on, let's get you to a chair." Summer took Dorothy by the elbow to help her up.

Dorothy shook herself from her friend's grip. "No. We have to get that bag off of Angelica."

"It's a crime scene now." Summer's tone was calm and soothing, but Dorothy could see her friend trembling. Or maybe it was herself who was shaking? "The police will be here any second," Summer added. "See, someone just showed up. Over here!" she called, over Dorothy's shoulder.

A young woman in dark clothes jogged up, frowning. Officer Caputo, Dorothy remembered. She recognized her from the last crime scene she and Summer had stumbled into, when a librarian was murdered in their very own Hibiscus Pointe library.

The last crime scene. How was it possible she'd had to use such an awful phrase, even to herself?

"What's happened here?" the officer asked. Judging by the black pantsuit, crisp white button-up shirt, and bright gold badge at her waist, she was now *Detective* Caputo.

Goodness, Dorothy thought. And she'd thought the young woman was fresh out of the academy.

"That missing person we called 911 about, Angelica Downs?" Summer stepped back and pointed toward the storage—now body—bag. "It's too late."

"Mmm," Detective Caputo said, with a brief glance in the direction of the deceased. "How long?"

Well, she was certainly all business. The detective's pale eyelashes didn't even flicker. But that was her job, Dorothy reminded herself quickly. Detectives were trained not to show emotion.

"Forty-five minutes, maybe?" Summer's voice was definitely unsteady. She was trying to be brave, Dorothy could tell, and not just for the police.

"An hour." Dorothy straightened her shoulders. She needed to pull herself together immediately. What good would she do poor Angelica as a nervous wreck? She and Summer had already failed her once.

Actually, that wasn't true. Summer had wanted to call for help right away. She was the one who had utterly failed Angelica. And now the poor woman was dead.

"Okay. I need you two ladies to stay right here, until I say you can leave. Got it?"

Dorothy and Summer both nodded.

Detective Caputo took a few steps away, and spoke in clipped tones to someone on her phone. "Gosh, she's cold," Summer whispered.

"It's her job to be efficient." *And ours, too*, she nearly added. They were detectives, after all. Amateurs, of course—but still…

In no time at all, it seemed, the backstage area at Waterman's on the Bay was swarming with activity. Emergency personnel, crime scene photographers and investigators, the coroner, and… Gladys Rumway.

"I need deets on everything that happened before I got here, Dorothy." Gladys leaned over Dorothy's folding chair. Her well-padded fist held a Waterman's pen poised above a matching Waterman's paper beverage napkin.

"Deets?" Dorothy said.

"Someone got killed, Mrs. Rumway," Summer said. "Is that enough detail for you?"

"Shh, dear," Dorothy murmured. "Don't be rude. It won't help things."

"I wasn't talking to you, missy." Gladys's pink-rimmed, beady eyes narrowed even further, giving her the appearance of an enormous—and furious—gray guinea pig. "You know, I find it really interesting that you and your snotty cheerleader nose have fallen over another stiff here in Milano. What's the body count for you now, three? And how long have you been in town, camping out like a princess at Hibiscus Pointe? *Very* interesting."

"Summer and I both found Angelica," Dorothy said. How dare Gladys refer to Angelica as a "stiff"?

"And I'm not *camping*," Summer added. "I pay rent. Well, my dad does, and I pay him. You can check that with Jennifer Margolis in Resident Services."

"You bet your skinny patootie I'll have a chat with Jennifer," Gladys said. "And Helen Murphy, our Residents Board president, is a good friend of mine. We don't need any low-class troublemakers like you stinking up the HP."

"Fine, Mrs. Rumway," Summer said. "You guys can find yourselves a new Aquatics Director, then, and you'll have to actually pay her. She'll probably flunk you on your Beginner swim test, too."

"Please, both of you." Dorothy held up her hands. "Stop this silly bickering. It's not respectful to Angelica, and it isn't helpful toward finding whoever did this dreadful thing, either."

"Oh, I'm already on that, Dorothy," Gladys said. "Don't you worry. I was on the horn to my cousin Merle down at the Milano PD the minute I heard someone got bumped off."

Bumped off? Dorothy held her tongue. There was no point in objecting to Gladys's unfortunate phrasing. She had the sensitivity of a fence post. Her cousin Merle was a volunteer clerk in the file room. Sometimes he answered the phones, if things got extra busy. Occasionally, he did provide some useful information, but Gladys never let her and Summer forget it. She fancied herself quite the detective.

"Whaddaya say you and me team up together, Dorothy?" Gladys leaned in even closer, and Dorothy suppressed an involuntary shudder. "You know, just to solve this case a little faster. I don't need a partner, really, but it'll give you a good excuse to dump your freeloading string bean friend here. She's dragging you down."

"Thank you for the offer, Gladys," Dorothy said. "But no."

"Ma'am? Who are you, and why are you back here? This is a crime scene. See the yellow tape? Authorized persons only."

Dorothy breathed a sigh of relief, as Detective Caputo jerked her head at Gladys, indicating the door.

Most likely, the Milano Police would solve the crime, anyway. They were a very well-regarded department across the state, and Dorothy had full confidence in their top-notch detective team, led by Senior Detective Shane Donovan.

Perhaps she and Summer had simply gotten lucky in solving those other cases, Dorothy thought. But in her heart she knew that wasn't true. The two of them worked hard on their investigations, and they'd run into considerable danger several times. And if they could lend assistance to the Milano PD in solving Angelica's murder...

"Oh, I think you'll be glad I'm here, Detective." Gladys waved the scribbled napkin in Caputo's face. "I'm already working the case, see?"

The detective's expression didn't change. "Do you have any information you can give us about the deceased?"

"Not yet," Gladys said. "But I will."

"Were you present in this room at any time today, or did you notice anything unusual out in the dining section, before or during the show?"

"I notice a lot of things," Gladys said.

The detective seemed unimpressed. "Please go back and wait in the dining room," she said, nodding toward the door again. "We'll be taking contact information from everyone in the building very shortly, as possible witnesses. Thanks for your patience."

"You're making a big mistake, Detective. I have connections down at the PD. Unlike some other people in here." When the detective remained silent, Gladys stomped from the backstage area, muttering under her breath. On her way, she knocked a container of colorful baubles to the floor with her gigantic, multi-buckled purse, but she didn't seem to notice.

"Do you need us to leave the area, also?" Dorothy asked Detective Caputo. "Summer and I will be happy to wait with the others." Maybe they could question a few people themselves, in case anyone had noticed anything out of the ordinary—or seen Angelica.

Stunning as the senior model had been, had anyone really noticed her? Dorothy wondered. Besides Monique, of course. And where was the boutique owner right now, anyway? Now *there* was someone who had been extremely visible this afternoon—practically every minute.

"You two can wait here," Detective Caputo said. "We'll interview you first. The coroner will remove the body very shortly. I'll be back."

"At least we'll get out of here soon," Summer said to Dorothy, as the detective walked briskly over to speak to a pair of crime scene investigators. "We need to find Zoe Z and her agent. And my phone."

"I'm more worried about Frankie Downs, back at Hibiscus Pointe," Dorothy said. "Angelica seemed so worried about her mother. She might be in danger, too."

"Shouldn't we tell…"

"Absolutely." Dorothy stood up so quickly, she felt a little dizzy. But she wasn't going to wait too long to get help this time. They needed to inform Detective Caputo about Frankie, and Angelica's obvious concern, right away.

Finding a body stuffed in an over-sized garment bag had muddled her thinking.

She and Summer had almost reached Detective Caputo, who was now conversing with a young woman
carrying a fingerprint lifting kit, when Roland Cho
burst through the curtain leading to the dining room.

"Stop everything!" the designer shouted, rushing
past a Waterman's security guard. "Nobody move!"

SUMMER NABBED ROLAND CHO by his velvet jacket sleeve
as he tried to plow straight through her. "Whoa, dude.
What's the problem? You're not supposed to be back
here."

He glared at her, and straightened his purple blazer
as she loosened her grip. "Look what you've done,
Blondie, you crushed the fabric. I'll be sure to send you
the dry cleaning bill. And I have every right to be in this
room. I'm the celebrity guest designer for this show."

"What's going on here?" Detective Caputo asked,
coming up with a frown.

"I'm Roland Cho, and I need to see the body," Roland
said. "Before you cart it away to wherever it's going."

Beside her, Summer heard Dorothy draw in a sharp
breath. *"Really,"* her friend said. She sounded ticked
off again.

"Negative on that, sir," the detective said. "Sorry."

Caputo didn't sound sorry. Zero emotion at all. No
wonder she'd gotten promoted so fast. She made her
boss, Detective Donovan, look like a stand-up comedian.

The designer drew himself up to his full height,
at least half a foot shorter than Summer. That was if
you counted his gelled, spiky hair, which looked like
ombré artificial turf. "I need my property back. Angelica Downs was wearing a Roland Cho original."

Wow. Roland was even colder than Caputo. What a jerk.

"Any items on the deceased's person will be returned at a future date," Detective Caputo said. "The team here is taking plenty of photos, and then the medical examiner will bag everything up for evidence."

"I can't afford to have my valuable jewelry in storage for who knows how long," Roland said. "My designs are meant to be worn. And *sold.*"

Summer glanced over her shoulder. The coroner had placed a sheet over Angelica's body and an assistant was helping her transfer it into another bag. Not a cheerful green-and-pink striped one this time. A long, black bag marked "City of Milano."

"Wait! I just need to check one thing." Roland rushed over, knocking into the metal gurney waiting to transport Angelica to the morgue.

Detective Caputo lunged after him, but the designer was already peering over the coroner's assistant's shoulder. "I knew it!" he said, pointing to the pale hand that was just visible outside the sheet. "It's gone."

"What's gone?" Dorothy asked, as she and Summer joined the group by the body.

"My bracelet. My best piece, *Stars of the Sea.* It's been stolen!" Roland covered his face, flashing a full set of purple tips with a rhinestone in the middle of each nail. Totally tacky, in Summer's view.

"Perhaps it fell off during…the struggle," Dorothy said. "I'm sure Angelica tried to fight off her attacker."

Summer bit her lip. Dorothy looked as if she were about to cry. She wished she knew what to say to make her feel better, but she couldn't think of anything super comforting at the moment.

It was true. Angelica had to have known she was going to die. And who cared about a stupid bracelet right now, anyway?

Roland Cho, obviously.

"She put up a struggle, all right." Detective Caputo nodded toward Angelica's still, white hand. "She's got several broken fingernails, see? Judging from the placement of the plastic bag, the killer must have come up from behind and surprised her."

Dorothy's mouth opened into an O, but she quickly closed it again without saying anything. Summer patted her on the shoulder and tried not to think about Angelica's last moments on earth.

"The team has searched the entire perimeter," the detective added. "No sign of any bracelet."

"So the person could have killed Angelica for the bracelet, if it's really valuable," Summer said to Dorothy.

"It is," Roland said.

"But why didn't she just hand it over to the guy?" Summer asked, ignoring him. "That's what I would have done. I mean, it's just a dumb bracelet, right?"

"Obviously, you know nothing about art," Roland said, as the coroner and her assistant wheeled Angelica's body toward the foyer. He seemed even more miffed now. "That bracelet was due to be auctioned for big bucks in New York next month. We've already had interest from some top celebrities."

"Like who?" Summer asked.

The designer actually sniffed. "You wouldn't know them."

"Hey, I just might," Summer said. Their agents probably had her dad's office on speed dial. She'd never had much use for celebrities herself. That was one of the reasons she'd moved to Milano.

The other reasons were nobody's business.

Dorothy gave Summer a tiny warning nudge, and turned to Detective Caputo. "If you're ready to begin interviewing us, Detective, we'd like to have a private word with you, if possible. It's important, and it directly concerns Angelica."

The detective gave a short nod. "Okay. Let's go over to those chairs in the corner, and let the team finish up here." She beckoned to an officer who was taking measurements on the floor. "Get Mr. Cho's contact info and have that security guard escort him out."

Yep. Next to Caputo, Detective Donovan was a real marshmallow.

She hadn't heard from the guy for a while now. What was the deal?

Much as she hated to admit it, things hadn't started off too well with the two of them, relationship-wise. If she could even call it a relationship.

Their so-called first date at the all-you-could-eat meat restaurant—Brazilian steakhouse, she corrected herself—was pretty much a disaster.

She'd been so excited that they would finally have a chance to spend some time together, which had nothing to do with a murder case. But nope.

When they'd finally made it to the steakhouse place, he'd gotten some emergency call, thrown down a bunch of cash for dinner and a cab, and left her stranded with a table full of lamb chops and shish kebabs.

All she'd ended up with from their big night out was a ginormous doggy bag of leftovers to bring home. She and Dorothy had eaten amazingly well for a whole week.

After *that*, the detective had been busy with some new investigation. Or so he said.

And now she had no phone again, so Detective Donovan couldn't call or text her at all. But he knew where she lived, right?

She'd never had to wait for a guy to make a move. Not once, in her entire life, that she could remember. And she wasn't going to start with Shane Donovan, no matter how much she liked him. She hardly knew him, anyway. There was just something about the guy...

Yikes. Summer snapped herself back to attention. Dorothy had been telling Detective Caputo about Angelica's mom, and how she lived over in that special section at Hibiscus Pointe. The memory care unit. What was that place called again?

Hibiscus Glade. No, *Glen*.

"Okay, Mrs. Westin, we'll look into it," Detective Caputo said, making a few notes on her tablet. "I'll make a call over to the Glen to check on Mrs. Downs, and alert the staff, until I can get there in person to talk to her."

"Thank you, Detective." Dorothy nodded, but Summer noticed that she was slumping a little.

"Are you okay?" she asked.

"I'm absolutely fine," Dorothy said.

Caputo frowned. "It's been a busy afternoon, Mrs. Westin, and you've been through a lot. If you want, I can interview you and Ms. Smythe-Sloan here—" the detective jerked her head in Summer's direction "—later. I think we have all we need from you both right now."

Ms. Smythe-Sloan. Summer thought of Detective Donovan again. Hopefully he'd show up soon to take charge of the Downs investigation. For some reason, Caputo really annoyed her.

And vice versa. Summer had no idea why. One thing she did know: Caputo and Donovan had to be the world's worst, most uptight detective team.

Almost as bad as Josh and Lexie, the detective partners on her fave TV show, *Citizen's Arrest*. Oh...no. Those two were also an undercover couple. And cop partners dated each other all the time, didn't they? Was it possible...

"You know, it *would* be wonderful if Summer and I could leave now, Detective," Dorothy said. "I have to admit, I *am* feeling a tad tired."

Her friend's voice sounded weak and wobbly, but her eyes were bright and alert. It was pretty obvious, to Summer, anyway, that Dorothy just wanted to get out of Waterman's ASAP.

She was pretending to help her across the room when Roland Cho reappeared backstage, followed by the apologetic-looking Waterman's security guard. Again.

Jeez. That guy could get a job with Hibiscus Pointe. He'd fit right in.

"I know who stole my *Stars of the Sea* bracelet," Roland announced loudly, sweeping the curtain open wider behind him. "And she's right back there in the restaurant."

Everyone left at the crime scene followed the designer's finger with their eyes.

Summer sucked in her breath. *Esmé.*

FOUR

"ESMÉ WOULD *NEVER* steal anything. Is that Roland Cho guy serious?" Summer seemed ready to pummel the celebrity designer straight through the black-and-white floor.

"Of course not." Dorothy patted Summer's arm in what she hoped was a calming gesture. "You know that, and I know that, and I'm sure Detective Caputo—" she glanced back at the detective, who was stony-faced, as usual "—would never believe it, either."

"Wanna bet?" Summer said, as Detective Caputo motioned to an officer with a clipboard and dispatched him toward the restaurant. "How can Roland get away with accusing a totally innocent person of something like that? The bracelet was super ugly, anyway."

"Keep your voice down, dear," Dorothy murmured. "Please. We don't want to make things worse."

Too late. Esmé was moving toward the backstage area like a highly motivated hornet, sparing the officer with the clipboard half the distance.

"Why didn't she just leave when she had the chance?" Summer tried to wave her away, but Esmé either didn't see her or ignored the warning. "She's headed toward Caputo. We'd better go see what's up." She immediately turned, and started jogging in the same direction as Esmé.

Dorothy scrambled after Summer, who looked as

dangerously determined as her friend. At this rate, they'd never get over to check on Angelica's mother at Hibiscus Glen. But the detective had said she'd make a call to the staff, and if Esmé was in trouble, too…

Summer beat both her friend and the furious designer to Detective Caputo. "Don't believe him, Detective," Summer said, a bit more forcefully than necessary. "He's crazy. I know Esmé really well, and she's totally trustworthy."

The young detective's eyes slid toward Summer for less than a second. "I'll handle this, thanks."

"Of course, Detective." Dorothy wished Summer would stop bouncing around on her toes like that. She was such a tall girl, it was doubly distracting.

"Hey, I'm the one with the stolen property here." Roland Cho threw Summer a disgusted look. "And FYI, I have a big tip for you, Detective. I caught this sneaky intern—" he jerked his head toward Esmé "—red-handed earlier, with my priceless missing bracelet in her hot little paws. Along with the pearl and amethyst necklace I created just for this occasion, *Moon over Milano*."

Oh, no. Dorothy's heart missed a beat. Roland's so-called tip could easily establish a motive for Esmé in Angelica's murder. Did he realize that?

"That is so not true." Summer crossed her arms over her chest and looked at her friend. "Tell him, Esmé."

"I didn't steal anything," Esmé said. Was it Dorothy's imagination, or had the young woman hesitated just a bit before answering? "I found the pieces out of their boxes by mistake and I only held them for a second or two. I put both of them back, right away."

"Only because I caught you," Roland said. "Later, when I was busy out there with the show, you saw your chance and stole my *Stars of the Sea* piece again, didn't you?"

"No, I didn't. You're making me look bad." Esmé definitely sounded more nervous than angry now. Detective Caputo brought out her tablet again.

That wasn't a good sign.

"Okay, let me make sure I have this straight," the detective said to Esmé, tapping the screen. "You had the jewelry in question in your possession at some point this afternoon?"

"Not for very long," Esmé said. "Like I told you, less than a minute."

"I see," Detective Caputo said. "Let's start with your address, please."

"She's an intern," Summer put in. "It's her job to accessorize the models' outfits. Right, Esmé?"

"Her job, before she was fired by me earlier this afternoon, was to make sure the models' dresses fit properly," another, distinctly nasal voice spoke up. "And I saw her trying to steal Roland's jewelry, too."

Could there be any worse time for Monique to finally show up, from wherever she'd been for the last hour? Dorothy didn't think so.

"What time was it, exactly, that you were terminated from your job today?" Detective Caputo asked Esmé, in an uncharacteristically interested tone.

"I wasn't fired," Esmé said, her eyes flashing again. "Monique here told me I had to stay until she said I could go. So then I quit."

"That's true," Summer added, nodding emphatically. "Dorothy and I heard the whole thing."

Well, *this* situation was going to take a while to sort out, Dorothy told herself. She felt badly for Esmé, of course. But she and Summer needed to get to Frankie quickly, before there was another possible tragedy.

She caught Summer's eye and gave her a slight nod toward the door. Summer shook her head, clearly reluctant to leave Esmé, but finally tore herself away.

"Summer!" Esmé called after her, frantically gesturing. "Call me," she mouthed, very clearly. Then, with her back still to the detective, she added one more word: *Zoe.*

"Do you think Esmé was just reminding us to check up on Zoe for her?" Summer asked Dorothy, as they headed toward the door.

"Possibly." Dorothy's tone sounded unusually grim. "Or she was trying to tell us something much, much worse."

"Whoa, wait a sec." Summer stopped short near a potted Norfolk pine draped in white twinkle lights. Why did anyone bother turning those on in the daytime? What a waste. "You mean, Zoe might be the one who swiped Roland Cho's bracelet, and... Oh."

"That's right," Dorothy said. "I'm afraid she could very well be a suspect in Angelica's murder."

"I'm not sure I buy that," Summer said. "I mean, yeah, I don't really know Zoe personally or anything. According to all the tabloids, she was a pain on the set of *Life with ZeeZee,* and even Esmé, her own cousin, says she's a brat. But murder... I don't think so. She's just a kid. Kids do dumb things."

She sure had, when she was in her teens. Actually, she still screwed up sometimes. Not on purpose, obviously.

"I believe you were the one who was worried about Zoe," Dorothy reminded her. "And she and her dining companion—we need to think about the agent's possible role, also—did disappear at the same time as Angelica."

Summer sighed. "I know. But still…"

"Not to mention, Esmé had already told us there had been some kind of issue involving Zoe before we arrived."

She couldn't argue with Dorothy on any of those points, Summer told herself, as she watched the twinkle lights flash on and off in the sunny hallway. Zoe was obnoxious, but also kind of pathetic. It was hard to imagine she could be an actual murderer.

Reality TV—show stars, especially the younger ones, were always messed up. They had no idea what was real and what wasn't sometimes. And living in LA didn't help a whole lot, with all the craziness there.

The worst thing was, some of those D-list kid celebrities thought they were a lot more important than they actually were. Between the computer-altered photos and fake stories in the tabloids and online, plus all those relentless paparazzi, most of those kids didn't get that their whole lives were bogus.

Brutal.

"Summer?" Dorothy was frowning at her. "Are you with me here?"

"What? Oh, sorry." Summer shook the fake Hollywood dust off her brain. "I was thinking about Zoe. There's something else that's bugging me, besides the idea she's too young and clueless to be a cold-blooded murderer."

"We can't rule anyone out, dear," Dorothy said. "Not yet. And certainly not until we have any kind of proof they're innocent."

"I thought it was innocent until proven guilty," Summer said.

Dorothy smiled. "Well, technically, that's correct. In a court of law, certainly. But we're just gathering information for our investigation at this point. We don't have much to go on."

"I guess you're right," Summer said. Dorothy was usually right. "But I still don't think a celebrity, not even a reality one, would kill for a piece of jewelry. Especially if it wasn't that cool a piece in the first place. They'd just get another bracelet or whatever from some other up-and-coming designer. Plus, actors get tons of free swag in those goody bags they give out backstage at award shows."

"Unless they were desperate for money, perhaps," Dorothy said.

"Maybe." Summer tried to think back on the latest gossip she'd heard about Zoe Z and her family. Hadn't there been some article on the *PartyWood* blog about ZeeZee going bankrupt? But again, you couldn't believe everything you read.

Or any of it, for that matter.

"What do you know about Zoe's agent?" Dorothy asked. "Do you think she could be, at least in some small part, encouraging her client's poor behavior?"

"Aleesha's been in the biz about ten years or so," Summer said. "I've never heard anything really bad about her, though. Her clients seem to think she's okay. Probably because she hangs out with them a lot and keeps them out of trouble."

"Not this time," Dorothy said.

Another good point, Summer thought. "My dad tried to date her a couple of years ago," she said.

"Even though he thinks all agents are money-grabbing leeches."

"Your father sounds like quite an interesting person," Dorothy said.

"Mmm." Summer had never heard Syd called "interesting." A lot of other things, but not that. "So should we go see Frankie first, or find Zoe and Aleesha first? At least we know where Frankie is."

"Hopefully," Dorothy said. "I'm sure by now Detective Caputo has already spoken to the Hibiscus Glen staff, and they're keeping careful watch over her."

"Right." Summer sure hoped they were better at their jobs than the Hibiscus Pointe security guys. "Hold on, I'm going to check really quick for my phone in the dining room, okay?"

"I'll wait here," Dorothy said. "Try to hurry, dear."

"I'll be back in two seconds," Summer promised.

Dorothy looked even more tired now, she noticed. Was she just upset about Angelica, or was something wrong? Her friend needed to take it easy, but Summer knew she wouldn't. Not when a killer was on the loose in Milano.

She needed to step up her game so Dorothy didn't overdo things, she told herself as she pulled open the French doors to the dining room. The tricky thing was to make things easier on Dorothy without her realizing it. Otherwise, she'd probably be mad.

The noise level in the dining room was at DEFCON 5, with all the luncheon ladies jabbering excitedly about the tragedy behind the curtain. Other guests seemed quiet and nervous, a bunch more were dabbing their eyes with monogrammed handkerchiefs, and several tables of fashion fans had started helping themselves to bottles of pricey wine from the holiday garland-draped rack.

Nadine and some of the waitstaff looked on help-lessly as Gladys passed around a handy gizmo from her purse that just happened to have a corkscrew attachment.

Major points for you, Mrs. Rumway, Summer thought. You had to admire that kind of moxie. That's what Dorothy always called it, anyway. Rochelle, her third stepmom, called it chutzpah.

Someone had cranked the cheerful holiday music again, in a futile effort to calm people down. Detective Caputo's team needed to speed things up on the info-gathering front, or the whole restaurant could be destroyed by a bunch of little old ladies.

No, that wasn't what she'd meant. Totally un-PC, and Dorothy would kill her. A bunch of really energetic seniors.

Summer tried to make herself invisible by taking the long way along the wall as she headed toward the table she and Dorothy had shared by the window. That seemed like ages ago.

While she was at it, she should check by Zoe and Aleesha's table, too. Maybe one of them had dropped something that would offer a clue as to why they'd been having lunch at Waterman's.

It couldn't really have been because Zoe wanted to meet her, right? How could the girl have known she was going to be at a fashion show lunch today, anyway? It was supposed to be a surprise for Dorothy, so the only person she'd told was her friend Dash, when they were at that club Beach Patrol the other night.

They'd been sitting at a funky tiki bar on the second

level, the one with the hula dancers flashing orange-and-green lava lights. And she'd had to kind of yell a little over the pounding music from the dance floor.

Was Zoe Z hanging out there, too? Um…well, maybe. Summer might have been paying more attention to the electric blue drinks than the other clubbers around them.

Summer checked her and Dorothy's table, and every inch underneath it. She even got down on her hands and knees, in case she was missing anything. But her phone was hot pink and the biggest one you could buy, so it was pretty safe to say it was now officially gone.

Someone had to have snagged it. That was super annoying. Had she left the Find My Phone app on, or turned it off so no one could track her? She couldn't remember.

There was nothing left at Zoe and Aleesha's table except a lingering blanket of expensive but gross perfume. If she stayed here any longer, she'd need a gas mask.

The tunes suddenly died, right in the middle of a rousing sleigh bell accompaniment. A badly timed *pop* sounded from one of the tables as someone uncorked a bottle.

"Ladies, may I have your attention again, please?" Martha Kirk, the tinsel-draped Milano Women's League president, waved her long silver arms at the front of the dining room.

Summer tried to flatten herself against the window and began to edge, very slowly, back the way she'd taken.

She needed to get back to Dorothy before her friend gave up on her and called an Uber.

"In light of the terrible tragedy here this afternoon, the Milano Police have informed me that we'll need to stay here at Waterman's a bit longer, until they've been able to take down all of our names and contact info. They're working just as fast as they can, and they expect that they'll be done with these initial interviews within the hour. In the meantime, please try to be patient and give these nice officers your kind cooperation."

The luncheon ladies were beginning to talk among themselves now. Some of them didn't look too happy about the wait. And she'd thought Roland Cho was cold. Where else did these people have to be right now, anyway?

"I know many of you have questions about possible refunds for the fashion show," Martha went on.

Seriously? Summer thought, repulsed. *That* was the burning piece of info people wanted after one of the models had been murdered backstage?

"But there's good news," Martha went on. "I wanted to let you all know as soon as possible, so you can change those busy engagement calendars right now, that our Christmas on the Catwalk show will go on as planned, at a new time and locale."

Loud murmurs of approval ran through the crowd. Several women actually clapped, Summer noticed, doubly annoyed. Why didn't they just cancel the whole stupid thing, out of respect for poor Angelica?

"Our show will be incorporated into the fabulous Silver Belles Holiday Fashion Show on Friday, over at the Majesty Golf and Tennis Club. Today's tickets will be honored over at Majesty for any of you who don't already have tickets to that event. Just give our hostess Nadine your name on the way out, and she'll make sure you're on the list."

"YES!" Gladys Rumway jumped up from her table

and executed an actual fist pump, before trying to slap high-fives with some ladies around her. Most of them just looked confused.

"Isn't that wonderful?" a woman in front of Summer said to her luncheon companion. "Those tickets have been sold out for months. Herb drove me over there on July Fourth weekend, as soon as they went on sale, and we were still too late."

"Well, the show is only two days away," the other woman said. "That doesn't leave us much shopping time. All the stores will probably be packed, too. Should we head over to The Waterfalls as soon as they let us leave here?"

Incredible, Summer thought.

"As you know," Martha went on from the front of the room, "all of these exciting events are part of Milano Fashion Week. We're thrilled that Roland Cho will also be one of the celebrity designers participating in Silver Belles, so none of us will miss out on his wonderful jewelry."

On cue, the miniature, spiky-haired designer burst through the curtain and appeared beside Martha, waving and bowing. Everyone applauded.

Summer tried hard not to celebrate when she saw that his velvet jacket sleeve still had the crush mark on it. Good.

He sure didn't seem that broken up over his priceless missing bracelet now, as he stood there in front of all those little old ladies—enthusiastic seniors—soaking up the love.

Now was the perfect time to make her exit, while everyone was focusing on Roland. Summer gave up on hugging the wall and breezed her way through the rest of the dining room to the French doors.

The hostess was on her phone, which she quickly tried to hide as Summer came up to the hostess stand. "Hi, Nadine. Can you please put Summer Sloan and Dorothy Westin on the list for the Silver Belles fashion show at Majesty?"

"Of course." Nadine paged her way through her reservations book to a blank page at the back. "You ladies heard that it's a charity event?" She gave Summer a fake pity smile as she uncapped her Waterman's pen. "Majesty has generously agreed to honor all of today's guests' tickets, as Martha announced. I must tell you, however, there is a highly suggested additional donation of one hundred seventy-five dollars per person for the Golfers Fund. Will that be a problem?"

Seriously? Summer thought. Did Nadine think she and Dorothy weren't good for it? True, she was a little short on cash again, thanks to the J.O.B. situation, but she could charge both tickets to her emergency credit card.

This was definitely an emergency. It wasn't like she was dying to go to another dumb fashion show, but someone already had. There was a murder to solve.

"No problem, Nadine," Summer said. "Sign us up."

FIVE

"SO WHAT DO you think we should say to Angelica's mom, exactly?" Summer asked, as she and Dorothy stepped into the elevator in the lobby at Hibiscus Glen.

"I guess we'll just have to play things by ear." Dorothy pushed the button for the top floor. "I'm sure the poor woman has already been given the terrible news, but we don't even know whether she's capable of understanding what happened. Either way, she may not want to speak with us right now."

"Well, we couldn't blame her for that," Summer said.

Dorothy nodded. "We just have to remember, the most important thing we can do is make sure Frankie stays safe."

Summer frowned up at the red numerals that lit up above their heads as they reached each floor. "I wonder why the top floor button says 'HG.' Isn't the whole place Hibiscus Glen?"

"No," Dorothy said. "This entire building is actually called Hibiscus Falls. Hibiscus Glen is the memory care unit. The rest of the floors have regular condos."

"Huh." Summer was still frowning. "I've never met anyone around the Pointe who lives over here. Do they get to use the pool and dining room and stuff in the main complex?"

"I'm really not sure," Dorothy admitted. "I do know they have a small dining room downstairs, for residents who can't cook for themselves, or prefer not to, and there's also a twenty-four-hour nurse on staff. I suppose you could call this building more of an assisted living facility."

"You mean, people live on the downstairs floors and then have to move upstairs later?" Summer asked.

"Not necessarily," Dorothy said. "It does seem to work out that way for some residents, though."

"Oh." Summer bit her lip, looking for all the world like Dorothy's daughter Maddie, when she was around the same age.

Mothers were not supposed to outlive their daughters. Not under normal circumstances, anyway. But sometimes Life had other ideas. Maddie had died too young; Angelica had also passed before her time. She and Frankie now shared a sad bond.

Dorothy pulled herself back to the present. These were not the types of thoughts that helped one focus on a murder investigation. "Assisted living isn't a bad thing, you know," she told Summer. "And neither is choosing to enter a memory care facility. People have to decide for themselves what is best for them and their families."

"I know," Summer said, with a sigh. Her eyes were on the numbers again. "But when I get old, I hope I'm just like you."

Old? She wasn't old, just old*er*. Good gracious. How and when had *that* happened? But her friend meant well.

"Thank you, dear." In spite of their somber mission, Dorothy felt greatly relieved when the HG button flashed and the elevator doors opened to Hibiscus Glen's brightly lit reception area. She really didn't want to dwell on the pros and cons of various senior living arrangements. Dorothy knew how lucky she was to be in good health, with sufficient funds—if she was very careful, of course—to live in a comfortable community like Hibiscus Pointe.

Many others were not as fortunate.

"Hello, ladies," the curly-blonde receptionist in the pink scrubs greeted them cheerfully as they approached the counter. "Are we visiting someone today?"

Summer looked at Dorothy.

"Yes, we are," Dorothy said, clearing her throat. The air-conditioning was much stronger here than it had been in the stuffy elevator. "I'm Dorothy Westin, and this is my good friend Summer. We're both residents here at Hibiscus Pointe. I live in the Gardens, you see, and…"

"I'm at the Towers," Summer put in, to speed things up.

"How nice." The receptionist, whose desk nameplate read "Valerie," beamed. "And who are you here to see?"

It was probably best to be straightforward, under the circumstances, Dorothy decided. "Well, we're hoping to speak with Frankie Downs, if she's available," she said.

Valerie's smile immediately faded. "Ohhhh," she said.

"I'm sorry, but Frankie isn't able to have visitors today," another blonde woman said, coming up beside Valerie. She was older, with red tortoiseshell glasses and "Lucinda Worth" printed on the Hibiscus Pointe staff ID clipped to her navy blazer breast pocket. "Is this something urgent?"

Dorothy hesitated. Should she let on that she and Summer knew about Angelica's death? They still had no idea what Frankie's level of understanding might be, as she was a patient—*resident*, she corrected herself quickly—here in the memory care unit, or how

Frankie was taking the news. "It's a condolence call," she said, finally.

"We were really sorry to hear about her daughter," Summer said. "We knew Angelica."

"Wasn't she just the sweetest lady?" Val said. "We didn't know her long, since Frankie just moved in a few weeks ago, but she was so concerned about her mom."

Lucinda was watching her and Summer carefully, Dorothy noticed. Sizing them up, it seemed. Well, it was doubtful the two of them would appear to pose much of a threat to Frankie's safety.

"Frankie has had a very tiring day, and she hasn't been told the news yet," Lucinda said. She lowered her voice. "We don't have the authorization to do that. Protocol, you know. But the appropriate person will be here soon."

Detective Caputo? Dorothy wondered. Oh dear. The detective might not be the first person she'd pick to deliver such heartbreaking news.

"Frankie has been in unusually high spirits today," Val said to Lucinda. "It might not hurt for these ladies to visit her for just a few minutes. Maybe she will recognize them." She turned back to Dorothy and Summer. "Do you know Frankie very well?"

"Oh, yeah," Summer said. "She's my godmother. I've known her all my life. She always used to give me candy when I visited her."

Dorothy tried not to roll her eyes. Summer loved to make up ill-advised details like that. The habit usually got them both into hot water.

"Oh, you're practically family, then." Val glanced at Lucinda, who shrugged and finally nodded. "Why don't you ladies come with me? I'll take you to Frankie. I think she might be in the activities room."

Summer grabbed two or three brightly colored lollipops from the faux-crystal candy dish on the counter and grinned at Dorothy behind Val's back as they dutifully followed the receptionist toward the double doors at the end of the hall.

On the other hand, sometimes Summer's little white fibs worked out just fine.

Two-nine-seven-eight. Two-nine-seven-eight, Summer repeated to herself, trying to memorize the numbers the receptionist pushed into the key pad on the wall beside the door to Hibiscus Glen.

Wait, that was her age—her real age—plus Dorothy's. Easy-sleazy. "Um, why do you have a code on the outside of the door?" she asked Val.

The blonde woman smiled as a click sounded and she pushed down on the bar to open the door. "For our residents' security, of course," she answered. "We also have a keypad on the inside of the door. Same code, but backward."

"You mean the residents have to remember it to get out?" Summer asked. Wasn't this a memory care place?

"Well…yes," Val said. "The first code is backward for the way out, and also to activate the elevator: eight-seven-nine-two. Just ask at the nurses' station if you forget, and they'll write it down for you."

"So all the residents are locked in here, then, pretty much?" Summer said. Well, that was suck-o. And probably illegal or something. Did they have any idea what they were signing up for when they moved into this place?

"Shh, dear," Dorothy said.

Val kept smiling, as she led them down the swirly-patterned hall. "We don't like to think of it as 'locked in,' exactly," she said. "It's really just another safeguard for our residents. Some of them might wander off and get lost. Or worse."

"Oh, right. Sorry." Well, that made sense, she guessed. She felt Dorothy shudder beside her, and she quickly shut up. Obviously, she had a lot to learn about this memory stuff, and she needed to be more sensitive. It was just the sort of stuff she'd never really thought about.

"Between us, we had a little incident with Frankie earlier," Val said. "Luckily, we were able to locate her before she got too far."

Summer traded glances with Dorothy.

The whole place smelled like lemons and bleach. The odor was so strong it was making her nose twitch and her eyes burn, a zillion times worse than the chlorine in a rec center pool. What if Dorothy ended up in a place like this someday? What if she herself did?

No way. That wasn't *ever* going to happen, to either of them. She hoped not, anyway.

Summer tried not to glance into any of the open rooms as she trailed Val and Dorothy down the hall. The residents had photos of themselves and their families outside of their rooms, probably to help them remember which one was theirs. Some of the doors had holiday cards and wreaths or glittery blue and silver stars and cardboard menorahs.

Well, that was nice. She stopped to look at an old black-and-white photo of a beautiful woman in a lace wedding dress. Beside her stood a handsome man in a white navy uniform. The couple was smiling.

They looked so happy. Could the woman remember her wedding day now?

"Excuse me, please. This is my room." A very elderly man, probably in his nineties, tapped Summer on the shoulder. He was carrying a little bowl of red and green carnations.

"Oh, sorry." She jumped away quickly, and the man stepped past her into the room. She couldn't help sneaking a peek, as he brought the flowers to a frail but smiling lady in a wheelchair by the window. "For you, my love," he said. "I nicked them from the dining room."

Tears filled Summer's eyes. How sweet. The couple in the photo outside the door was still together, here in Hibiscus Glen. There was even a homey-looking double bed with a cream-chenille bedspread against the wall, and a pair of men's socks on the floor.

"Summer?" Dorothy said, behind her. "We lost you. What on earth are you doing?"

"Nothing," she said, brushing a tear off her cheek before her friend could spot it. "Sorry."

"Don't cry, dear, I know you're upset about Angelica," Dorothy said, as they hurried to catch up to Val, who was waiting for them at the end of the hall.

"Mmhmm," Summer said. Dorothy had really good eyesight. Jeez, she never missed anything.

"But keeping Frankie safe and solving this awful murder will help us both feel better," Dorothy added, in a whisper.

"Right," Summer said. This was a new thing for her lately, the crying. She hated it. Before she'd moved to Milano, her life had been one long, no-tears formula.

She needed to get back to that zone ASAP. Focusing on just herself and her own problems was so much easier.

"You ladies will just love our activity room," Val said cheerfully, as they reached the last set of double doors. Hopefully it was the last one, anyway, Summer thought.

She tried to stay patient as the receptionist punched in another set of numbers on still another pin pad. They probably didn't have half this much security at the White House.

The doors opened to a huge space that was so bright Summer couldn't see anything at all for a second or two.

"My, how lovely," Dorothy said. "I love solariums."

"We call it our Florida room." Val practically clapped in delight. "The residents adore it and the sunlight is so good for them."

It *was* a cool space, Summer had to admit. Kind of like…well, a fish tank, with glass windows on three sides. In the corner, a fake white Christmas tree with white angel ornaments made a loud, annoying buzzing sound as it rotated on its stand. Someone needed to fix that.

"Which one is Frankie?" she asked.

Val looked confused.

"She hasn't seen her godmother for years," Dorothy said, quickly. "Isn't that right, Summer?"

Oops. "Oh, yeah," Summer said. "I think I was about six, maybe." That's how old Juliette-Margot was, so the age just popped into her head. She had a feeling that was also probably how old she'd been when she'd last seen her Grandma Sloan, whose condo she was living in now.

She didn't remember anything about her grandmother. Her dad and whatever gold digger bimbo he was married to at the time—or was it her mom, Harmony?—had brought her and Joy to Florida to visit once.

Was her grandma living at Hibiscus Pointe back then? This place had been built in the eighties or something, so…yeah, probably. She didn't remember much about it, except for the pool. It had seemed so much bigger when she was a kid.

And now here she was again in Florida, starting her whole life over. What would Grandma Sloan think of that? Had she been as nice as Dorothy? She hoped so.

Dorothy was kind of like a grandma. Except they were friends and detective partners. Maybe it was better not being related for real. In her experience, that caused way too many problems.

"There's Frankie now, poor dear," Val said, pointing toward a table of four seniors at a green felt-covered table across from the angel tree.

Luckily, two of the seniors at the table were men. That left a frail-looking woman snoring in a wheelchair with a purple afghan over her lap and another one who was dealing the cards. She looked like Angelica, sort of, except she was super tiny and her hair was blue.

Not the same almost-lavender shade of blue Summer had seen on some of the other older ladies around Hibiscus Pointe. More like the mom's on *The Simpsons*.

"Frankie looks just the same," Dorothy said, smiling at Val. "She hasn't changed a bit, has she, Summer?"

"Nope," Summer said. "She always was an amazing card dealer."

That had to be true, at least. The tiny woman in the magenta, stretch-velour pantsuit was flipping cards around the table like a Vegas blackjack pro. "Aha!

Looks like you're all in, Stanley," she said, turning up
one of the guy's cards as he smiled over her shoulder
at the wobbly Christmas tree. "You, too, Myrtle," she
added to the sleeping woman on her right.

"What about me?" the second man asked, sounding
a little anxious. "Am I in?"

"Bet on it," Frankie said, taking a queen of hearts
from the turned up cards in front of him. "And Sweet
Lady Luck, would you take a lookee at this." She
grabbed another card, an ace of hearts, from Stanley's
pile and added them both to the ten, jack and king of
hearts in front of her. "Royal straight flush. I win again.
Hard to believe, huh?"

"That's nice." The second man fiddled with a button on his red-and-green argyle cardigan as Frankie
swept her companions' small, teetering stacks of nickels and dimes into a canvas bag attached to the walker
beside her chair.

Jeez. Summer knew a few things about Texas Hold
'em from hanging around those high roller rooms in
Vegas. One of her jerk exes—a long story—got banned
for life for counting cards. But even if she'd known zero
about poker, it was mucho obvious Angelica's mom was
a total cheater.

"Frankie, honey, what are you doing?" Val said, hus-
tling toward the table.

Instantly, the teensy, blue-haired woman tried to grab
back all the cards. "Bingo!" she called loudly.

Summer tried her best not to burst out laughing,
as Val started scooping the coins from Frankie's basket and dumping them back onto the table. "That's my
money," Frankie said, throwing her arms over as much
of her winnings as she could.

"No, Frankie, you can't take everyone's dimes," Val said. "Game time is just for fun. You do want to have fun with all your nice friends here, don't you?"

"Fun? Ha!" Frankie looked disgusted. "You should serve drinks in this place. Now *that* would be fun." She frowned at Val. "I won that money fair and square. Who the heck are you, anyway?"

"I'm Val. You remember me, don't you? Of course you do."

"Oh dear," Dorothy said to Summer in a low voice. "I'm afraid we won't get much information about Angelica from her mother."

"I don't know about that," Summer said. "She definitely knows her poker."

"I'm just glad she's in a nice, safe place like Hibiscus Glen," Dorothy said.

This place was safe, all right. Maybe a little *too* safe.

The receptionist knelt down beside Frankie's chair. "I'm Val," she repeated. "I come by and say hi to you every day, remember? And guess what?" She pointed over her shoulder at Summer and Dorothy. "You have some nice visitors."

Frankie immediately stiffened and her eyes darted in their direction. "What? I don't want visitors. Never seen those two before in my life."

Dorothy walked over and extended her hand. "Hello, Frankie," she said smoothly. "I'm Dorothy Westin from Hibiscus Gardens, and I knew—" she glanced at Val "—I mean, I *know* your daughter Angelica."

"Angelica?" Frankie's thick, dark-penciled eyebrows shot up.

Well, that sure got her attention, Summer told herself. Were those brows black or navy?

LISA Q. MATHEWS   69

"And this is Summer," Dorothy added, motioning to her.

Summer dutifully came up next to Dorothy and gave Frankie the same big smile she usually reserved for Helen Murphy, the Hibiscus Pointe Residents Board president. "Hi, I'm your goddaughter," she said. "Remember me?"

"Hmm," Frankie said, her eyes narrowing. "I might."

Yikes. Why was Angelica's mom staring at her in that weird way? It was almost like she could see through her or something.

"I can't be sure. Let me get a closer look at you." The woman reached out and grabbed Summer's wrist, pulling her all the way down to eye level.

Ouch.

"Oh, yeah. Sweet little Summer. I remember you *real* well." Frankie leaned in even closer, and dropped her voice to a raspy whisper. "You need to get me out of here, honey. Right. Now."

SIX

"WELL, HELLO THERE, Dot! Fancy meeting you here."

Startled, Dorothy turned away from the poker table to find her good friend Ernie Conlon and his wife, Grace, directly behind her.

Oh, no. This was terrible. What were the Conlons doing at Hibiscus Glen? Grace had been diagnosed with Alzheimer's some time ago, but the two of them still lived together in their condo at Hibiscus Gardens. Had Grace—or both of them—had to move here to the memory care unit?

Surely Ernie would have told her. They saw each other practically every day.

"I could say the same about you," she answered.

"We're here for the card game," Ernie said. "Grace loves coming here on Wednesday afternoons. You know, just for a break in the old routine at home."

Thank goodness. "Of course, how nice." Dorothy smiled at Grace, hoping the relief didn't show on her face. Ernie's wife, serene and well-coiffed as always, smiled back.

Dorothy knew some of the residents at Hibiscus Pointe were under the impression that she and Ernie were involved in some kind of romantic entanglement, which was completely ridiculous. Ernie was married, after all, and neither of them would ever do anything that might be hurtful to Grace, who was a lovely person. And Ernie was devoted to her.

Nevertheless, Dorothy couldn't help feeling glad she was still dressed in her nice outfit from the Waterman's fashion show. Not that Ernie cared a whit about fashion, of course. As usual he was wearing his Hibiscus Pointe polo and checkered golf pants—the colors of choice today were red, black and yellow—and Grace had a festive candy-cane-striped bow tied to her wheelchair.

"Mind if we join you, everyone?" Ernie rolled Grace's chair up to the table next to Frankie and Summer. "What's our poison today, Frankie? You pick."

"Texas Hold 'Em." Frankie's eyes slid to Val. "I mean, *bingo*."

Why was Angelica's mother holding on to Summer's wrist like that? Dorothy wondered. Good heavens. Her friend seemed to be trying to tell her something, frowning and jerking her head toward Frankie.

Val's beeper went off, and the receptionist glanced down at her waist. "Oh, darn, that's Lucinda again," she said. "I have to go, everyone. Nice to meet you, Dorothy and Summer. Do stop at the front desk and say goodbye when you're done with your visit."

"Thank you," Dorothy said. Was it possible Detective Caputo had arrived to talk to Frankie and the staff? Should she follow Val to find out, or would that be too obvious?

Ernie settled in at the table on the other side of Angelica's mother. "Okay, Frankie, deal 'em out," he said, rubbing his hands eagerly.

Dorothy tried not to smile. Really, was this Wednesday afternoon poker game outing for Grace, or Ernie? The man was as much of a card shark as Frankie.

Fortunately, Angelica's mother had to let go of Summer's wrist to deal the cards. Quite expertly, too, Dorothy noted, as Frankie snapped the cards into a perfect bridge and waterfall before shooting them around to each player at the table.

Summer moved to a safer distance, rubbing her wrist.

"Ten dollar ante," Frankie said to Ernie. "You, too, Goddaughter," she added to Summer.

"Um, I don't think I have any cash on me," Summer said.

That was probably true, Dorothy thought. Summer never seemed to carry any form of payment other than her father's no-limit credit card.

"No problem, Summer my girl, I'll spot you," Ernie said. "Come on, we need more players."

Summer glanced her way, and Dorothy gave her an encouraging nod. Maybe a nice, friendly card game would keep Frankie busy while she followed Val back to meet the detective. And Summer would be there to make sure Angelica's mother stayed safe.

Hopefully she knew how to play poker. Dorothy had never even cared for bridge, which was highly popular with so many of the ladies at Hibiscus Pointe. She suspected Frankie Downs had little use for the game either.

The woman had to have some of her faculties intact, at least, with her considerable card dealing prowess and enthusiasm for poker. Hopefully later she would be able to give them information about her daughter, no matter how trivial the details. It was possible Frankie might even reveal whether someone had threatened the two of them—and identify that person.

Dorothy excused herself and hurried back toward the reception area. Luckily, she caught up to Val in time to slide through the doors behind her, as she'd neglected to note the numbers for the pin pad code.

"Mrs. Westin, do you need something?" Val asked, as they walked briskly down the hall together. Dorothy was glad she'd worn her best AeroLite shoes.

"Oh, no, thanks," Dorothy said. "I thought perhaps I dropped my reading glasses out by the desk. Without them, all those cards are a blur."

"I hear you," Val said, pointing to her own glasses perched on top of her head. "That Frankie has such an obsession with cards, doesn't she? Poker is too complicated for many of the other residents to follow, I'm afraid. I've tried to get her interested in bingo instead, but she just won't bite—not even if we play for nickels."

"Frankie seems very sharp," Dorothy said, still trying to keep pace with the receptionist.

"Well, sometimes she is," Val said. "And sometimes she's way out there. She certainly is very…determined." The blonde woman's face turned a darker pink. "I really shouldn't discuss resident health issues."

"Heavens no, of course not," Dorothy said. "So sorry. I'm sure Detective Caputo is on her way by now to speak to her about her daughter. If I could be of any assistance in telling Frankie the terrible news, I'd be most happy to join them. Summer and I found Angelica, in fact, so maybe…"

Val stopped short in the hallway, and stared at her with an expression of horror.

Oh dear. It had been a huge mistake to bring up her and Summer's involvement, Dorothy realized. She had just shown her hand more fully than the unwitting members of Frankie's poker club.

To her surprise—and relief—Val's eyes filled with

tears. "You poor thing, Mrs. Westin, finding Angelica," she said. "I never get used to witnessing the end of life myself, but it's part of my job, unfortunately."

Mine, too, Dorothy thought, but she wasn't about to say so. Instead, she nodded sympathetically. Probably the less she said right now, the better.

Val checked both ways down the hall and leaned closer to Dorothy. "It's not Detective Caputo we're waiting for to break the news to Frankie," she said. "It's Violet. You must know her—Frankie's younger daughter, the real estate agent? Sort of an odd duck, if you ask me. I've only met her once, and I don't think the two of them are that close."

"Ah," Dorothy said. Well, that was interesting. *How close were Violet and her sister Angelica?* she wondered. Was it possible there had been some issues between them, too?

"She's driving down from Vero Beach, so she should be here in another hour or so." The receptionist blushed even pinker this time and covered her mouth with her hand. "Sorry, I shouldn't have said that about Violet being a little...different. I'm sure you are much better acquainted with her than I am, since you're a close family friend."

"Absolutely," Dorothy said. Or, at least, she and Summer would plan to make Violet's acquaintance very soon.

SUMMER WAS HAVING a hard time concentrating on the Hibiscus Glen poker game. For one thing, Frankie wasn't easy to keep up with. Plus, she and Ernie kept arguing over the rules.

"Hey, you forgot to put down the burn card," Ernie said to Frankie.

"I did not," Frankie said, dropping another stack of

coins into her walker bag. "We don't need to have one, anyway."

"Ernie's right, Frankie," Summer put in. "The dealer always puts a burn card face down before the flop." She was careful not to add, *That way, we can be sure you aren't trying to cheat.* It might not be such a hot idea to tick her fake godmother off right now.

What had Frankie meant about busting her out of this place? Val had said she'd tried to escape earlier today. Did Angelica's mom just hate it here or did she know she was in danger? Or was she just crazy? And why the heck had she chosen her as a possible accomplice, anyway?

But the biggest question was, should she help her? She really needed to talk to Dorothy, but she had taken off like a shot and left her with Angelica's card shark mom.

Dorothy had to have had a good reason, though. Had Detective Caputo shown up already? If so, she was okay with just staying here and playing poker.

Hopefully Shane Donovan would come back from wherever he was soon to take over the case.

Or at least call her.

"So sorry I had to step away, everyone," Dorothy said, returning to the table. Summer thought she looked a little out of breath. "Have I missed anything?"

"Not much," Ernie said, sounding grumpy. "Frankie's been making things up."

Frankie shrugged as he gave Dorothy his chair and went to get another one from the next table. "Dealer's rules."

"Dorothy, can I talk to you alone for just a second?" Summer asked. "I need to…"

"Mrs. Westin!"

Great, Summer told herself as Val the receptionist waved from the doorway and hurried toward them.
What did *she* want? She and Dorothy were never going
to get anywhere on the investigation, at this rate.

"I found your reading glasses!" Val sounded super
pleased with herself as she pulled a beaded chain holding a pair of rhinestone glasses from the pocket of her
scrubs.

Ugh. Dorothy would never wear anything as unflat-
tering as those. She wouldn't let her.

"Thank you, Val," Dorothy said, as the receptionist came up next to her and triumphantly placed the
glasses on the green felt table. "But I'm afraid those
aren't mine." Why did Dorothy look so guilty?

"Oh." Val let out her breath like a deflated pink balloon.

"Those are *my* glasses," Frankie said, frowning.

Doubtful, Summer thought. She was wearing another, equally ugly pair on top of her head right now.

Maybe Angelica wasn't worried about Frankie because her mom was in some kind of danger, Summer
told herself. It could have been because Frankie had no
clue what she was doing anymore, and was a danger to
herself. The fact that Angelica ended up being killed
could have just been some horrible coincidence.

"So how's the big game going, everybody?" Val
asked in a perky voice, scooping up the glasses again.
Frankie didn't seem to notice.

"It's my turn to deal," Ernie said. "Come on, fork
over the deck, Frankie. Pretty please?"

Frankie held the cards against her chest. "Nope."

Summer looked at Dorothy. Had she come to the
same conclusion about Angelica's mom? It was hard

to tell. Dorothy's face had zero expression as Frankie continued to bicker with Ernie.

"Oh, no, this isn't good," she heard Val say in a low voice to Dorothy. "We don't want her in a mood. Especially right before she hears...the news. Violet is on her way."

Frankie suddenly stopped arguing and sat straight up in her chair. "News? What news? And what do you mean, Violet's coming? She'd never show up here unless it was something bad."

Now Dorothy's face had plenty of expression—mostly horror, Summer decided—but just for a nanosecond. "There, there, Frankie, dear," she said, patting the woman's arm. "Your daughter will be here soon, and you two can talk. Would you like me to get you a nice cup of water from the cooler?"

Frankie threw the cards on the floor. "I don't want to talk to Violet. I don't want her anywhere near me. And somebody better spill the beans quick on whatever it is you're all hiding."

"I'm not hiding anything except my winning hand here," Ernie said. "Grace isn't, either. Nobody is. Right, Dot?"

Dorothy looked guilty again. Summer knew she probably did, too. But the worst of them had to be Val. The Pink Lady stood behind Dorothy's chair, jittering like a cocktail shaker. How could she have been so stupid, blabbing like that?

"I'd better go get Lucinda," Val said.

"No one's going anywhere," Frankie said. "Not until I get an answer."

Summer saw Angelica's mom slide her walker a tiny

bit closer with her foot, under the table. Was she going to try to make another break for it?

"Oh, this is terrible." Val was literally wringing her hands now as she looked at Dorothy for help. "I'm going to get fired. We have to tell her now."

"Darned straight you do," Frankie said. "Don't even bother trying to bluff. I always know when people are lying."

So do I, Summer thought. *Pretty much always, anyway.* And she was a zillion percent sure now that Frankie didn't have a memory problem. She was putting on some kind of weird act.

The fake antique grandfather's clock in the far corner chimed four o'clock and Val abruptly quit sniveling. "My gracious, it's medication time for Mrs. Edelman. She likes me to grind the pills into applesauce for her, so I'd better go." She backed away from the table, giving them all a wobbly smile. "Why don't you ladies chat with Frankie about…the situation," she added to Summer and Dorothy. "Since you're family friends and all."

The receptionist scurried toward the door like a crazed pink Easter bunny, almost tripping into the wall as she lunged for the keypad.

"I'm waiting." Frankie tapped the green felt table, as the revolving Christmas tree suddenly groaned and came to a creaky stop.

Uh oh. Summer didn't want to look at Dorothy. This was not going to end well.

Her friend cleared her throat. "Frankie, there's been an accident," she said. "We were waiting to tell you until Violet could be here with you. I still think that's a much better idea…"

Frankie turned to Summer. "You're my goddaughter, aren't you? Out with it." Her chin pointed up in a definite challenge, but Summer could tell the woman was scared. Really scared.

She took an extra deep breath. "Why don't we go somewhere else where we can sit down?"

"We are sitting down," Frankie pointed out, but her voice sounded a little less sharp now.

"Dot, what is going on?" Summer heard Ernie say, in a low voice. "What accident?" Dorothy shook her head to discourage him.

Frankie was right. She deserved to know. "Come on, Godmother," Summer said, helping Angelica's mom out of her chair. "Here's your walker. If you go back to your room with me—" she fumbled in her bag "—I'll give you some lollipops. I brought them just for you."

No need to mention she'd picked them up at the reception desk. But she doubted a lame bribe would work, anyway.

Frankie took the lollipops Summer held out to her and dumped them in her canvas walker bag on top of all the dimes and nickels. "Okay, let's go."

"I'll come with you two," Dorothy offered quickly.

"No need," Frankie said, as she shuffled toward a hallway off the activities room, with Summer beside her. "My goddaughter here always takes good care of me."

I do? Summer thought. Well, that was nice of her to say. But how was she going to break the terrible news to her about Angelica? She reached to help guide the tiny woman, but Frankie slapped her hand away and started down the hall so quickly that Summer had to hustle to catch up with her.

"Hey, wait, put that thing down," she said, as Frankie lifted the walker above her head and took a sharp right turn down still another long, carpeted hallway. "You might get hurt."

Frankie snorted, and Summer gave up. Fine. She'd just have to catch her if she fell.

It seemed like a long way to Frankie's room. Most of the residents had their doors open, probably so the staff could keep a better eye on them. One lady in a wheelchair with a holiday bow in her hair gave Summer a cheerful wave, and she waved back.

Wait a minute. They'd taken a few turns, and they were almost at the end of the last hall now. "Frankie, where are we going?" she asked. "We must have passed your room. We need to talk, remember? It's really important."

"I don't want to hear any news," Frankie said. "We're going someplace else first. Here we are." She stopped in front of a large red door. "Open it, please."

"That's an emergency exit," Summer said. "There's an alarm and everything."

"Big deal. I've already done it once today, and you can help me move a lot faster. By the time anyone shows up we'll be miles ahead of them." Frankie shook her walker. "You're busting me out of here. Then maybe I'll listen to whatever it is you're so eager to tell me."

This was nuts. Frankie already knew the news had something to do with Angelica—and that it probably wasn't good. Didn't she care? Or did she just not want to face it?

Maybe, if Angelica put her mom in here to keep her safe from a killer who was after both of them, Frankie already suspected the worst. If the murderer knew she was here in Hibiscus Glen, he or she would probably come here next. And neither the staff nor the cops would believe a supposedly crazy woman's story that someone was out to get her. Was that why Frankie was so anxious to escape?

This might not be the world's most fabulous place to hide, but Angelica's mom would probably be safer here than running around out in Milano somewhere.

"Open the door," Frankie demanded. "When they look back, you'll be on the security cameras letting me out."

"Open it yourself," Summer said, crossing her arms.

"I have a gun."

Now Frankie was the one who was bluffing. Summer hoped so, anyway, as she eyed the bulging bag on her walker. This was a gamble she did not want to take. But she didn't have much choice.

She lunged past the tiny woman to cut her off from the emergency exit. Unfortunately, she hit the bar by mistake, and she muttered under her breath as the alarm began to sound through the hallway.

A heavily muscled forearm reached over her shoulder and pulled the door shut. "Going somewhere?" a deep voice said.

SEVEN

"I WASN'T HELPING her escape or anything," Summer told Detective Donovan, as the door alarm in the memory unit finally quit blaring. "I swear, this isn't how it looks."

"It never is with you, is it?" The detective sighed, and ran a tired hand through his dark brush cut. Then he turned to Frankie, who looked as annoyed as Dorothy's cat, Mr. Bitey, when she locked him in his cat crate to take him to the vet. "I was very sorry to hear about your daughter, Mrs. Downs. My condolences."

"Condolences?" Frankie's whole face dropped. "What do you mean? Angelica's really...*dead?*"

Oh, nooo. Summer muttered under her breath again. This was no way for the poor woman to find out her daughter had been murdered. "Dorothy and I were going to tell you before but..." she began, then stopped. What was the point? She'd just sound lame again.

Someone should have told her. Waiting for her other daughter to show up had been a stupid idea.

"I'm afraid so." Detective Donovan used his professional voice but she saw the flash of sympathy in his intense blue eyes. "I apologize, ma'am, for giving you bad news this way. I thought you knew."

"I'm really sorry, too, Frankie," Summer said, as Angelica's mom slumped against her with a muffled wail.

She patted the full-out sobbing woman on the shoulder and looked over at the detective for help.

He just stood there looking uncomfortable. "We've got to get her to her room," she told him, above Frankie's head. "She needs to lie down."

"I don't want to lie down. I want to know what happened. Where is Angelica? I want to see her."

Detective Donovan cleared his throat. "I'm not sure that's possible right now."

"You're wrong about my Angie," Frankie said, stepping away from Summer. "I'm getting my purse with my money and my cigarettes and then you two are taking me out of here, right past that simpy Val's nose. We're going to clear up this big misunderstanding real soon."

At least she wasn't crying anymore. Now she just looked ticked off. Summer wasn't sure whether that was better or worse. Then Frankie whirled around and zoomed back down the hall like she was off to the races at Santa Ana. Summer immediately jogged after her.

"Come to think of it, going back to her room may not be such a good idea," Detective Donovan muttered, striding along behind Summer.

"Too late," she said, as the three of them reached the open door of Room 308. Obviously, he was clueless about old people. Or maybe all people, come to think of it. Especially almost-girlfriends, who might appreciate a text or call or check-in every once in a while.

But that wasn't important anymore. All she cared about right now was the case. And maybe-crazy Frankie.

She glanced back over her shoulder and stopped for a second when she spotted the old black-and-white photo hanging outside the door. It showed a tiny, dark-haired woman in a polka-dot blouse with two pigtailed little girls. It might have been taken in the fifties or some-thing, judging by the retro swoop of her hairstyle, the heavily penciled brows and dark lipstick.

There was another photo hanging next to it, but that one was colorized. It showed a tall woman with flam-ing red hair wearing a navy blue coat and holding a folded American flag. She was surrounded by a bunch of dark-haired police officers in dress uniform who looked super solemn.

A funeral, obviously, with an honor guard. Or maybe they were family members, because they all looked alike. The woman in the middle wasn't Frankie Downs, but all of those guys with brush cuts seemed weirdly familiar.

Uh oh. No way. Summer peered closer at the photo behind the glass as Frankie and the detective headed into the room. Was that family…?

"What, the card game's over already?" a husky woman's voice said from inside the room.

Yep, she'd been right. Frankie's roomie was Peggy Donovan, the detective's piece-of-work grandma. What was *she* doing here?

Summer was pretty sure Peggy lived near Dorothy over at Hibiscus Gardens. And the woman's memory, unfortunately for Summer, was perfectly fine. Shane's grandma wasn't a big fan of hers, for no reason at all.

Except maybe that she'd sort of dated her darling grandson.

And maybe also that she'd interrupted a stupid tennis tournament by mistake and wrecked Peggy's chances of winning the Ladies Wheelchair trophy.

But probably mostly that she wasn't sweet, perfect Jennifer Margolis, the Hibiscus Pointe resident services

manager. Peggy already had her picked out to make
Shane an amazing, goody-two-shoes wife.

"Can't you go back and play another couple of
hands?" Peggy was saying to Frankie, as Summer
squeezed into the room behind the detective. She tried
to make herself as invisible as possible.

"I was trying to visit with Shane Junior here," Peggy
went on, "before he up and ran out on me without a
shred of explanation."

Summer heard the detective give a very tiny sigh.
"Nana, please."

"There's no privacy in this heck-hole whatsoever,"
Peggy added. "It's worse than prison."

"No, it's not," Frankie muttered, heading over to the
nightstand next to the empty bed and yanking open the
bottom drawer. "But don't worry, I'll be out of your
carrot-juice hair in a jiffy, if I can ever find my purse."

"What?" For some reason, Peggy didn't sound happy
that her roommate was planning to take off. "Where are
you going? You can't just leave, you know."

Well, Shane's grandma definitely wasn't going anywhere. The woman's wheelchair, her usual mode of
transport, was folded up against the wall and her left
foot was encased in a ginormous black splint.

"Nana," Detective Donovan said. "We have a situation here. And no one is going anywhere." He turned
to Summer. "Except you, Ms. Smythe-Sloan. I'll take
things from here, thanks."

Summer's face burned. "I'm trying to help." He was
treating her like some stranger, not someone who'd
already helped him solve two murder cases. And he
wasn't hot enough to get away with it.

Okay, so maybe he was. But she wasn't going to let

that little fact keep her from finding Angelica's killer. Plus, she and Dorothy had to make sure Frankie, loony or not, stayed safe.

"Now, hold on just a New York minute," Peggy said to her grandson, as Angelica's mom kept moving around the tiny room, opening more drawers and slamming them shut. "You're on vacation, remember? You don't need to be the big hero down at the PD for once. You need to be here taking care of *me*." She pointed to her ugly black boot. "I'm completely helpless."

Talk about a play for attention, Summer thought. She would never stoop to acting like that. Unless it was for a case, of course.

"He thinks my daughter is dead," Frankie said, peering under her pillow. "But she isn't."

That shut Shane's grandma up fast. For about two seconds. "The nice dark-haired lady who brought you in here or the blonde one?"

"The nice one." Frankie was feeling around the lumps in the diamond-print bedspread now.

"That's not good, if my grandson says she's dead," Peggy said. "He never lies. So what happened, Shane?" She twisted back toward Detective Donovan too fast and jerked her ankle. "Ouch. Out with it, Junior."

"It's not officially my case and I'm not at liberty to share any details right now," he said. "With *anyone*." He glanced over his shoulder at Summer.

"Pfft." Peggy gave a dismissive wave.

Summer silently seconded that. "Okay," she told everyone. "I'm, um, leaving now."

None of them seemed to care or even hear her. Peggy was peppering her grandson, whose lips were clamped in a thin line, with questions like bullets as Frankie triumphantly pulled a tiny black drawstring handbag from an empty plastic vaporizer. "Got it!" she announced.

Jeez. Everyone in this entire room—except her, of course—was bat crazy. Summer started to back her way slowly out the door.

There was nothing she could accomplish here right now. Frankie was safe with Detective Donovan and she needed to find Dorothy so they could follow some other leads.

Of course she felt totally sorry for Angelica's mom, who was about to find out for real that her daughter was dead. But now definitely wasn't the right time to question Frankie. They'd never get anywhere, anyway, with Peggy and her precious grandma's boy around.

Plus, she and Dorothy needed to find Zoe Z, who'd been lurking around backstage at Waterman's right before Angelica was killed. That girl had some explaining to do, especially since Esmé was probably in jail by now because of her.

"Bye, Goddaughter!" Frankie called to Summer, cheerfully, as she stuffed the little black bag into her bra. "See you later."

Much later, hopefully. Summer forced a smile before she turned and fled down the swirly Hibiscus Glen carpet.

DOROTHY HOPED IT hadn't been too terribly rude of her to leave Ernie and Grace alone at the card table with the non-players, all of them dozing. But Summer had disappeared with Frankie for what seemed like quite a long time, and Violet had to be speaking with the staff by now.

A food service aide was struggling to balance a tray

load of tall drinks in foam cups as she pushed the buttons on the keypad lock outside the reception area.

Perfect timing. "Here, let me hold those drinks for you," Dorothy told her, reaching for the tray.

"Oh, thanks so much," the aide said. "I need to bring them to the family conference room, stat."

"Happy to help." Dorothy slid into the reception area behind the aide and headed straight to the desk. A glance into the glass-walled meeting room to her left told her that Angelica's sister had indeed arrived.

The petite woman with the tight helmet of blonde hair, voluminous pieces of gold jewelry and crisp navy suit had to be Violet. She was speaking and gesturing across the conference table in a highly animated fashion to a nervous-looking Lucinda.

"Mrs. Westin?" The receptionist's voice was practically a whisper as she slid open the plastic divider at the reception desk. "I don't think you want to go in there right now."

"I wouldn't dream of it," Dorothy said. "What seems to be the trouble, if I may ask?"

Val beckoned her closer. "Violet wants to take Frankie back to Vero Beach with her tonight," she said, in a confidential tone. "But Lucinda thinks that's too soon, under the circumstances."

"Of course," Dorothy murmured.

"Besides, only Angelica was authorized to sign their mom out, and we'll need to make sure all the paperwork is in order," Val went on. "The Hibiscus Glen physician on call has to give his okay, too, and his answering service said he hasn't returned their page yet."

"Ah," Dorothy said. No doubt he was still out on the

golf course, with half the other doctors in Milano. "Will Violet talk with her mother soon?"

"I hope so," Val said. "We just don't know how Frankie may react. She can be a little...volatile sometimes." She nodded toward the conference room. "Like someone else in there."

Oh dear. Violet seemed more angry with Lucinda than upset about her sister's untimely death. Right now she was making little stabbing motions in the air with her long red fingernails.

The Downses certainly were an interesting family, Dorothy thought. Trying to work with Frankie and Violet for the case might be trickier than they had anticipated. "Summer and I thought it might be best to continue our visit with Frankie later, under the circumstances."

"Do you want me to run in and let Violet know you're here?" Val asked.

"Oh, no," Dorothy said, quickly. "Please don't bother her right now. You don't happen to know where she's staying in Milano, do you?"

Val leaned through the plastic divider. "Well, she wanted to take Frankie straight home to Vero Beach, like I said. Lucinda recommended one of the Hibiscus Pointe guest condos, but Violet said if she had to stay, it'd be at the Milano Grand."

"Ah," Dorothy said. The Florida real estate market had to be very profitable right now, for her to afford such a luxurious hotel. Why wouldn't Violet simply use her sister's home in town, wherever that might be?

Perhaps, if she and Angelica were estranged, Violet didn't have a key. Or possibly it would be too upsetting for her to stay there, now that Angelica was gone.

Judging by the way Violet was clearly arguing and gesturing at poor Lucinda, Dorothy guessed the former was the more likely scenario.

After thanking Val and promising she'd be back soon, Dorothy quickly headed toward the elevators and punched in the last exit code posted above the buttons.

She couldn't wait to get out of Hibiscus Glen. No wonder Frankie wanted to leave. Sometimes she forgot how truly lucky she was. Thank goodness she had her health, and her memory. *Not to mention my life*, she added silently, thinking of Angelica again.

Once she was safely outside in the balmy, Floridian-winter air, Dorothy settled herself on the visitors' bench to the left of the sliding entrance doors.

"Oh my gosh, I am sooo glad to be out of there." Summer dropped onto the bench beside her and blew out a breath that ruffled her sunny-blonde side bangs. "Poor Frankie."

"And where is she right now, exactly?" Dorothy asked. "How did she take the news about Angelica, once you explained everything to her?"

"Well…" Summer hesitated. "I didn't really get a chance to say a whole lot."

Dorothy listened patiently as she launched into a long story that included Detective Donovan and his grandmother Peggy, plus Frankie searching for her purse. "So I guess Detective Donovan is pretty much handling things," Summer finished. "I mean, it's Detective Caputo's case, but he's the one who's watching Frankie right this second."

"Well, the important thing is, she's safe," Dorothy said. "I didn't have much luck on my end, either. I just hope her daughter isn't going to take her back to Vero

Beach before we get a chance to talk to her." She told
Summer about Violet's arrival, and the real estate agent's
eagerness to remove Frankie from Hibiscus Glen. "Did
you run into Violet on your way out, by any chance?"

"Nope." Summer said. "Sorry. I guess I was moving pretty fast. But it sounds as if maybe that was a
good thing."

"Mmm." Dorothy took a lace-edged hankie from her
purse and dotted her forehead. The humidity was getting
to her, after the stiff air-conditioning inside the building.

"You look kind of tired, Dorothy," Summer said.
"Why don't you go back to the condo and take a nap?
I'll catch up with Esmé, wherever she is—hopefully not
downtown at the station—and figure out how to find
Zoe Z. That girl can't hide anywhere for long."

"All right." Dorothy agreed a bit more quickly than
she'd intended. It had been a long day so far, and her
peach cardigan felt uncomfortably clammy. "We can
meet up later this evening for a case strategy session.
I told Ernie I'd meet him for dinner, but I might just
order in tonight."

And maybe have a little conversation with Angelica's
sister, she added silently. Which might be a bit easier,
she had to admit, without Summer's help.

Even though Dorothy hadn't met Violet yet, something about that woman's attitude wasn't sitting well
with her.

EIGHT

SUMMER PULLED HER orange MINI to a screeching stop outside a pink sandstone, multi-level building a few blocks from the beach. The sign on the decrepit lawn—if you could call the sandy lot with the brown grass and the beer bottles a lawn—said "The Milano Arms."

What a perfectly awesome time for her phone to disappear again.

This was the way detectives had to operate before cell phones, she reminded herself, as she jumped out of the car and immediately had to kick a plastic bag with a big smiley face on it off of her foot. Well, fine. But it sucked rotten eggs.

If she wasn't such a nice person, and a really good friend, she might have said the same thing about Esmé's apartment building.

If it was, in fact, where she lived. The whole way over from Hibiscus Pointe, Summer had tried to remember what Esmé had told her about the place. It was pink. Not too far from the beach. Really old and a total dump.

Well, this place definitely qualified.

"What do you want?" a scruffy older man asked from a retro striped lawn chair on the slab of concrete that was supposed to be the porch.

Gross. With all that chest hair and saggy skin, he could at least have put on a tank top.

"I'm looking for a friend," Summer answered, staring over his head at the brightly colored bathing suits and beach towels strung across the balcony. At least that way she didn't have to look at him. "Esmé?"

"No one here with any uppity name like that," the man said, with a chomp of his toothpick. "But I've got a beer over here by me with *your* name on it. Whatever it is, baby." He patted the white foam cooler beside him with a toothless grin.

"Shut your trap, Larry. You're a sleazy weasel." Esmé stuck her head out from a window three floors up and pointed toward a crooked set of crumbling concrete stairs at the side of the building. "Use those," she called to Summer.

Summer bounded up the steps two at a time, mainly to decrease the odds of stepping on a broken one and breaking her neck.

Esmé met her at the top. "I see you've met my charming landlord."

"Uh, yeah." Summer followed her friend down the breezeway to the half-open door of her apartment. "How'd you end up living here, anyway?"

She hadn't even known they had places like this in Milano. It made some parts of Hollywood look good.

"Don't ask." Esmé closed the door behind them and bolted the chain. "At least it's cheap. Want a drink or something? I was about to start happy hour here."

"Sure, what have you got?" Summer looked around at the tiny, almost-empty kitchen. Actually, it was more like a counter with a hot plate. No wonder.

Esmé opened the fridge, which also had practically nothing in it. It looked a lot like hers. "PBR," she said. "And a couple of hard flavored lemonades. Raspberry or grape fizz?"

"Raspberry," Summer said. Jeez. For a professional bartender, Esmé didn't have much of a drinks selection. She probably didn't like bringing her work home. Or, more likely, her friend was as broke as she was.

Design student interns didn't get paid any more than volunteer lifeguards.

"So what happened back at Waterman's after Dorothy and I left?" she asked, as her friend expertly popped the top off a bottle on the scratched counter and handed it to her. "I came by to check on you, and make sure you weren't in jail. That was going to be my next stop."

"Nope," Esmé said, hopping onto the stool beside her. "It was close, though. Monique tried her best, but that head cop woman let me go. For now, anyway."

"What is Monique's problem?" Summer said. "She was really mean to Angelica and she has it in for you, too."

"She's like that with everyone, trust me," Esmé said. "But I am totally fired from fashion week events now. So I'll probably flunk my design class. I was supposed to work the Majesty show on Friday night."

And now Dorothy and I are, Summer thought. Unless they got the case solved before that, of course. She could live without attending another fashion show for a while.

Esmé took a long swig from her bottle and made a face. "Ugh," she said, getting up to dump the fizzing purple liquid down the already-stained sink. "How do people stand this stuff?"

"How come you bought it, if you don't like it?" Summer asked.

"I didn't," Esmé said. "It's Enrique's. He's working right now."

"You live with a guy?" Summer looked around the

studio apartment. There was a futon with an old TV in front of it and a tiny area curtained off in the corner. That was pretty much it. "I didn't even know you were seeing anyone."

"I'm not, unfortunately," Esmé said. "Enrique's at MIFD with me and we split the rent. He's out most of the time with his boyfriend, anyway."

"Oh," Summer said. She couldn't help thinking about how Esmé was related to a bunch of reality TV stars like ZeeZee and Zoe Z, who lived in Beverly Hills or someplace. That didn't seem right.

"I know what you're thinking," Esmé said. "I don't have a fancy place like some other people in my family, right?"

Summer's face felt hot. It was probably redder than the hard raspberry lemonade. "I wasn't thinking that."

"Yeah, you were. But that's okay." Esmé reached for a bag of cheese puffs at the other end of the counter and tore it open. "I didn't want my whole life broadcast in humiliating detail on national TV, that's all. I'm fine with being the poor relation. At least I have an actual life." She took a handful of puffs and held out the bag.

Summer shook her head. "No thanks. So what happened to Zoe?"

Esmé stopped crunching. "You didn't find her yet? I thought maybe that was why you dropped by. Why didn't you just call, anyway? Would have saved time."

"My cell's still missing," Summer said, with a sigh. "Nabbed from the table at Waterman's, I'm pretty sure."

"Zoe," Esmé said immediately. "The girl is a total klepto. That's why Roland Cho saw me with his precious jewelry. She swiped it backstage, and I yelled at her and took it away. I didn't want to rat her out to the cops when Roland was throwing his little tantrum and calling me a thief, even though she deserved it. The story would have broken the Internet, and Aunt ZeeZee would be so upset. We've all bailed Zoe out so many times."

"Jeez," Summer said. "That was really nice of you." Zoe was a brat, all right, but she had to admit, the teen drama queen wasn't the only rich kid who'd gotten some second chances. Being a celebrity, or even just related to someone in show biz, was rough. Especially when you were just a kid. "But why would she want my phone? She probably has an even better one."

Esmé frowned at her orange-stained fingers. "Oh, that's easy. She wants your contacts, and some way to impress your dad. Don't you get it? She's stalking you."

Summer's stomach dropped. She'd skipped the password protection on her phone because it was so annoying. The kid could read every single one of her texts, if she wanted. And go through her photos and old emails, and… Yikes.

"You don't think she'd try to blackmail me or something, do you?" she asked Esmé.

Her friend shrugged. "Dunno. She's pretty smart in some ways. And really dumb in others."

"She wouldn't be dumb enough to kill somebody, though, right?" Summer said. "Even if she wanted something badly enough?"

Esmé stared at her like she was nuts. "What? You actually think my cousin might go all crazy and *murder* you to get your dad's attention? That's pretty twisted. Wasn't that in a movie already, or something?"

"Sort of," Summer said. "But I wasn't talking about me. I meant Angelica."

"Oh. Right." Esmé frowned, then shook her head. "Nope. She'd never do anything like that. Zoe makes some bad decisions, and she's selfish to the max, but she's an okay kid underneath. Sort of. Aunt ZeeZee tried to bring her up right, before all the TV ridiculousness."

"Well, that's a relief." Summer studied her pedicure for an extra second or two. In a way, Esmé could have been talking about her. Joy, her older sister in New Jersey, always told her she was selfish—and never let her forget that she'd made some *really* bad decisions in her life.

She still did, sometimes. But she was working on it.

"We'll find Zoe," Summer said to Esmé. "I need to ask her some questions about what she may have seen backstage at the fashion show. And I want my phone back."

"She could be anywhere." Esmé twisted one of her braids. "That agent of hers hides her pretty well, though, between incidents."

"We know she likes to hit the clubs, right? So… I say the two of us go downtown tonight and find her."

"Works for me," Esmé said. "How about you pick me up around eleven and we'll get a bite first? Zoe won't show up anywhere before midnight."

"It's a plan," Summer said, hopping off her stool. "That'll give me time to talk to Dorothy about the case and then hit the pool for a few laps."

Esmé's phone buzzed from somewhere across the room. "Hope it's the little cuz, by some miracle," she told Summer, as she ran to answer the text. "Unless she's in trouble again."

That would sure make things easier, Summer thought. And then she and Esmé could just hit the town for fun.

"Nope," Esmé announced, glancing at the screen. "It's your buddy Dash. Uh oh. You were supposed to give his kid a swim lesson this afternoon."

Ohhhh. Summer felt terrible that she'd completely spaced on Juliette-Margot. And Gladys, her other Beginner student, too, but the Battle Ax could drown, for all she cared. That wasn't really true, actually, but she'd had a huge emergency today. A *murder*, in fact. And now she couldn't let people know if she'd be late for anything, because she had no phone.

What a pain. Zoe Z was going down. *After* she gave her back her cell—and spilled whatever she knew about what might have happened to Angelica.

AFTER A SOMEWHAT less than refreshing nap, Dorothy agreed to join Ernie and Grace for the five o'clock seating in the Canyons Dining Room.

It wasn't that she didn't want to spend more time with her friends this evening, of course. She still felt a bit guilty about deserting the Conlons with no explanation back at Hibiscus Glen. Poor Ernie thought something had happened to her.

Well, that was true, in a way. Dorothy had tossed and turned the whole rest of the afternoon on her tufted, extra-firm mattress, envisioning Angelica's disturbingly blue complexion under that awful dry cleaning bag.

It was a relief when the phone rang with Ernie on the other end. Not to mention, she hadn't had a bite to eat all day that wasn't sugar, and Hibiscus Pointe pot roast was the perfect antidote.

Plus, she would have a chance to explain to Ernie about the case. And even more importantly, maybe he could offer some helpful information about Frankie—

or Angelica herself. It was possible the two of them had met during one of Grace's visits to Hibiscus Glen.

"Good evening, Mrs. Westin." Walter, the longtime Canyons dining room manager, looked up with a smile from his reservations chart. "Mr. Conlon said you'd be joining his party tonight."

"Yes, thank you, Walter." Dorothy said. She easily spotted Ernie and Grace at their usual table, just under the potted palm in the center of the room. Grace's caretaker Rosaline was seated there, as well.

Ernie glanced toward the dining room entrance just then, and Dorothy gave him a little wave. She was about to follow Walter to the table when she spotted a petite blonde woman over her shoulder, pacing in the side sitting room off the lobby. The woman was wearing large designer sunglasses indoors, and talking animatedly on her cell phone.

Violet Downs. There was no mistaking that buzz of energy.

"Excuse me, Walter. I'll be back." Dorothy made an abrupt U-turn toward the lobby.

Except for Angelica's sister, and Jennifer Margolis diligently working at a computer behind the Resident Services counter, the elaborately furnished area was deserted. Fortunately, everyone at Hibiscus Pointe took dinnertime, the social peak of the day, very seriously.

Dorothy hesitated outside the sitting room. Violet hadn't seen her yet. Perhaps she could listen in on that phone conversation, just for a moment or two, and gather a bit of helpful information for the case.

"I'm sorry, that simply doesn't work for us," Violet was saying. "Time is of the essence here. Twenty-four hours, take it or leave it." She turned suddenly toward the door, and Dorothy quickly grabbed a brochure from the faux-Edwardian table beside her.

Hibiscus Pointe: Active Luxury Living at a Value YOU Deserve, she read intently. A perpetually smiling Helen Murphy, the Residents Board president, was featured on every page, it seemed. With groups of ladies holding tennis racquets, golf clubs and cocktails. And dining tête-à-tête or relaxing poolside with various handsome, presumably single gentlemen.

"Look, I can make this whole thing go away, okay?" Violet thankfully continued her conversation. "I'll hold up my end of the deal. But another matter has come up that I have to deal with first."

Another matter? Was she talking about her sister's murder? Or her memory-impaired mother? Violet Downs could very well be the coldest person Dorothy knew. What kind of deal had she made with the person on the other end of the line? And most of all, what did she mean, she could make it go away?

Dorothy shivered under her beaded white cardigan. What if Violet had, in fact, killed Angelica…and now she had her sights set on her own mother? That was a long shot, of course, but it was entirely plausible. Didn't the police always consider family members first as suspects? Perhaps the real estate business wasn't as lucrative as Violet wished, and she was after an early inheritance.

It was also possible she had read too many crime novels of late, but could Angelica have placed Frankie in Hibiscus Glen to keep her safe from her scheming sister? And an infuriated Violet had gunned for Angelica first?

On the other hand, if getting her hands on family

money was Violet's goal, she would have had to remove Angelica eventually, anyway. Chilling.

"Dot?"

Dorothy jumped, dropping the colorful Hibiscus Pointe brochure. Helen Murphy stared up at her accusingly from the floor.

Ernie reached down to retrieve the pamphlet. "What's going on?" he asked, rather loudly, as he handed it back to her. "You took off from the dining room like a bat out of Boise, just like you did this afternoon."

"Goodness, Ernie, you gave me a fright." Dorothy cleared her throat, and snuck a peek back into the sitting room. "Don't worry, everything's fine," she whispered, straining to hear Violet now. "Summer and I are working another case. I'd planned to tell you at dinner, but it concerns your friend Frankie's daughter."

"That one?" he asked, jerking his head toward the sitting room. "She was at Hibiscus Glen today, but I don't think she stuck around too long."

"You know, this place is lovely, but you two really should consider another community."

Dorothy and Ernie turned at the same time to find Violet standing in the lobby doorway. *Oh dear*, Dorothy thought. Had *she* been eavesdropping on *them*?

"I see you're looking into active living communities," Violet went on, nodding at the Hibiscus Pointe brochure in Dorothy's hand. "This is a very nice one, like I said, but between us, you can get a lot more bang for your buck across town."

Dorothy forced a smile. Should she offer the woman her condolences on the death of her sister? Or play along as an eager retiree in search of a little slice of paradise?

"Gotta call you back," Violet said into her phone,

disconnecting the call and turning her attention back to them. "I'm Violet Downs, and I happen to be a real estate broker up in Vero Beach. But I have an adorable, easy-maintenance waterfront condo right here in Milano with an extremely motivated seller—death in the family—that you have to see. Just came on the market."

"Really?" Dorothy murmured. "Sounds wonderful."

Except it wasn't wonderful at all. Dorothy didn't know yet where Angelica had been living in town, but was it *her* condo Violet was already hawking?

"Your husband looks like a golfer." Violet smiled at Ernie. "Those are very nice slacks."

Dorothy felt dumbfounded. What was worse, the real estate agent mistaking Ernie for her husband, or the fact that she was commenting on his golf pants?

"I'm Mrs. Westin's attorney, actually," Ernie said. "She doesn't buy anything without my approval."

Really. Dorothy frowned at her friend.

He shrugged. "It's a risky market out there. You need to be careful."

Violet pushed up her sunglasses, and Dorothy noticed that her eyes looked red and puffy. Had she been crying, after all? "It's not dangerous if you're working with the right real estate professional," she said. "So what do you say we take a drive over and see the place right now?"

The offer to walk through what could very well be Angelica's home was tempting, but Dorothy was beginning to feel dizzy from lack of food. And it would be dark soon. "How about tomorrow?" she asked.

"Perfect, Mrs. Westin." Violet made a rapid note on her phone. "I'll see you and your...*attorney*...around nine, then, how's that? Where are you staying, with friends or at a hotel?"

"Friends," Dorothy said.

"Hotel," Ernie said, at the same time. Dorothy felt her face grow warm. Violet raised her eyebrows.

"You can meet us at The Brooklyn Deli on LaVista," Ernie said. That was one of his favorite places, Dorothy knew, because the bagels reminded him of home. "And make it ten-thirty."

"Got it. See you then!" Violet hustled off toward the sliding doors at the end of the lobby, nearly knocking over a worried-looking Jennifer Margolis on her way.

Jennifer always looked a bit worried, of course. But right now the hardworking Hibiscus Pointe resident services director had even more concern than usual in her pretty brown eyes.

"Oh, Mrs. Westin, I couldn't help hearing just the last second or two of your conversation," she said, glancing after the tiny real estate agent in dismay. "You aren't planning to leave us, are you?"

"Absolutely not, dear," Dorothy assured her.

Not if she could help it, anyway.

NINE

SUMMER UBERED BACK to her condo in Hibiscus Towers later than she'd expected, after she and Esmé had accidentally discovered—and then polished off—the instant margarita mix and tequila in Esmé's roommate's half of the cupboards.

They could replace the stuff before Enrique even realized it was missing. Unless he was having a guest over or a party or something tonight—but hey, what were the chances of that, really?

Besides, she and Esmé had gotten stuff done for the case, Summer told herself, as she tossed her key card on the counter and dropped onto Grandma Sloan's flowered couch. They'd made a list of all the downtown clubs Zoe Z was likely to show up at tonight, so they could plan where to go. Basically, the Zoe list was the same as Summer's regular club circuit, which Esmé pointed out made sense, since neither of them would waste time at any lame places.

Plus, if Zoe really was stalking her, it made sense she'd pick the clubs where Summer hung out the most.

It didn't matter that the kid was underage. The bouncers let in anyone with a fake ID who looked halfway cool. And they'd recognize Zoe, anyway—tabloid publicity was always a plus, especially since no clubs were trendy for long.

After that, she and Esmé had debated for a while

whether Detective Donovan was worth the effort. First Esmé said yes and Summer said no. Then Summer said yes, and Esmé said no. Then her friend had pointed out the fact that since he wasn't calling her or anything, it didn't really matter.

Ouch. Esmé could be brutal like that sometimes. But Summer had to admit, she was right.

Summer rolled over onto her stomach and voice-activated her screening-room-sized TV. There was nothing on, really. And now the TV was reminding her that Detective Donovan had installed it for her, and…wait, wasn't she supposed to be somewhere?

Oh, no. Summer sat straight up again. She'd told Dorothy she'd come over to talk about the case. And there was no way for her to call and tell her friend she'd be late, because she'd gotten rid of Grandma Sloan's landline ages ago.

She shouldn't have had that last margarita. The tequila was definitely fogging her brain. Maybe if she had something to eat, and brushed her teeth really well, Dorothy wouldn't realize she was a tiny bit tipsy.

Summer slipped into her flip-flops and stumbled just a little on her way to the fridge. She and Esmé were going to have to Uber it again tonight, for sure.

Luckily, there were a couple of cartons of Chinese food in the fridge. They couldn't have been there more than a week. Two weeks, tops. Besides, you couldn't get food poisoning if the stuff had MSG, right? MSG protected you from everything, except Death Valley thirst and killer headaches.

Wait. What was that weird rustling noise? It seemed like it was coming from her bedroom.

Maybe it was just her imagination. Summer stood totally still, listening. It wasn't even dark outside yet, but the light from the fridge gave the kitchen a weird, creepy glow. It didn't help that she kept the living room drapes closed in the daytime, so she didn't have to see the dizzying view from a zillion floors up. She hated heights.

There was the noise again, louder this time. Summer very quietly removed her flip-flops, and tiptoed across the carpet toward the open bedroom door. Now she *really* needed her phone, to call the police if it turned out there was some kind of psycho in there.

She peered through the doorway in the dim light, ready to make a break for the front door if she needed to. Cautiously, she took one step forward, raising a flip-flop over her head. Not that it would make much of a weapon, but it made her feel better.

A small, blue-haired figure was bent over Grandma Sloan's dresser against the wall, with her back to Summer, peering intently at something in her hands.

Unbelievable. Frankie Downs had broken into her condo. What was Angelica's mom doing here? And how had she escaped from Hibiscus Glen?

On the other hand, maybe she shouldn't be too surprised about that. "Okay, Frankie," she said. "Put whatever you're holding there down."

The tiny woman whirled around. "Oh," she said. "It's you."

"Well, yeah," Summer said, crossing her arms. "I happen to live here. And you have a ton of explaining to do."

"I was just waiting for you to show up, that's all." Frankie slowly opened her fist to let the chain of a delicate necklace coil back onto the dresser top.

Summer frowned. That was the moonstone necklace her mom had given her on her tenth birthday, just before she took off for that hippie farm, or wherever she went that time. Joy had one just like it. "Why are you pawing through my stuff?"

"There was nothing else to do." Frankie shrugged. "You have some nice jewelry. Ever think about selling it?"

"No," Summer said, as Angelica's mom brushed past her into the living room. Actually, she had, but that was none of Frankie's business. She followed after her, flipping on a few overhead lights, and sighed in relief as her surprise guest settled on the couch.

"You need to change the channel," Frankie said, nodding toward the upset-stomach commercial on the TV.

"TV off," Summer told the black command tower in the corner. What was she going to do now? She still had no idea whether the blue-haired woman had all her marbles or not. And Frankie sure didn't seem to understand—or believe—that her daughter was really dead. Otherwise, wouldn't she be too upset to sneak into other people's condos?

"Come over here by me, honey." Frankie patted the couch. "We need to talk."

They sure did. But Summer wasn't sitting down. She didn't trust that con artist for a second. "How did you get in here?"

"Easy." Frankie held up a Hibiscus Pointe pool key card. "Found it on the sidewalk. Works on practically every door in this place."

Summer had to hand it to her. She used the same trick herself, more than she'd admit. "We need to get you back to Hibiscus Glen," she said.

"Nope." Frankie shook her blue head emphatically.

"I'm staying right here. I'm never setting foot in that place again."

Summer sighed. Now what was she supposed to do? She needed to drop by Dorothy's and then get ready to hit the clubs with Esmé and track down Zoe. Should she rat out Frankie and dump her back at the memory care unit? But then she and Dorothy might never have another great chance like this to question her for the case.

On the other hand, if anyone at Hibiscus Glen found out she was hiding Frankie in her condo after she'd gone AWOL, she'd be in major trouble. And she was in enough hot water as it was with the Residents Board for the under-fifty-five thing.

There was only one thing to do. "Okay, Frankie, you win," Summer said, slipping on her flip-flops again. "You're coming with me. But not to Hibiscus Glen, I promise."

"You know, you and I are a lot alike," Frankie said, as she stepped through the door in front of Summer. "It's probably because you're my goddaughter."

"Mmmhmm." Summer made sure the door was securely locked behind them, not that it did much good. She wasn't *anything* like Angelica's crazy mom.

DOROTHY HAD EXPECTED to find Summer at her door at some point that evening, but certainly not with Frankie Downs in tow.

"Don't ask," Summer said, as she tossed her bag on the breakfast bar and helped herself to a brownish banana.

Well, that was ridiculous. Of course she had to ask what Angelica's mother was doing in the company of

her detective partner—and not Val and the rest of the
staff at the memory care unit.

It took a few minutes for Dorothy to get the gist of
the situation, as Summer and Frankie kept talking over
each other. She'd tried to convince Frankie to return to
her lovely room at Hibiscus Glen, with her nice new
friend Peggy.

No dice, in Frankie's words.

"Can she stay here with you?" Summer asked. "Just
for tonight? I really have to find Zoe."

"Zoe who?" Frankie's ears pricked up like Mr.
Bitey's when he heard Dorothy open the cat food bin.

At the moment, the treacherous orange feline was
contentedly curled in Frankie's tiny lap. He'd never
demonstrated any type of affection like that to anyone, including Dorothy, since she'd adopted him from
the cat rescue a while back. Mr. Bitey was nearly as
large as Frankie, and equally stubborn.

"Summer, can you help me in the kitchen for a moment, please?" Dorothy said. "I'm sure I have some
snacks somewhere."

That wasn't true, and her cramped kitchenette
wouldn't afford them much privacy with its close prox-
imity to the living room, but she and Summer needed
to make a plan. They couldn't risk having Frankie stay
with either of them indefinitely. Violet—and the police,
no doubt—would be looking for her.

Not to mention, Frankie might have mental or physical health issues neither she nor Summer were aware
of. And Dorothy didn't care much for the idea of bunk-
ing with Angelica's mother for any length of time. Even
one night.

"What else can we do?" Summer asked, after she and

Dorothy had debated the matter for several minutes, in low tones. "We're stuck with her. For now, anyway."

Dorothy sighed. "Frankie can stay tonight, but first thing in the morning, she goes back to Hibiscus Glen. I just hope no one finds out we're harboring an escaped resident. Surely the memory unit is monitored with some kind of security cameras, don't you think?"

"Well, it's not like the rest of the ones around Hibiscus Pointe ever work." Summer pulled a stuffed pepper dinner from the freezer and extracted a baking sheet from the jumble of pans and lids and casserole dishes in the drawer under Dorothy's oven. "Here, you guys can cut up the pepper and make little apps, kind of."

"I guess that'll have to do for refreshments. Frankie probably didn't have any dinner tonight." Dorothy shot a glance through the kitchen at the older woman, who was petting a happily purring Mr. Bitey with her bare feet up on the coffee table. "It looks as if she's already making herself right at home. I just don't understand why she hasn't even mentioned Angelica yet. Especially under the…circumstances."

"I dunno," Summer said. "Maybe you can work on Frankie tonight while I go after the Zoe angle. We've got to get a break here somewhere soon, or we're cooked. Don't they say your best chances of catching a killer are in the first forty-eight hours?"

"Yes, I've heard that," Dorothy said, with a sigh. "Why don't you go get ready to meet Esmé, then, and I'll see what I can find out on my end."

She had a feeling it would be a very long night. For both of them.

"Okay," Summer agreed quickly, scooping up her

bag from the counter. "See you later, Frankie!" she called into the living room.

"Don't forget, Ernie and I are meeting Violet tomorrow morning at ten-thirty," Dorothy said in a low voice, as Summer bounded past her. "You'll need to take Frankie back to your condo by ten, at the very latest. Earlier would probably be better, so you won't run into as many people."

"Got it," Summer said cheerfully, from the door.

"Oh, and Summer?"

"Yeah?" Her friend poked her blonde head back inside the condo.

"Maybe you should take a cab tonight, dear."

TEN

SUMMER AND ESMÉ arrived at Inferno, the first club on their hot list, at just the right time. Late enough to be cool, but early enough to snag a seat at the private VIP bar on the top level. It didn't hurt, of course, that Summer's name was on their Regulars list.

Sort of like being on a TSA pre-check list or something, but way more fun. Now all they had to do was wait.

It also helped that, unlike Hibiscus Pointe, the security camera monitors at Inferno actually functioned. If she glanced into the little side room behind the slightly open velvet curtain to the left of the main bar area, she could see every single clubgoer who tried to get in—at every door, even the secret ones.

Zoe's butt was hers. And if for some reason the brat didn't show up, she and Esmé would go to the next place. Piece of cake. Not bad as far as stakeouts went, either. At least they could have drinks while they waited.

The VIP bar was known as Dante's—sort of like the top level in the place where killers ended up after *they* were dead. There was another, older club in Milano, a lot like this one, called Burn. But it had been shut down for a while by the health department.

"Haven't seen you two in a while. What'll it be, ladies?" The bartender, amazingly hot and casual in a V-necked black T-shirt and tight black skinny jeans, leaned in super close over the candy-red, sparkly mica counter.

Summer couldn't remember the guy's name. For help, she glanced over at the string of little holiday stockings and stars with employee names hung just beyond the velvet curtain, but they were too fuzzy to read this far away.

A weird touch for a trendy club. Kind of cute, though. No one except for the staff was supposed to see it, anyway. Hopefully that curtain would stay open for a while longer, so she could keep watching the monitors for Zoe.

Esmé ordered a Jack and soda, and Summer decided on the lavender martini. She'd been tempted to try one of the flaming drinks, but they were slightly over her budget. She needed to pace herself tonight, anyway. The margaritas she'd knocked back earlier had given her a throbbing headache.

"On the house," the bartender said, as he set their cocktails in front of them. "Enjoy the holidays."

"Thanks." Summer threw him a grateful smile. Maybe she should have ordered a flaming drink after all. Rats.

"So what's the plan when Zoe gets here?" Esmé stirred her drink, and took a taste off the straw. "Do we just grab her and hustle her out of here?"

Oh. Summer hadn't thought much yet about the actual logistics. She'd figured maybe the three of them would just talk, but the music was starting to get a lot louder.

She also hadn't factored in the possibility of Zoe's usual entourage. How could she and Esmé get rid of them? Not easily, she was pretty sure. Glommers-on tended to stick super close to their celebrity BFFs—

especially when it was time to close the bar tab, if the club even bothered to keep one.

On the other hand, this was Milano, not LA, right? Even the clubgoers tended to be a few years older, which was how she and Esmé got away with clubbing at twenty-nine. Twenty-*six*, Summer corrected quickly. Would any of Zoe's friends even want to party in this town? Probably not, unless it was on the beach.

There was a decent chance the leeches didn't even know their celebrity cash cow was here.

"Guess we'll just have to play things by ear," Summer said to Esmé.

The club began to fill up fast, but luckily not on the Dante's level yet. They had started their third drinks, and Summer had just taken her eyes off the monitors for a nanosecond, when Esmé gave a little gasp. "Zoe's here," she said. "She's heading up in the security elevator, wearing a sequined red ball cap. Cueing entrance in three, two…"

"Expecting me?"

Summer turned on the red velvet bar stool to see Zoe Z shaking out her long, sleek dark hair. She had to admit, Zoe looked gorgeous tonight—and a lot more sophisticated than her age in that bright red Lycra bodysuit that clung to every one of her curves in a major way. With her serious red eyeliner, she didn't look like the spoiled little kid on *Life with Zee Zee*. She looked more like…well, ZeeZee herself.

"Put on a coat, girl," Esmé snapped. "You look like a tramp."

"Chill, Esmé," Zoe said. "She's just jealous," she added to Summer.

Summer frowned. Esmé looked great, in her opinion—and the bartender's, too, she could tell. Underneath that orange-and-silver patterned, short and flowy dress, Esmé had some killer curves herself. She also had the kind of natural style you couldn't buy on Rodeo Drive.

"Have a seat, Zoe," Summer said, dragging up another stool with the open toe of her gold stiletto pump.

The bartender immediately materialized. "The kid here will have a diet cola," Esmé told him.

"I don't drink anything diet," Zoe said, with a disgusted look. "It's bad for you."

"Make it regular, then," Esmé said to the bartender, before turning back to her cousin. "So okay, be straight with us, girl. Where did you take off to this afternoon? And where's Aleesha? She's supposed to be keeping an eye on you."

"Oh, she's back at the Milano Grand," Zoe said, with a shrug. "Asleep. I left her a note."

"We're glad you showed up, Zoe," Summer said, to head Esmé off. She didn't want her friend to say anything else to annoy the brat. The kid couldn't leave until they were done questioning her for the case. *And* she wanted her phone back.

Almost as if Zoe had read her mind, the girl reached into a side pocket of the shiny red knapsack she'd tossed on the bar. "Hey, look what I found," she said, producing Summer's phone. "I think it might be yours."

"Thanks." Summer snatched the cell from Zoe's red-tipped paws. "You took this from my table at the Waterman's fashion show, didn't you?"

"What? Of course not." Zoe gazed back at her with wide, innocent eyes. "You're so paranoid, just like my cousin over there. I told you, I found it. I just held on to it for you, so no one would steal it."

Or go through all my private stuff, Summer wanted to add. "Awesome," she said.

"I charged it up for you, too," Zoe said. "So you can use it right away. Oh, and I added my name to your contacts. How come you don't do any social media?"

"That is so none of your business," Esmé said. "I can't believe you…"

"It's okay," Summer said, holding up a hand. "I have, like, zero friends," she said to Zoe. "It's really sad."

"That's such a lie," Zoe said. "By the way, who's that dark-haired guy with the Navy SEAL bod in your photos? He's totally adorbs. If you don't want him…"

Summer squeezed her eyes shut. Okay, now Zoe was officially ticking her off. "He's too old for you," she said. "So anyway, I've got a couple of questions for you, and they're really important. One of the models at Waterman's, an older lady, got murdered today."

"I know," Zoe said. "Too bad."

"Yeah," Summer said. "But here's the thing. You were backstage. Right? And Esmé here saved your butt over that bracelet you were planning to lift, remember? And…"

"I wasn't going to steal it," Zoe said. "I told you, my cousin is totally paranoid. I was just looking at the stupid bracelet for a minute."

"And the necklace," Esmé put in. "I swear, you have zero common sense. You're practically on *parole*, after your last crazy stunt."

"That was a traffic accident," Zoe said. "They don't count. And for the record, I was *not* trying to run anybody over. I wasn't even driving, my friend was. She swore it all over the place, but no one listened to her."

"Maybe because the paparazzi have pictures?" Esmé said. "Hello?"

This was getting way out of hand. "Okay," Summer broke in. "Back to the fashion show. Did you notice anything at all backstage that seemed weird? Did you talk to any of the models? The one who got killed was named Angelica."

"I didn't talk to anyone." Zoe studied a small crack in her gel manicure. "And I remember that lady. She seemed kind of nice. I felt sorry for her because she kept getting yelled at by that Monique witch."

"Can't argue with that," Esmé murmured.

"What was Monique chewing her out for, exactly?" Summer asked.

"Nothing, really," Zoe said. "She was just screaming around, and then the model lady tried to say stuff back but Monique drowned her out. I don't remember much, because I was checking out the jewelry over by the garment bags. You know, near where the model ended up dead. And then Roland Cho ran over and accused me of *stealing*. Which I would never do, FYI. I mean, maybe I might borrow something, just temporarily, but that's it."

Like her phone. Summer remembered now that she'd seen that shoplifting episode from *Life with ZeeZee*. It hadn't been pretty, but ZeeZee had fixed everything so Zoe only got a warning from the cops. But that was a long time ago.

"I got even with that loser designer on Twitter, though," Zoe added. "My friends are *never* going to buy his stuff."

"Great." Esmé sighed. "There goes my nonexistent design career. For good."

"So how come you and Aleesha left the fashion show?" Summer said. "Because people thought you were trying to steal... I mean, *borrow*...the Roland Cho jewelry?"

"No." Zoe rolled her eyes, looking super annoyed now. "I just went to the dumb show in the first place so I could meet you, since I might be working with your dad soon and everything. And you were snotty to me, so I told Aleesha we were leaving."

Summer frowned. What? She was never snotty. Or maybe she had been, a little. "Sorry," Summer muttered, even though she wasn't.

"But mostly, Aleesha and I bailed because the fashion show was lame. What were you doing there, anyway? I mean, you're old, but not *that* old."

Gee, thanks, Summer thought. "I was having lunch with a friend," she said.

"So I've answered all your questions now, right?" Zoe stood up. "And I gave you back your phone, which you should thank me for. I think maybe you owe me, actually. Maybe you could introduce me to your dad or something."

"I'll consider it," Summer lied. "But I may have more questions for you if things come up, okay?"

"No problem." Zoe shrugged. "I'm going to stick around town for a while. The beaches are pretty cool, even if the clubs and the fashions stink. But hey, maybe we could go to the Majesty show together on Friday. That one's not supposed to be too bad. You have my number in your contacts now, remember?"

"I think we're done here," Esmé said, signaling for the check. The bartender just smiled and shook his head, before slipping her his number on a matchbook. Esmé gave him a little smile back and tucked it in her purse.

"Not bad, Cuz." Zoe looked impressed. "Well, nice running into you guys. I'm headed to Aquamarine," she added, tucking her hair into her red cap again.

"No, you're not," Esmé said. "Summer and I are taking you straight back to the hotel. And while we're at it, I can give Aleesha a piece of my mind."

"She works for me," Zoe said.

"She works for your mom," Esmé said. "You don't want Aunt ZeeZee heading down here, do you? That's just what she'll do if…"

"Ladies." The bartender was frowning now at the security monitors behind the velvet curtain. "I think we're about to get some extra company, if they make it past the bouncers."

Uh oh. A huge crowd of guys with cameras and teen girls—Zoe and ZeeZee fans, probably—was pushing against the velvet rope at the front of Inferno. And yikes, the back entrance, too.

Time to go.

"I hate it when this happens." Zoe sighed, pulling the brim of her baseball hat lower over her face.

Liar, Summer thought. She wasn't sure the little diva was telling the truth about what had happened backstage at the fashion show, either. How had Zoe known that she and Dorothy had found Angelica's body near the garment bags, if she'd really left the restaurant?

Summer chugged the last of her lavender martini as she headed out of Dante's behind Esmé and her brat cousin. Her dad's production company still had a TV division. Maybe she should give ol' Syd a heads-up for a hot new reality show: *Zoe Z: Behind Bars.*

ELEVEN

"THERE, THERE. HAVE another nice drink, you'll feel much better." Dorothy felt terrible as she handed a sobbing Frankie a second tall glass of Milano's finest tap water.

"Don't you have anything a little stronger?" Frankie asked, with a loud hiccup. "Like, scotch, maybe?" She drew the sleeve of her billowy purple blouse across her blotchy face in a futile attempt to wipe away her tears.

"I'm afraid not," Dorothy said. "Just peppermint tea." She wished she had something more potent right now herself, because finally convincing Frankie that her daughter was dead—murdered, no less—had been an enormously sad and difficult task.

"I can't believe Angelica is really gone," Frankie said, stumbling back into the living room and dropping into Dorothy's favorite chair. "My poor, gorgeous baby."

As if on cue, Mr. Bitey jumped up onto the distraught woman's lap and curled into as tight a ball as he could manage, his huge hind paws hanging down over the seat.

Dorothy perched on the edge of the couch. "Frankie," she said, carefully. "We want to try to help the police find out who did this to Angelica, Summer and I."

Frankie's chin snapped up. "My goddaughter?"

Dorothy smiled and nodded. "That's right." She had no idea what Frankie's true level of understanding was, but it seemed the woman took comfort in being related to Summer in some way. "So maybe you could tell me a little more about Angelica." She paused. "I've been... out of touch with the rest of the family lately. For quite some time, actually."

It would never do to say that she'd never even met any of the Downses before today, no matter how much Frankie remembered.

"Well, she was a looker, as you know," Frankie said. "But she never let it go to her head. I put her in modeling school when she was five, but she'd already been the Thurber Detergent Baby for years."

"My," Dorothy said. Everyone knew the beautiful, dark-haired Thurber Baby's face, way back when. Her own mother had been a loyal Thurber customer for as far back as Dorothy could remember.

"Angelica didn't like having her picture taken, or walking around in front of crowds," Frankie went on. "But she went along with it, and modeled 'til she was twenty-one or so, because we needed the money. I had a little side business in New York, but we ran into... some hard times."

Frankie wiped more tears from her eyes. "Too bad my other daughter, Violet, wasn't as good looking. She takes more after me, I guess. That one wanted to model like her older sister, but she never got much attention from the bookers. It made her tougher, though. She put herself through college and business school and now she's making a fortune in real estate."

"I see," Dorothy said. She wasn't sure whether to feel sorry for Violet, but at least Angelica's sister had found her niche. "So all of you ended up together here in Florida," she said.

"Well, not together, exactly," Frankie said, with a

shrug. "Angelica married a young man with no money, a photographer, and they traveled the world on pennies. He died in an unfortunate war zone incident, trying to get his big break, and my daughter remarried a much older man with a place here in Milano. I think she just wanted to forget everything, and she was happy enough. But after he died she got lonely and brought me down here too."

"How nice for you both," Dorothy said. At least Angelica was probably never bored, with her mercurial mother to care for.

Frankie gave Mr. Bitey a distracted scratch under the chin. "Then I had a few health issues, and the bills started eating up what was left of Angelica's money. So she went back to work again. Some scout from the Page Models spotted her in a laundromat downtown. She did some magazine work, a lot of ad stuff for seniors down here, and…" She stopped and sighed. "Fashion shows. I can't believe one of them got her killed."

Dorothy leaned forward. "Frankie, do you have any idea who might have wanted to harm your daughter?"

"Nope." Frankie noisily swirled her rapidly melting ice cubes. "She was an angel. Kept to herself most of the time, and she took real good care of me. Not that I needed it, or anything."

"Of course not," Dorothy murmured.

"We even took a few trips to Vegas together," Frankie added, her expression brightening slightly. "Those were some good times. Hit the jackpot once or twice, too."

Well, that wasn't terribly surprising. Frankie had seemed like quite a gambler, dealing cards as she had back at Hibiscus Glen. "Did Angelica have any…romantic interests?" Dorothy hinted delicately, smoothing her badly wrinkled skirt over her knees. It was getting very late, and she fervently wished she could change into her nightie and cozy robe. But questioning Frankie for the case was much more important than her own selfish comfort.

She jumped as Frankie suddenly slammed her glass down on the antique side table beside the chair, unceremoniously dislodging Mr. Bitey. "That's it!" the woman cried. *"Cherchez la femme!"*

Dorothy quickly recovered her composure at Frankie's outburst. *"Pardon me?"*

She knew what the rather sexist French expression meant, of course—"look for the woman." Was Angelica's attacker definitely female, then?

"That horrible Monique woman," Frankie said. "She's the one who took my perfect angel away from me."

Dorothy sat up straighter on the couch. "Do you mean the Monique who's the owner of Monique's Boutique downtown? She was one of the sponsors of the fashion show."

Frankie waved. "That's the one. Terrible store. Angelica worked there for a real short time, before that witch boss of hers got too jealous."

Of Angelica's beauty? Dorothy wondered. Maybe Monique didn't have Angelica's model looks, but she was attractive enough, in a highly style-conscious way. And surely, women of a certain age would have the maturity to celebrate their individual differences, wouldn't they?

"Even Monique's husband—*ex*-husband now—couldn't stand her. Somehow she got it in her head that the husband was having an affair with Angelica, because he kept coming by the store to see her. Or so

Monique said. My angel would never have a fling with a married man."

"Mmm," Dorothy said. Sometimes mothers weren't the best judges of their daughter's love lives, and it was best to keep quiet. She had learned that the hard way with her own Maddie. "So where is Monique's former husband now?" Maybe she and Summer should talk to him.

"Who knows?" Frankie said. "I think he moved back up to Michigan or something, to be near his sister. Don't think I ever even knew his name. Roderick, maybe? He could be dead—" her eyes quickly filled with tears again at the word "—for all I know."

"How about your other daughter, Violet?" Dorothy asked. "I'm sure she's upset about Angelica, too, and wants the best for you."

Frankie snorted. "Violet? She wasn't close with Angelica, and she doesn't care about me, either. All that one cares about is money."

"But she wants to bring you home with her to Vero Beach," Dorothy reminded her, gently. "It's such a lovely place, you might be very happy there."

"I know you mean well and all, but forget it, Dorothy," Frankie said. "Violet doesn't want me to live with her. She wants to stick me in another place like Hibiscus Glen, but cheaper, and throw away the key. She can't wait for me to croak, so she can get my money."

"Now, now, I very much doubt that," Dorothy said, in what she hoped was a soothing tone.

"Well, I don't give a fig about Violet," Frankie said. "I only care about Angelica, and finding out who took her away from me." Her tiny body began to shake with sobs again, so violently that Mr. Bitey sunk his claws into Dorothy's favorite chair to hold on.

Dorothy went over to pat Frankie's shoulder, and detach her determined feline from the ripping fabric. "If it's any comfort to you, Frankie, I know what it's like to lose a daughter much too soon," she said.

Frankie immediately stopped crying. "Really? What happened?"

Dorothy glanced toward the small photo of Maddie on the side table, the last one ever taken of her, as far as she knew. It showed her tall, slender blonde daughter standing in front of a small prop plane, her hair blowing in a gusty wind. "Her name was Madeline, but she always preferred Maddie," she said.

"Glad she went with the nickname," Frankie said. "I've never liked Madeline, either. I'm a Francine myself. Blech."

Dorothy ignored the rude remark. The elderly woman was not in possession of all her faculties, she reminded herself. "Maddie was a storm chaser. There was an accident, and she tried to save someone's life."

That's what she and Harlan had been told, anyway. Dorothy had always suspected that there were other details, but she would probably never know the full story. Harlan had been more accepting, of course. Knowing wouldn't change the result, he'd always said. Their beautiful, impulsive daughter was gone, but they would see her again someday.

How she missed them both.

Dorothy quickly willed the threatening tears away, before they spilled over and upset Frankie further. Angelica's mother was looking at her now with an unreadable expression.

Harlan was right. What was past was past, and couldn't be undone. But if she could help this poor woman learn the truth about her daughter, maybe they would both feel better.

"You know what?" Frankie said, finally. "You're a good person, Dorothy Westin. If anyone's going to find out who killed my Angelica, my bet's on you."

"Thank you, Frankie," Dorothy said. She wished she shared that same confidence. But one thing she was quite sure of: she and Summer would give the case their best shot.

TWELVE

Summer awakened to a loud banging on her door. Jeez. That was *so* annoying. What time was it, anyway? It had to be the middle of the night. She'd just gotten home.

She felt around for her phone, which she kept under her pillow for safekeeping while she slept, and squinted at the screen.

Ten-oh-five. And someone was still going to town on the door, at the same tempo as the pounding in her head. The bell must be broken again.

"I'm on my way already!" she called, rolling off the bed and padding toward the living room in her tank top and PJs. At least she'd changed out of her club clothes when she came in. Her hot green tube dress was in a heap in the tub.

"Summer, did you forget?" Dorothy stood outside the door, dressed in a freshly ironed, light blue linen suit. Her favorite hummingbird pin was fastened to the lapel.

Behind her friend, Frankie was yawning widely in a powder pink tracksuit Summer recognized as Dorothy's. It was way too big for her. Angelica's mom looked as tired as Summer felt right now.

Oops. She was supposed to show up at Dorothy's this morning to get Frankie. Where was Dorothy going, again? Oh, yeah. She and Ernie were going to view Angelica's condo. Well, Dorothy was pretty sure it was

Angelica's, anyway. If not, at least she'd get to find out more about Violet.

"Sorry, but I have to run, dear," Dorothy said. "Ernie is already downstairs." She held out a little plastic container of doughnuts from the Hibiscus Pointe continental breakfast buffet. "Frankie wasn't hungry earlier, but I figured you'd both want some of these. If you have some coffee, you'll be all set. So I'll let you know how everything went when I get back."

"Okay," Summer said, taking the doughnuts and stepping aside to let Frankie in. What was she going to do with her? She was hardly even awake yet.

She felt bad for Frankie, she really did, but Angelica's mom couldn't stay *here*. She was pretty sure Dorothy felt the same way about having Frankie hang out at her place. Besides, if anyone found out they were hiding her—well, not *hiding*, exactly, but whatever—they'd be in trouble.

What would Caputo think? Or, even worse, Detective Donovan? He'd probably never speak to her again. And it wouldn't be professional. Not that she and Dorothy were technically pro detectives, but still…

"I hope you have a comfy bed for guests, Goddaughter," Frankie said, as soon as Dorothy was gone. "I am not a morning person."

"Me neither," Summer said, with a sigh. Hopefully both of them could just go back to sleep until Dorothy showed up and they went over to Hibiscus Glen.

An hour later, though, she was still tossing and turning on Grandma Sloan's extra-firm mattress, unable to fall asleep again. Frankie was snoring in the other bedroom, but that wasn't the problem. Why did she feel so bad about selling Angelica's mom out? Because that was what she and Dorothy would be doing.

Summer's cell gave a muffled ring under the pillow. Great timing. She needed a distraction.

"Hey, Cali Girl," her friend Dash said. "What happened to you yesterday?"

Aargh. Right. She'd missed Juliette-Margot's swim lesson. "Dash, I am soooo sorry. Dorothy and I have a new case, and I got caught up. And then my cell phone got stolen by one of our suspects but I just got it back and..."

Luckily, Dash was a good listener and an awesome friend, as usual. He totally understood when she told him the whole story. But she felt really bad about letting Juliette-Margot down. The kid was only six, and really looked up to her, for some reason.

"Hold on a sec, Dash, okay?" Summer sat up and glanced into the guest room. Frankie was still snoring away in there, big-time. If she snuck out for a little while to take Juliette-Margot to the pool, it would probably be okay.

The kid could only go swimming early in the morning and late afternoon, though, because Dash and Julian, her other dad, were worried about her getting sunburned. Even though Juliette-Margot wore, like, 100 SPF and Summer had bought her a special sun-protected surf suit.

Well, the two of them could do something else, then. Ice cream, maybe. Juliette-Margot loved ice cream. So did she. Even for breakfast.

"Sure," Dash said, when Summer asked him. "I've got a lunch meet-and-greet with a potential client, and

Julian would probably appreciate a break. He's been working really hard lately."

Both guys had, actually. Dash had a super successful design biz and Julian was a workaholic lawyer. But Juliette-Margot was always their top priority. They adored that kid.

So did she.

Feeling a lot more energetic after she hung up with Dash, Summer took a few long swigs from the water bottle next to her bed and bounded into the bathroom. Maybe she'd wear her new black sundress with the crisscrossed back this morning. Juliette-Margot would like it. Her mom was a runway model in Paris, so the kid had fashion in her genes.

Summer left a doughnut and a note on the nightstand for Frankie, in case she woke up, and tiptoed out of the condo.

Unfortunately, Juliette-Margot wasn't ready for ice cream yet. Breakfast in the Hamel-LeBlanc household this morning had included strawberry waffles, courtesy of Dash. He'd packed a to-go offer for Summer, too.

"So what should we do?" she asked Juliette-Margot, glancing into the tiny backseat of the MINI. "Anything you want. We could visit your turtle friends at the zoo, if you want."

The little blonde girl adjusted her enormous white sunglasses. "Juliette-Margot would like to go shopping, *s'il vous plaît*." She snapped open her pink patent-leather purse with the bow on top and held up one of those fake plastic charge cards that came in the mail with credit card come-ons.

"You got it," Summer said, pushing the ignition key. It cracked her up that the kid always referred to herself in the third person. Dash said she'd started to talk that way when she was two and still hadn't grown out of it. She also tossed in a bunch of French words or phrases whenever she could, maybe because she'd never met her Parisian-native mom.

Shopping was a good choice. Much better than the Turtle Lagoon. Maybe she could pick up something to wear to the Majesty fashion show tomorrow.

Her cell rang, and Summer pushed the voice button on her steering wheel.

"Hey there," Esmé said. "I hope you're feeling better this morning than I am."

"I'm fine," Summer said, glancing into the backseat again. "Juliette-Margot and I are headed downtown."

"Well, good, because I have some info for you. Remember when you asked me last night who booked the Waterman's gig for Angelica? Turns out all the models came from the PAGE Agency's senior division. The place is right on South Fifth, if you want to drop in. No sign, but it's a little pink building with black shutters. They never answer their phones or email. Too many model wannabes."

"Awesome, thanks," Summer said. "We'll check it out. Talk to you later, okay?"

Well, that was interesting, she thought as she clicked off. PAGE had offices in New York, LA, Miami, Milan and Paris. Who knew they had a division for senior models in Milano? "Have I got a surprise for you," she told Juliette-Margot. "You're gonna love this."

It was easy enough to find the pink building, but a parking spot, not so much. She and Juliette-Margot had to hike a few blocks. On the way, a lot of people smiled at them, because their black dresses were almost identical, by total coincidence. Juliette-Margot's dress was a little longer, but it looked super cute on her. She had great taste, that kid.

Summer couldn't wait to see her in a few years. Dash and Julian were going to be in for quite a ride.

After a quick stop at Beanz for a to-go iced coffee to wash down the last of the cold strawberry waffles, Summer and Juliette-Margot climbed the three flights of stairs to the PAGE reception area.

The whole place was done in black and white, with a hot-pink floor. There was one uncomfortable-looking slab of a couch with a glass frame and a glass coffee table with not even one magazine on it. That seemed kind of weird for a modeling agency. And who sat on a glass couch, anyway? Unless they weighed zero pounds, maybe.

There were a bunch of blown-up magazine covers on the wall, though, along with a few very un-senior head shots. The young models, a few of them shirtless guys, stared down at Summer and Juliette-Margot in an intimidating, hungry way. Some of the women didn't have shirts on, either.

Maybe bringing a kid here wasn't such a hot idea, Summer told herself. But she'd been around this kind of stuff when she was Juliette-Margot's age—younger, actually—and it hadn't been such a big deal.

Anyway, Juliette-Margot had seemed thrilled when they came in. But now, as they approached the reception desk, Summer saw she'd sucked in her cheeks and pasted some kind of bland, uber-focused look on her face. And where did she learn that weird walk? It was more like a grown-up strut, actually. Yikes.

No time to worry about that now. "Hi," Summer

said to the pale, angular young woman behind the desk. "Marta," her name plate said. "I'm a friend—well, I mean, I was—of one of your models and I'm here to speak to someone about…"

"You can fill out an application online," Marta cut her off. "Or, if you really want to, you can do it here in the office, I guess." She handed Summer a pink clipboard with a single piece of paper clipped to it. "Measurements, date of birth, any previous modeling experience. We'll need to see your portfolio, tear sheets and a professional head shot to scan into your application, too."

"No, that's not what I meant," Summer said. "My friend was Angelica Downs and I need to…"

"Look, I'm sorry for your loss," Marta broke in again. "I really am. We're all going to miss Angelica here at PAGE, too. But I can't give you any special treatment."

"Juliette-Margot's mother is a very famous model," the little girl spoke. "In Paris."

"Yeah?" Marta's thick eyebrows quivered like twin squirrel tails. "Listen," she said, turning back to Summer. "I can save you a lot of time and disappointment. I don't know who your mom is, or why Angelica sent you here, but you're way too young for our senior division."

Well, duh, Summer thought.

"And way too old for our main division," Marta went on. "Our cut-off for Cover Girls is twenty-one and that's really pushing it. And, no offense, but we're definitely not looking for the next Christie Brinkley. The All-American, wholesome blonde beach girl look has been out for decades. We're only signing edgy. And—" she nodded toward Summer's milk-and-sugar-filled iced coffee "—well, *thin*. You probably already know, the camera adds twenty pounds."

Summer's mouth dropped open. Seriously? She had made her point. She didn't need to be insulting or anything.

"Your kid here, though, she may have potential." Marta smiled at Juliette-Margot and pressed a button under the glass desk. "Nancy, I have a STAT referral from Angelica Downs."

Immediately, a freckled, middle-aged woman with no makeup, wearing designer jeans and her hair pulled back in a preppy ponytail, appeared in the doorway of the office behind Marta. "Hey, come on in," she said, zeroing in on Juliette-Margot and giving her an even bigger smile than Marta had. "I'm sure I can help some friends of Angelica's." She looked at Summer over Juliette-Margot's head. "Terrible news, huh? We're just devastated here. But the fashion shows must go on, right?"

Right, Summer thought as she followed Juliette-Margot into Nancy's office. At least until they found Angelica's killer.

THIRTEEN

"SO GLAD YOU two could make it this morning. You're the perfect couple for this place, I can already tell. It's going to go fast, of course, but you're the first ones to see it. I have exclusive right to sell, by the way."

"The condo is for me," Dorothy reminded the overly enthusiastic Violet. "We told you earlier, I believe, that Mr. Conlon is my attorney."

Beside her, Ernie gave a distinctly self-satisfied chuckle. Dorothy frowned at him.

"Of course he is." Violet winked at Dorothy, and ushered them in through the door of Angelica's condo.

It was definitely Angelica's place, because "Downs, A.M." had been listed next to 3-A on the foam directory board in the lobby.

"The Flamingo Pass properties weren't designed on quite as grand a scale as Hibiscus Pointe's," Violet said, as she brought Dorothy and Ernie into the tiny living room. "But it's a very good value. The only slight drawback is that this particular condo doesn't have a spectacular view."

Ernie pulled back one of the striped satin drapes, revealing a looming, gray cinderblock wall. "Yowza," he said. "You're telling me."

"Extra fire wall protection," Violet said, smoothly. "And just think of the considerable savings on the listing price and condo fees, right off the bat."

"What about the pool?" Ernie asked. "Mrs. Westin is a dedicated swimmer."

"Oh, it's being renovated right now," Violet said. "Charmingly retro. But it will be lovely once construction is completed."

Ernie was doing an excellent job of distracting the overzealous real estate agent, just as Dorothy had asked him to on the short drive over to meet Violet at the Brooklyn Deli. She tried to listen with one ear as she made a quick scan of Angelica's home.

At first glance, all signs indicated that its former inhabitant had been a woman of modest tastes. But the artwork—intriguing, but mostly eighties-era pop art, which Dorothy knew next to nothing about—white fur rugs and expensive leather furniture hinted otherwise.

The basic layout was similar to that of Dorothy's own two-bedroom garden condo, but close to half the size. The kitchen was even smaller, but much better equipped than hers. She surreptitiously cracked open the fridge, which was well-stocked with various juices, French cheeses, fresh fruits and veggies, and a bottle or two of sparkling mineral water.

Nothing very exciting there, but clearly Angelica had enjoyed a healthy lifestyle. There was one black ashtray set on the counter, shaped like the Ace of Spades. That had to be Frankie's. How long had Angelica's mother been staying at Hibiscus Glen? The bed in the guest room had been stripped of its sheets, and the closet was a tumbled mess.

The Milano PD must have been through here, looking for clues. Perhaps they had already removed any items of possible interest for the case. So far, the condo had offered a blurry snapshot of Angelica's daily life, but not a terribly useful one.

"As I mentioned, the seller is extremely motivated," Violet was telling Ernie. "We could put in an offer today, before this steal hits the market, and block any other potential bids. So what do you say? You two—I mean, Mrs. Westin—could be all moved in here in maybe three weeks, tops."

"That's motivated, all right," Ernie said. "So who is the seller, anyway? Did the person who lived here die?"

Oh dear. Dorothy hoped her friend's question wouldn't upset Violet. Angelica was her sister, after all, and blood was thicker than water—money or no money. Unless the bereaved relative was a cold-blooded killer, of course.

"I assure you, Mr. Conlon, this is not a stigmatized property in any way," Violet said. "There have been absolutely zero deaths on the premises. Unlike a lot of other places you might look at here in Florida," she added, in a slightly dropped voice.

Dorothy half-froze in the doorway to the master bedroom. How incredibly heartless. And downright morbid. What was *wrong* with this woman? She could very well be a certified psychopath.

"And not to worry, it's not haunted, either," Violet went on. "No ghostly visits or bumps in the night." She gave a short, tinny laugh. "Hope you're not too disappointed. Some people love a good fright."

Dorothy had a good mind to march back out there and tell Violet exactly what she thought of her utter lack of sensitivity. But that would blow her cover, tenuous as it was, and get her and Summer nowhere for their investigation.

Maybe she should have been direct with Violet Downs in the first place, instead of becoming embroiled in this silly charade. But then she might not have had this opportunity to access Angelica's home. Legally, at least.

She didn't notice much of interest in the master bedroom, either. Angelica must have loved seafoam, because the room was done in an ocean theme. Blue-green bedspread, blue pillows, a wavy-print armchair and a glass bottle of seashells on the dresser. Little pieces of blue, green and ivory sea glass dotted the windowsill behind a filmy white curtain.

How sad that Angelica had died in a frothy seafoam dress. It must have been her favorite color.

Two framed photographs stood on the nightstand, behind a small clock radio. Dorothy went over to peer at them more closely.

The first showed Angelica and Frankie holding up cocktails on a rooftop in a glittering city. Las Vegas, Dorothy guessed, recalling the trips with Angelica that Frankie had mentioned fondly. The mother and daughter indeed looked as if they were having a wonderful time. It was possible Frankie was a bit tipsy, judging from her wobbly smile.

Yes, there was a tiny Eiffel Tower in the background, and the Statue of Liberty. Dorothy squinted to read the lanyard badges hanging from the women's necks. The names *Angelica* and *Frankie* were clearly visible, but she couldn't make out the rest of the words, except for one. *Gem.*

Interesting. Had Angelica and Frankie been attendees at a jewelry show or trade convention? And could it be just a sad coincidence that Angelica may have been murdered over a piece of stolen jewelry?

The other photo showed Angelica and Violet as young girls, standing back to back. They were probably about fourteen and ten. If Dorothy hadn't known Angelica was already a model by then, she would never have guessed. In the photo, she looked like a shy, dreamy child. But hadn't Frankie said her older daughter never cared for having her picture taken?

Violet, on the other hand, stood with her arms crossed, gazing defiantly toward the photographer. The blonde girl was half Angelica's height, but looked as if she might have been able to take her older sister in a tussle. Her saddle shoes were scuffed and she'd attached a glittery pin—a bird, maybe, or a butterfly?—to her sweater to hide a ragged hole in the yarn.

"I know you'll be impressed with the closet space in here," Violet said, from the doorway.

Dorothy spun around to find the real estate agent staring at her with that same, steely gaze she'd noticed in the sibling photo. Oh dear. She probably looked very guilty.

But weren't most people a bit snoopy when they toured homes for sale? It wasn't any worse than, say, investigating a hostess's medicine cabinet at a dinner party.

"Oh, yes, closet space is a top priority for me," Dorothy said, heading over to open the accordion-style doors. "I have *so* many clothes, I'm afraid. And shoes, naturally."

That was a fib, of course. Though she probably owned a lot more items than she needed for a halfway decent wardrobe.

She pulled on the closet doors, and one of them unhinged from the track above her head.

Violet was beside her in a flash, blocking the closet. "That can be fixed very easily," she said. "I'll talk to the super—I mean, the *valet* about it right away. Did I mention what a fabulous staff they have here at Flamingo Pass?"

"No, I don't believe you did." Dorothy craned her neck to see past the real estate agent's well-coifed blonde head, as the irritating smell of hairspray assaulted her nostrils. The closet was stuffed with neatly hung blouses, dresses and slacks, as well as an extensive collection of hats and neatly labeled accessory boxes. Many of the clothes still had pink Monique's Boutique price tags hanging from them.

A lone diamond earring lay on the carpet, an inch from the toe of Dorothy's AeroLite pump. She bent to scoop it up, planning to leave it on the dresser, but Violet took her lightly by the arm.

"You know," she said, guiding Dorothy out of the bedroom, "It might be better to see the closets on your next visit—or the final walkthrough, even. It's hard to appreciate the scope of the space with all the previous owner's clothes in the way."

"Oh, I'd love to see them, though," Dorothy said, glancing over her shoulder. "She must have been a very stylish dresser."

"She was," Violet said. "Too bad neither of us is tall and skinny enough to wear those dresses, or we'd be the belles of Milano, wouldn't we?"

"Mmm," Dorothy said, trying not to let her frustration show. Was that a good-sized black safe next to the overloaded shoe rack, half-hidden under a tangle of fallen scarves? It looked as if the door was open, but she couldn't really tell in the semi-darkness of the closet.

"You know, I'd definitely like to get another look at that bedroom closet," she said.

"Oh, we'll get the whole thing cleaned out for your next visit, and fix that pesky door, too," Violet said. "That way you can really get an idea of all the space. It's so hard to tell at the moment, isn't it? Now let's find that nice attorney of yours and start talking some numbers."

Dorothy could have sworn she heard Violet smack her lips. But why had the real estate agent mentioned the closet earlier, and then refused to let her see it? She doubted it had anything to do with a broken door.

Unless, perhaps, it was the door to an open safe.

THE VISIT TO the PAGE Modeling Agency had been a total bust, Summer told herself, as she swung the MINI into Dash and Julian's circular drive. As far as the case was concerned, anyway.

Nancy the booker had given her zero information about Angelica, claiming privacy rules for their models—even deceased ones. All she would say was that Angelica had been one of her favorites—so sweet, always professional—and that she had already told the police everything she knew about the model's private life and her last, unfortunate booking.

Which was, apparently...zilch.

Oh, well. At least Juliette-Margot had gotten something out of their visit. As in, a modeling contract. Were her daddies going to be surprised.

"So," Dash greeted them at the door, with his easy, toothpaste commercial smile. "How did things go? Did you bring me any ice cream?"

"Not exactly," Summer said.

"Guess what, Papa?" Juliette-Margot shot into the

grand foyer like a popped champagne cork. "Juliette-Margot is going to be a real, live model!"

Dash looked back at Summer. "Do all little girls have that crazy fantasy? It's some kind of stage she'll grow out of, right, like ponies and chicken pox?"

She hovered uncertainly in the doorway. "Um…" It might not have been such a stellar idea after all, taking Juliette-Margot to PAGE. "Well, nothing's final or anything, because they need parental permission and all, but your daughter here may actually be the world's new top kid model."

"What?" Dash paled under his dark tan. "Please tell me you're joking."

"Actually, I'm not," Summer said. "I had to stop by PAGE for the case, and she wanted to go, so I thought…"

"Well, you thought wrong," Dash said. "If Julian finds out you two even stepped foot in that place, he's going to blow a gasket."

"Why?" Summer said. Juliette-Margot was bouncing down the hall with joy now. "It's making her so happy."

Dash ran a hand through his wavy, sun-bleached blond hair. He looked like a model himself. "You don't understand. Julian and I agreed that we wouldn't put her in the biz. She can decide for herself later. When she's thirty, maybe."

"That's too old," Summer said. The receptionist at PAGE had made that a thousand percent clear to her, even though she wasn't interested. And she was nowhere near thirty.

"Exactly," Dash said. "We just don't want her to have that kind of childhood. No one who grows up with a bunch of cameras in their face turns out normal."

For a second, Summer thought of Zoe Z. He might

have a point there. "I'm sorry," she said. "I told you, we didn't sign any papers or anything."

"I know, but…" Dash nodded over his shoulder at Juliette-Margot, who was twirling dizzily, her perfect little chin pointed toward the ceiling and her blonde curls bouncing. "What am I going to tell her? She'll be crushed."

"I'll talk to her," Summer said. "I'm the one who got her hopes up, I guess, so I should do it. Don't worry, she'll understand." *Someday.*

Dash sighed. "No, that's all right. You know how obsessed she is with the idea of her mom, and the whole model-in-Paris thing. Julian and I were going to have this convo with her eventually. It might as well be now."

Summer was pretty sure there was no way she could feel any worse. She was such a moron. Juliette-Margot had never even met her supermodel mom, so of course she wanted to be just like her. Maybe the kid was even hoping to impress the infamous Margot.

Summer knew a lot about moms, and she'd never been a fan. Her real mom was a hippy-dippy space shot, and she'd had so many stepmoms it was hard to keep track of them. Of all people, she should have realized how Juliette-Margot might feel.

She'd make it up to her, Summer swore to herself. Then she remembered something, and reached into her bag. "Hey, Dash, this may not help much or anything," she said, "but the lady at PAGE gave us two tickets to the Majesty holiday fashion show. Dorothy and I are already going for the case, so maybe you guys could come with us."

Why was Dash staring at her like that, as if she'd lost

her mind? He loved fancy Milano events, and Juliette-Margot would get a kick out of it, too.

Oh. Right. The models. "Sorry," she mumbled. "Stupid idea."

He shook his head, but to her surprise he chuckled a little and took the tickets. "We'll see how things go," he said. "Maybe I can deal with this impending crisis before Julian gets home from court. I'll call you later, okay?"

"Okay." Summer impulsively leaned over and gave her friend a quick hug before she hightailed it out the door and down the front steps. "Let me know how JM takes everything," she said, over her shoulder. "If I can help or do *anything* at all, just…"

"No worries, Cali Girl," Dash cut in. "Bye for now." He closed the heavy oak door.

Summer headed toward the MINI, still feeling terrible. Nothing was going right for her lately—nada. She'd messed up big time with Juliette-Margot and Dash. Her love life was nonexistent, not that she cared that much. And, worst of all, she and Dorothy had gotten nowhere on the case so far. It was like they were running in circles.

But it was only the day after Angelica Downs was murdered, she reminded herself. It just *felt* a lot longer than that. They still had time to find her killer. They were only halfway to that forty-eight hours before the trail got cold.

Oh, no. Summer ducked into the car and grabbed her cell from where it had fallen between the seats. What time was it now?

Almost one o'clock. Dorothy and Ernie had to be back from meeting Violet at Angelica's condo by now.

LISA Q. MATHEWS   145

And Dorothy had probably already shown up to get Frankie, who had to have been awake for hours.

Yikes. Summer hoped Dorothy had gotten her something to eat. The donut probably wasn't enough. With luck, Dorothy had taken Frankie back to her place—or else they were both just waiting for her to get back.

Summer floored it over to Hibiscus Towers, bracing herself against all the annoying speed bumps. For once she got a primo spot in the parking garage, so she was back at her place in seven minutes flat.

The door was wide open. Uh oh. Dorothy would never leave it like that.

She stepped carefully into the condo, edging against the wall so no one could sneak up on her. Some game show was blaring from the TV, but Frankie wasn't in the living room. Or the kitchen, the bathroom or either of the bedrooms. Summer glanced at her dresser top, and breathed a sigh of relief when she saw the cash and jewelry she'd left on it were still there.

But there was something else on the dresser, too. Her November cable bill, which she hadn't gotten around to paying yet. She couldn't remember where she'd left it, but it wasn't on the dresser, or she would have noticed.

Summer frowned as she picked up the envelope. Yep, Frankie had left her a note. A really short one.

Thanks for the donut.

FOURTEEN

"WHAT DO YOU mean, you *lost* Frankie?" Dorothy stared at Summer, hoping she hadn't heard correctly.

Summer twisted a sun-bleached strand of hair as she sat in Dorothy's favorite chair, her long, toned legs draped over the arms. "Well, I didn't lose her, exactly. She just…left. I'm really sorry."

Dorothy rubbed her temples. She'd had a feeling something like this might happen, if she left that slippery Frankie with Summer. Her detective partner meant well, but she was easily distracted. She should have postponed her and Ernie's appointment with Violet, and taken Angelica's mother straight back to Hibiscus Glen.

And why, oh, why had she let Ernie talk her into that nice lunch at the Double Deckers Sandwich Shop? If she'd returned to the complex earlier, and headed directly over to Summer's condo instead of home to change and rest… The list of "if onlys" seemed endless.

"Don't worry, we'll find her," Summer said. "She couldn't have gotten that far. I kept my eyes peeled on my way over here, but I bet she's headed to town. Maybe she took the Hibiscus Pointe Shuttle. No one ever checks IDs or anything on it."

"I'm not sure whom we should tell first." Dorothy sank onto the couch, dislodging a disgruntled orange blur of fur. "The memory care unit staff, or the police. Or even Violet."

That last choice was out of the question for her, of course, or her cover as an eager Milano home buyer would be blown. Summer could step in, but once Violet spoke to the staff at Hibiscus Glen, they'd both be cooked.

"I don't think we should tell any of them," Summer said. "Technically Frankie isn't even a missing person yet."

"I'm afraid she is now." Dorothy reached for the Hibiscus Pointe Emergency Alert bulletin on the coffee table in front of her. "I found this under my door when I got back."

"Oh." Summer gazed at the blurry but recent photo of Frankie, taken at a holiday party, below the word "Missing" in large, bold type and a brief physical description. "We're supposed to contact Jennifer if we've seen her, though. Not the police."

"Frankie could be in serious danger," Dorothy said. "If not from Angelica's killer, which is a very definite possibility, then maybe from herself. As I said earlier, we're hardly mental health professionals."

"Frankie's mind is perfectly fine," Summer said. "Or almost fine, anyway. She's already made it pretty clear she doesn't want to go back to the creepy memory place, and if she does she'll never stay there. Plus, we know she doesn't want to talk to her other daughter, anyway. And so far, it seems like she's been taking care of herself just fine."

Dorothy sighed. Summer was so good at rationalizing sometimes. But this was indeed a dilemma. Why had they ever hidden Frankie, even for one night? Another "if only" to add to her list.

"You know," Summer said, "we don't really have

any new info to give anyone. I mean, they already know she's missing. And she isn't here now."

Goodness. "Isn't that stretching things a bit, dear?" Dorothy said.

"Well, yeah, I guess so," Summer said. "But I think we're kind of losing our focus here. The only real way to keep Frankie safe is to find Angelica's murderer, right?"

Dorothy had to admit, the girl did have a point. And the sooner they solved this case, the better—not just for Frankie, but for all of them.

Summer's cell rang, and she slipped it from her pocket. "Sorry, Dorothy, I'd better answer this," she said. "Esmé, what's up?" she added, into the phone.

To give her friend some privacy for her conversation, Dorothy headed toward the kitchen to get them a few of the mini eclairs she'd brought home from her lunch with Ernie.

She couldn't help overhearing, though.

"You're kidding." Summer was frowning now. "Okay, listen, I'm here with Dorothy. We'll be there as soon as we can. Hang in there."

Dorothy immediately closed the lid of the cardboard pastry box. "What happened? Is Esmé all right?"

"She's fine," Summer said. "But she was calling from the Milano PD. Zoe's been arrested."

"For Angelica's murder?" Dorothy asked. My, the police certainly had wrapped up their investigation fast. She doubted they could even have gotten the lab work back on the evidence from the crime scene yet. Usually that took at least a week.

Zoe must have made a confession. How sad that she'd ruined her young life—and taken someone else's—in such a terrible way.

"Nope, not murder," Summer said. "Shoplifting."

"Thank heavens," Dorothy said. "Not that that's a good thing, either," she added quickly.

"She tried to lift a couple of cheap rings from Sparkle, that new jewelry place next to Monique's Boutique." Summer shook her head. "How dumb is that kid? Aunt ZeeZee threw a fit. She called Esmé from the plane on her way to the French Riviera to chew her out."

It seemed to Dorothy that it might have been considerably more appropriate for the TV star to have blamed Zoe rather than her niece. But still… "I understand that we need to support Esmé right now," she said. "But as you said, shouldn't we focus our efforts on finding Angelica's killer?"

Summer sighed. "Well, yeah. There's another thing, though. Detective Caputo stopped by Esmé's apartment to ask her more questions this morning. And then, when she went down to the station later to try to help with the whole Zoe thing, they wanted to take *her* fingerprints, too."

"Oh my. Did she agree?" Dorothy asked.

"Nope. She said she wanted to talk to her lawyer first. Except she doesn't have one."

"Perhaps Julian will offer his services, if we explain the story to him," Dorothy said. Lately, Dash's partner had been adding criminal law clients—including Summer, during their first investigation—to his caseload at Black and LeBlanc at quite a clip.

"I'll ask him," Summer said. "Maybe he's less busy during the holidays. I dunno, though. That guy is always working."

"Next stop, Milano PD." Dorothy grabbed a few napkins from the iron dragonfly holder on the counter and slipped an éclair or two from the pastry box in her purse. One never knew when one might need a little energy boost.

She and Summer would be sure to look out for Frankie on the way downtown. At this point, Angelica's determined mother could be just about anywhere.

And so could Angelica's killer.

"HI, MERLE," SUMMER greeted the timid-looking, older man behind the round security window at the entrance to the Milano PD. "You remember us, right? Summer Smythe and Dorothy Westin?"

She had never seen him before in her life, actually, but he had to be related to Gladys. Those beady, watery eyes and the giant, beaklike nose were a dead giveaway.

"We're very good friends of your lovely cousin," Dorothy added. "Neighbors, too, in fact."

"Gladys?" Merle shot up straighter in his office chair, on high alert. "Is she with you?" He looked around Dorothy to the front door.

"Nope," Summer said. *You can chill*, she wanted to tell him. "Anyway, we're here to see…"

Uh oh. She hadn't exactly thought this getting-into-the-station thing through on the way over here. They couldn't just say they wanted to talk to Esmé or Zoe. And the last thing she wanted was to have another fun convo with Caputo. The detective wasn't going to give her any updates or decent info on the case, anyway.

Not on purpose, at least.

"Detective Donovan," Summer blurted. She didn't want to talk to him, either, but chances were good he wasn't here, anyway. His precious grandma probably had him giving her a pedicure or something.

"What is this in reference to?" Merle reached for a yellow legal pad and pushed his wire glasses higher on his pelican beak, all business again.

The door behind Summer swung open, and a tanned, athletic-looking dad and his kid came through it with a yapping brown-and-white dog on a half-chewed leash.

"So, Merle." Dorothy leaned closer to the window, blocking his view. "Gladys mentioned you're a senior volunteer here, and a critical member of the department. It sounds fascinating. I'd love to find out more about the application process. I hear it's quite extensive."

"Nice dog," Summer told its owners, as she passed them on her way through the entrance. The dog bared its gnarly teeth at her.

He and Mr. Bitey would be a great match.

Summer hurried past the main area of desks, file cabinets and busy office workers to the back of the open room, where she knew those orange plastic visitor benches were located. She knew exactly where people brought in for questioning and stuff had to wait. And think about their stories, very carefully. She'd learned that herself once or twice, the hard way.

No Zoe. No Esmé either. Was that a good thing or a bad thing?

"Well, hello there." A broad-shouldered, sandy-haired officer with a moustache smiled at her as she peeked cautiously into one of the side offices. "Are you here for the Citizens Police Academy?"

"Gosh, no," Summer blurted, then wanted to kick herself. That would have been the perfect cover.

"So who are you looking for?" the officer said. "Or maybe I can help you."

Summer glanced around the busy stationhouse. Still

no sign of Zoe or Esmé. Or Caputo, luckily. "Um, is Detective Donovan here?"

"You're in luck, young lady. I just saw him come in a couple of minutes ago." The officer, whose nametag said, "Sgt. Kash," stepped out from behind his desk. "I can take you over there. I'm headed that way myself."

"Super," Summer said, forcing a smile. "Thanks."

She knew exactly where the detective's office was, of course—she'd actually thrown up in it once—but she kept up the clueless act until they arrived at the door.

"Donovan, you've got a visitor," Sgt. Kash announced. "A real pretty one, too, I might add."

Summer's face burned as Detective Donovan looked up in surprise from the papers on his desk. His usual navy blue blazer was tossed on a side chair, and his "World's #1 Son" mug was filled with steaming black coffee, as usual.

So he was a nana's boy *and* a mamma's boy. Well, at least he was a family guy. Most women considered that a good thing, right?

"Don't do anything I would do, Detective." Sgt. Kash chuckled, and left. Good.

That's when Summer noticed the other person in Detective Donovan's office, glaring at her from the visitor's chair across from the desk. Who else? Caputo.

Detective Donovan cleared his throat. "Ms. Smythe-Sloan," he said. "What a surprise."

"Hi," she said. "I was just…in the neighborhood."

Well, that sounded stupid. As in, what neighborhood? Downtown Milano?

Caputo stood up with her iPad. "If you don't need me for anything else, sir, I'm headed out. Roberts and I need to follow up on those leads I mentioned."

He nodded. "Thanks, Detective. Keep me posted."

"You got it," Caputo told him. "*You* again," Summer heard the junior detective add under her breath, as she brushed past her. "Give it up."

Summer's mouth dropped open. What was *that* supposed to mean? Give up the case? Or any hope of a semi-relationship with Shane Donovan? Or maybe both.

"So hey, I'm glad you came by," the detective said. "Sit down." He motioned toward the visitor chair.

It was still warm from Caputo's mean, skinny butt. Ugh.

"Detective Caputo was just filling me in on the details of everything I missed while I was off," he went on. "Between my crazy caseload lately, and traveling, and my grandma, I've been a little out of touch with... well, everything."

Like me? Summer wanted to say.

"But I, uh, was planning to call you and see if maybe you wanted to try again. You know, for an evening out or something."

"You mean, an actual date?" Summer said. "No work? No grandma?"

The dimple that always showed up when he smiled appeared, just for a second. "I can't promise that. But hopefully. Nana can be pretty demanding sometimes."

Well, *that* was the understatement of the year. Summer caught herself pressing her already beat-up nails into the plastic seat. *He's just a guy*, she reminded herself. *No big deal.*

"I love her, though, and she's the only grandma I've got." He shrugged. "So what do you say? Anywhere you want to go. Surprise me."

"Okay," Summer said. That probably hadn't come

out sounding very excited, but maybe that was a good thing. "When?"

"How about Saturday night?" he said. "I'll pick you up at seven. I'd say tomorrow, but I have to accompany Nana to some golf club holiday fashion show she's over the moon about. Apparently it's the event of the season."

"I'm going to that, too," Summer said. "With Dorothy." She almost added, *For the case*, but luckily she stopped herself from that in time.

"Great," he said. "We can suffer together."

"Deal," she said, smiling for real as she stood up from her chair. She was kind of looking forward to this big-time show now. "Sorry, but I'd better go. Dorothy's outside, waiting for me."

"Well, thanks for stopping by," he said. The dimple showed up again, deeper than the last time. "See you tomorrow."

Summer stopped at the door. "I heard my friend Esmé was in here today," she said. "She didn't do anything wrong, I can tell you that for sure. And I don't think Zoe Z had anything to do with what happened to Angelica Downs, either."

The dimple immediately disappeared. "Caputo is in charge of the investigation," the detective said. "Let's leave it at that, okay? The evidence will support the facts, in the end."

"So *is* there any evidence, then?" Summer knew she was pushing it.

He sighed. "Not much, so far. The crime scene was unfortunately contaminated with all those people running around. We're pursuing a few possible angles we have left, though."

"Oh." Summer waited, but the detective didn't offer

anything else. Talk about unhelpful. "See you at the show," she said finally, and stepped out of the office without looking back. Hopefully she wouldn't run into Sgt. Kash—or Caputo—on her way out.

She absorbed herself in checking her text messages as she made her way back through the main room. That way she wouldn't make eye contact with anyone—and she could pretend she was invisible.

Esmé was at work now, bartending at Chameleon. And she'd texted her that Zoe's overworked lawyer back in LA had negotiated some kind of deal to spring her from the holding cell. Esmé had no idea where the kid was now, but there were paparazzi camped outside the restaurant, in case she showed up.

Summer sighed. At least neither her friend nor the brat were in jail. Too bad her and Dorothy's visit to the Milano PD had been pretty much a bust for the case, info-wise.

But for her and a certain awkward, annoying, but hot detective, things might just be looking up.

FIFTEEN

"COME ON OUT, Dorothy. Let's see what you've got."

Dorothy sighed as she took a last glance in the ornate, gold-framed mirror in the frilly dressing room of Monique's Boutique. Not a single dress in the entire walk-in closet worth of outfits Summer had collected for her seemed right for the Majesty Holiday Fashion Show.

Or right for *her*, anyway. Was her choice of wardrobe really that important? Summer had pointed out that they needed to blend in with the well-dressed guests, of course, but all this fuss seemed downright silly. Their focus should be on finding Angelica's killer.

"You can't go wrong with a little black dress," Summer said, as Dorothy reluctantly stepped out into the outer dressing lounge.

Emphasis on the little, Dorothy thought. "It's much too short," she said.

"Nah." Summer shook her blonde head from her perch on a satin striped divan. "You're just not used to that length. It looks really nice on you, I think. You've got great legs."

That might be true, Dorothy had to admit. All that swimming over the years had served her well. But still…

"Try the sparkly blue one," Summer said, pointing back into the dressing room. "That's going to be my favorite, I think."

"I'm not sure beading is really my style," Dorothy

said. "To tell you the truth, I was perfectly comfortable in that coral sweater and skirt set yesterday."

Summer's mouth dropped open. "What? No way. You *cannot* be an outfit repeater. Especially only two days later, jeez. And it's an evening event."

"I suppose you're right." Dorothy drew the curtain carefully shut on her private dressing area.

"Ow," she heard Summer say, sounding annoyed, as Monique pushed her aside and poked her head through the curtain. "How are we doing in there, Mrs. Westin? I've brought a few more dresses I know you'll just love. These are a bit more high-couture."

Dorothy tried not to think about the rainbow of dresses already hanging from the gold hooks all around her as she took the new batch. "Wonderful," she said. *And exhausting.*

This was ridiculous. But there was a reason they had chosen Monique's Boutique.

Summer appeared again behind Monique. "Wow, these are all such great outfits," she said, her mouth quirking slightly. "How are you ever going to choose, Dorothy?"

Very easily, Dorothy wanted to inform her. Every one of these pricey dresses was going straight back to the racks. As soon as they got some information— any miniscule piece whatsoever—out of the boutique's sharklike owner, they were leaving.

"That black dress is just stunning on you," Monique said. "And it's marked down for the holidays. Imagine how perfect it would be for New Year's Eve. You do have plans, don't you?"

Dorothy truly hadn't thought that far ahead. Last year's festivities had included a nine-thirty champagne or cider toast and balloon drop in the activity room at the top of Hibiscus Tower B.

"We're shopping for the Majesty fashion show tomorrow," Summer said. "You'll be there, right, Monique?"

The boutique owner gave a dismissive wave. "Oh, of course. Our entire Parisian holiday collection will be featured." She dropped her voice. "So many people were disappointed to miss the full premiere at the Waterman's show yesterday."

Especially those who were suffocated to death with a dry cleaner's bag, Dorothy thought. *Or questioned as possible murder suspects.* But what a stroke of luck for her and Summer's investigation that there was a second opportunity for Monique to unveil her questionable fashions—and for all the same people to gather.

"Hey, now that you mention it, Monique," Summer said, gathering up the dismissed dresses and replacing them with all the new ones she had collected. "Do you have any idea what happened to that really nice model Angelica, before...well, you know. She went backstage with you after you guys left our table, right?"

Monique didn't bat an eye at the question, Dorothy noticed. "Yes, she did," the boutique owner said. "She'd spent far too much time chatting. But then she disappeared somewhere, and missed her cue. I have to say, I was rather put out about it. Angelica was a former employee of mine, and I approved her for the Waterman's job only as a favor."

"A favor?" Summer said, as Dorothy pulled another overly tight dress over her head. Now she'd need to redo her hair before tomorrow.

"Well, she was practically destitute after losing her position here at the boutique," Monique said. "But I was forced to let her go for unprofessional behavior. It was too bad, because she'd received ample compensation and a more than generous employee discount. I'm not sure she even deserved a second chance, frankly."

"What did she do wrong?" Summer asked, before Dorothy could stop her.

Monique gave a hard yank on the striped bolero jacket with god-awful fringe Dorothy was still struggling to bring down over her shoulders. "Let's just say some women are driven to desperate measures after they run through all their dead husband's money and have to find a new sugar daddy." Her lips, bright orange today, pursed in high disapproval.

She had to be referring to Angelica's alleged pursuit of her former husband, Dorothy told herself. Was she trying to justify her poor treatment of a woman who was now sadly dead? Or was she offering an explanation of why someone might be driven to murder?

Like herself, for instance.

"I was willing to look past that kind of behavior to allow Angelica to be hired in a different capacity," Monique said. "On a very limited basis, just a few holiday shows to start."

"So she was going to model at Majesty tomorrow, too, then?" Summer's eyes met Dorothy's in the mirror.

"That's right," Monique said, with a put-upon sigh. "She was the perfect model for our exclusive, ermine-trimmed Christmas gown over there, too." She gestured toward a ghastly heap of poufy red netting, fur and taffeta strung on a satin-padded hanger. "Such a pity."

Summer visibly shuddered, and Dorothy briefly considered the idea that the fringe nightmare currently draping her shoulders might not actually be the ugliest vestment on the planet.

"Tell me, Monique," Dorothy said. "Did Angelica have any visitors when she worked here, people stopping by the store to talk to her?"

Monique sniffed. "Other than unavailable men, you mean?"

Oh dear. Dorothy hadn't meant to bring up the ex-husband again. "Did she ever seem nervous or frightened in any way?" she rephrased.

"I really can't recall." The boutique owner's tone was evasive. "So what do you think, Mrs. Westin? Which of these lovely garments will you take home? I'm sure we can arrange a very nice discount should you decide to purchase multiple items."

"Go for it, Dorothy." Summer could barely contain her glee at the hilarity of the situation, it seemed.

"I'll think about it," Dorothy said. "Overnight, perhaps." Or over the next millennium, more likely.

"But the Majesty show is tomorrow night," Monique said. "I can't promise any of these outfits will still be available by store closing."

"Mmm," Dorothy said, closing the curtain.

"Other than our regular customers and one man of questionable character I prefer not to name, the only person I ever saw Angelica with was her mother," Monique offered, as the silence grew in the dressing room. "The elder Mrs. Downs was in here many times. She's a huge fan of the store, I'll say that. But with all that time spent away…" Her voice trailed off delicately.

"Away where?" Summer said, immediately.

"Well—" Monique lowered her voice "—she was

briefly incarcerated in Nevada, I believe. Angelica never confided in me, but that's what I gathered."

"What was she in for?" Summer asked. Behind the curtain, Dorothy stayed silent. Her sleuthing partner was fishing for leads, and she didn't want to distract Monique.

"Mrs. Westin, have you made a decision?" Monique called into the dressing room. Dorothy had to admire her equal sense of focus.

"Not yet," Dorothy said. "So difficult to choose."

"Maybe if you could tell us a little more about Angelica's mom," Summer said. "I had no idea she was such a…um, criminal. That's horrible."

And that criminal had been staying in Summer's condo, Dorothy thought. Although not for long, it had turned out. Perhaps that was a good thing.

"Well, I have no idea why the elder Mrs. Downs went to jail," Monique said, "but I'm sure it was something especially shady. And one never knows how far the apple falls from the tree, if you know what I mean. That's another reason why I had to let Angelica go."

"Wow," Summer said. "Well, thanks, Monique. Dorothy will take the black dress," she added. "And maybe some accessories, too. Can we go look at all the jewelry you've got?"

What? Dorothy buttoned her light sweater as quickly as possible over her boatneck T-shirt and threw open the curtain, stepping out of the dressing room at the same time as a woman in a much larger size of the same fringed bolero jacket Dorothy held over her arm.

"Well, well, well," Gladys said. "Looks like we have the same excellent taste, Dorothy."

How long had Gladys been in there, listening with

her giant ears? Dorothy was guilty of the very same thing, of course. But that was different. Or was it?

"You're not going to wear *our* jacket to Majesty tomorrow, are you, Dorothy?" Gladys said. "That'd be a real fashion faux pas, ya know what I mean? You should go with the black dress, like your Big Bird friend said. It's real chic on a skinny person like you, and it'll come in handy for all those funerals, too."

Dorothy was about to reply when Summer reappeared in the dressing lounge, looking distressed. "What is it, dear?" Dorothy asked. "Is something wrong?"

Summer dropped back onto the satin chaise. "It's practically the worst thing ever. I just got a phone call. From the booker at PAGE Models."

"PAGE? What did they want?" Gladys said, eagerly. "Was it something about Angelica? Spill it, Beanstalk."

Both Summer and Dorothy glared at her. "It's none of your business, Mrs. Rumway," Summer said.

"Anything for the Downs investigation *is* my business," Gladys said. "I'm related to a member of the Milano PD, remember? Plus I signed up for the next Citizens Police Academy. I'm practically on the force already."

Dorothy had a feeling Gladys and the Milano PD differed on their definitions of "members of the force." Mercifully, Summer just rolled her eyes at Dorothy and kept her mouth shut.

"Come on, Dorothy. We need to look at shoes for you, too." Summer pulled her out of the dressing lounge and headed them both in the direction of one of Monique's clear plastic tower displays of evening shoes and furry bedroom kitten heels.

"So what information did the modeling agency offer

on Angelica?" Dorothy said, dropping her voice. Monique had spotted them from the cash register, and her eyes were already gleaming with the prospect of another sale.

"They wanted me to fill in for Angelica at the Majesty show, can you believe it?" Summer said. "A lot of the models have been dropping out because of what happened at Waterman's."

"Well, I think it's a wonderful opportunity," Dorothy said.

"You're kidding, right?" Summer said. "That'd be, like, a joke."

Dorothy smiled. "Don't worry, you'll do a wonderful job."

"I don't want that kind of job," Summer said, frowning. "Even if it pays more than volunteering at the pool. And Detective Donovan's going to be there. With his grandma. It'd be the worst idea ever."

"Sometimes we have to put our personal preferences aside for an investigation." Dorothy nodded toward the pink-and-black Monique's Boutique bag Summer was carrying for her, with that frightfully short black dress and what looked like several tissue-wrapped pieces of jewelry. "Don't you agree, dear?"

SUMMER STOOD IN front of Grandma Sloan's bedroom closet, which was now majorly jammed with both of their clothes and shoes—so full that the accordion wood doors were about to break, even though she kept them open.

"I hate to say it, Cali Girl, but your whole bedroom is starting to look like something out of one of those hoarding shows," Dash said, from his safe perch on the edge of her unmade bed.

"Yeah, I know," Summer said. "I'm going to clean the whole thing up and totally organize it, as soon as I have time." Which she never did. But that was okay, because solving murders was a lot more important than having a perfect closet. And anyway, Dash was super picky, because he was an interior designer and didn't even believe in dressers. He and Julian and Juliette-Margot each had walk-in closets twice the size of her entire condo.

"Try the zig-zag dress again, Mademoiselle Summer," Juliette-Margot said. "With the white hoop earrings and white envelope purse, *s'il vous plaît.*"

"Okay." Summer bit back a grin, but did as she was told. She had to admit, the kid had a definite eye.

"Detective Donovan likes black and white," Juliette Margot added, crossing her arms over her mint-green dress with the tangerine sash. She had matching Mary-Janes, too. How many pairs of those did she own, anyway? And they were never scuffed.

"Hey, how do *you* know what colors Detective Donovan likes?" Summer said. "Not that I care, by the way."

Behind her, Dash snorted.

"Juliette-Margot reads the fashion magazines," the little girl said, in a perfectly serious voice. "All men appreciate the contrast of black and white. The zig-zags are slimming and sophisticated and draw the eye away from most figure flaws. Not that you have any of those," she added, quickly.

"Thanks, JM." Summer rescued the matching jacket for the Donovan Dress from the floor and glanced over her shoulder at Dash. "You guys have created a little fashionista monster," she told him.

"Not guilty." He held up his hands in defense. "Julian and I had nothing to do with it, I swear. Mother got her a subscription to *Vogue* for her sixth birthday."

"Not the black-and-white choker," Juliette-Margot added, as Summer reached toward one of her favorite necklaces. "It is too much with the earrings. Remember, you must put three accessories on and take one off. Two, if you have an accent piece." She stuck out her left wrist, showing off a gold bracelet with a tiny dolphin charm.

"Got it," Summer said. "Nice bracelet." Juliette-Margot beamed.

"Not to rain on your parade," Dash said, "but aren't you getting a little too dolled up for this gig? Most models show up for work looking like they rolled out of bed. Or from a club."

"I know that," Summer said. "I just want to look nice, that's all."

"Uh huh." Dash smiled in an annoyingly smug way. "You're still trying to impress this Donovan guy, aren't you?"

"Noooo," Summer said, concentrating on the stubborn earring wire that refused to go through her earlobe. "Well, maybe," she said, when Dash raised a skeptical blond brow. The earring finally went in with a nasty pinch, and she reached for her cosmetics bag on the dresser. The bag was mostly empty at the moment, since all the shadows and liners and mascaras and lipsticks she owned were scattered everywhere.

"No makeup," Juliette-Margot said. "You must have a fresh face so the stylists can have a blank canvas to create the perfect look."

Summer tried hard not to bust out laughing. Dash's daughter was one crazy determined kid. Impulsively, she turned around from the mirror and messed up Juliette-Margot's blonde curls with one hand, before she remembered how much she'd hated the way grown-ups did that when she was the same age. "Sorry, JM," she said, as the kid carefully patted her hair back into place. "Maybe you should lay off the *Vogue* for a while, though."

"I couldn't agree more," Dash said. "So do you want us to give you a ride over to the club, Cali Girl? I promised Juliette-Margot we'd get there early to get a seat in front."

If she didn't take her car, there was a decent chance Detective Donovan might offer her a ride home from the show—or, even better, take her out. After they'd dropped off his grandma, of course. "Thanks, that'd be awesome," Summer said.

THE MAJESTY GOLF and Tennis Club looked amazing as Dash pulled the Mercedes up to the well-staffed valet stand in front of the main entrance. It was almost getting dark, thanks to the cloudy December day, and the palm trees lining the drive, along with the huge porch columns, were wound in white twinkle lights.

"It's like a real-live fairy land," Juliette-Margot said, pressing her face up to the window in the back seat. She sounded like an actual kid now. "And oooh, look, it is snowing!"

"What?" Summer peered out the passenger window as Dash gave the valet his keys—and probably a few not-so-subtle suggestions about the best place to park his precious car. Juliette-Margot was right. It was practically a blizzard of fake snow out there now.

"Cool," she said. She hated real snow, unless she was in Aspen or someplace skiing, but this kind was okay. The stuff melted in two seconds in Florida or back home in LA, but it looked pretty while it lasted. "Guess Santa will be here soon," she added.

"Juliette-Margot does not believe in Santa Claus," the little girl said, with what sounded like a semi-disdainful sniff.

"Gee, that's too bad," Summer said. "Are you sure? He brings lots of presents if you're on his Good list, you know. You were good this year, weren't you?"

"Juliette-Margot is always good," she said. "But Santa never brings her the real present she wants."

Summer twisted around in her seat. "Oh, yeah? What's that?" If Dash and Julian had already done their shopping, she'd get whatever it was for the kid herself. In fact, maybe she'd do that, anyway, as long as it wasn't that pony Juliette-Margot was always talking about.

"Juliette-Margot would like to meet her *maman*. Margot."

Ohhhh. That might be even harder to come up with than a pony. "Well, I don't know," Summer said. "She's probably super busy over the holidays."

"Models do not work on Christmas," Juliette-Margot said.

Good point. What could she say to *that*? Summer wondered. Luckily, one of the maroon-and-gold uniformed attendants opened the front passenger door for her just then, and she was saved from having to come up with an answer.

The kid needed one, though. She'd definitely have to

talk to Dash about this. But right now, unfortunately, it was time to go humiliate herself in a super-public way.

Summer had never been in the grand lobby of Majesty Golf and Tennis, just in the tony pro shop, but it was pretty awesome. The elaborate domed ceiling was so far up, she and Juliette-Margot had to really tilt their heads back to see it. And then there was the enormous Christmas tree under the dome, kitted out with more white twinkle lights and a ton of gold and maroon ornaments. A giant silver menorah with three of its candles lit shone under a spotlight in an alcove beside a group portrait of the club's ancient-looking founders.

"Here comes the train." Juliette-Margot pointed to a Lionel engine pulling several cars and a cute red caboose along a set of tracks that circled the lobby molding above the arched doorways.

"Wow, they really do this place up for the holidays," Summer said. "Pretty cool, huh?"

Juliette-Margot wasn't paying attention to the decorations anymore. Some cheery classical music Summer almost recognized was playing from hidden speakers somewhere, and the little girl was twirling in her mint-chip colored dress, her arms in a circle over her head like a ballerina. "Juliette-Margot is the Sugar Plum Fairy!" she called.

"Um, okay," Summer said. "Very nice." A fairy. Well, that was super cute, especially for a kid who didn't believe in Santa Claus.

"From *The Nutcracker*," Juliette-Margot said breathlessly, as she twirled her way toward Summer. "You know, the ballet? Grandmère took Juliette-Margot to see it last year at Lincoln Center in New York City."

"Ohhh." Summer felt really stupid now. Grandma

Sloan had never taken her to see a ballet, but she'd sent her a little jewelry box once for her birthday. A tiny pink ballerina with a white net tutu twirled around like Juliette-Margot whenever the lid opened. And she was pretty sure the tinkly tune it played was the same music that was on right now.

"Dance with me, Summer!" Juliette-Margot threw her a winning smile as she tugged on Summer's arm and started dragging her across the luckily deserted lobby. "You can be Juliette-Margot's partner for the pirouettes, so she won't get dizzy."

"Okay, but just for a minute," Summer said, as the little girl twirled and twirled under her arm. "I have to go get ready for the fashion show."

Jeez, *she* was getting dizzy now. Where was Dash and everybody else, anyway? She hoped she hadn't gotten the time wrong. The models were supposed to show up at Ballroom A, wherever that was, by six, and it had to be...

Whoa, wait. Was that Frankie Downs scurrying past that big column by the palm court? What was she doing here?

Summer caught Juliette-Margot mid-twirl. "Hold up, JM," she said, over the music. "I just saw someone I need to talk to."

But she couldn't just leave the kid here by herself. She had no clue what had happened to Dash.

"Juliette-Margot does not see anyone."

Summer bit her lip in frustration. Had Frankie really just disappeared like that, or had she totally imagined Angelica's AWOL mom in the Majesty lobby?

She couldn't run after her with Juliette-Margot. But

maybe, if they just went a little way past the lobby, and she was super careful…

"Come on, JM," Summer said. "I'm not sure where your dad is, so let's go find the hair and makeup place."

Juliette-Margot's eyes were practically glowing at the chance to hang out backstage. Summer held on tight to the kid's hand and headed for the doorway where she'd seen Frankie—well, *maybe* seen her.

Where was Ballroom A, anyway? The fashion show organizers could have at least put up a sign.

They'd reached the last, huge white column in the lobby. Should they go right or left? There were a bunch of closed doors on both sides of the hall, all the way down, and plenty of potted palms for a tiny woman to duck behind.

"Ow." She winced in pain as a hard piece of metal suddenly jabbed into her back.

"Hold it right there, Goddaughter," Frankie said. "Or you and your little ballet friend will be dancing *Swan Lake*." She leaned closer to Summer. "Spoiler alert. The swan dies."

SIXTEEN

DOROTHY TWISTED AROUND in her velvet-backed chair. Goodness, the grand ballroom at Majesty Golf and Tennis was certainly filling up fast. It was a lucky thing Ernie had dropped her off early. She'd managed to snag an excellent seat, just a few rows behind the roped-off Reserved area.

The fashion show organizers had spared no expense in creating a luxurious and festive atmosphere, right down to the sparkling crystal snowflakes and multi-pointed stars hanging from the ceiling. The stage area at the front had been draped with heavy maroon-and-gold curtains that might have been borrowed from the Milano Metropolitan Opera House.

"Excuse me. Pardon me. So sorry."

Dash, looking extremely debonair in a white dinner jacket with black lapels, was doing his best to squeeze his way down the endless row of fashion show audience members toward the seats Dorothy had saved beside her for him and Juliette-Margot.

Summer's friend was frowning, which made him seem very unlike his usual, charming self. *Something is wrong*, Dorothy thought.

"Have you seen Summer and my daughter?" Dash asked, without taking a seat. "I was hoping Juliette-Margot might be with you."

Dorothy rose immediately. "No, but I'll help you look

for her," she said. "Perhaps Summer took her to see the models' dressing area."

Doubtful, she added to herself. *But possible.*

"I certainly hope that's it," Dash said. "But she knows how strongly I feel about steering Juliette-Margot clear of the modeling world."

He guided Dorothy through the well-heeled crowd still milling in the outer reception area, sipping champagne with strawberries. "Can you ask someone how to get to wherever the models are getting ready before they head backstage?" he asked. "No one would tell me. They thought I was some kind of stalker, I guess, even after I told them I was looking for my daughter."

"Well, security is extra tight, after what happened to Angelica," Dorothy said.

"I'm not sure that's very comforting." Dash's tone was grim as they entered the main lobby.

No one was eager to share the location of the models' dressing area, as Dash had found earlier, but Dorothy managed to wheedle the information from a harried looking young woman balancing several large bottles of water and a clipboard.

"Medication for my granddaughter," she said, hastily retrieving a flowered pill case from her pocketbook and holding it up. "It's very important that she have it right away."

"Well done, Dorothy," Dash said, as they turned a corner on their way toward Ballroom A.

"It's just aspirin," Dorothy said, trying to keep up. Gracious, this was another long hall. The Majesty Golf and Tennis Club had to have more function rooms than the Milano Grand.

"There's Summer!" Dash said, pointing straight ahead.

Sure enough, she was standing with her back to the doors of yet another ballroom. She had one hand on a door handle and the other on the arm of... Frankie Downs.

Thanks goodness, Summer had found Angelica's missing mother. But oh dear. Where was Juliette-Margot?

"Am I glad to see you guys," Summer said, as Dorothy and Dash came up.

Frankie looked considerably less enthusiastic, Dorothy noted. Even the tiny woman's distinctive blue hair sagged as she stood, slumped and clearly miserable, under Summer's iron grip. What on earth was going on here?

"Where is my daughter?" Dash looked frantic again.

"Don't worry, she's fine," Summer said. "No thanks to you," she added to Frankie, before jerking her blonde head toward the door behind her. "She's in there. If you hold on to this crazy person for me, Dash, I'll let her out."

"What is going *on* here?" Dash threw up his hands, bringing one of them down on Frankie's shoulder. "Why is Juliette-Margot locked in a conference room?"

"It's for her own safety," Summer said. "Trust me on that." She threw open the door to reveal Juliette-Margot sitting calmly on a velvet chair, clutching her purse on her lap.

The little girl rose, smoothed the skirt of her mint-green dress, and walked through the doorway. "Let's go, Papa, we will be late for the show," she said.

"Hey, I'm sorry, kid," Frankie said, lifting her chin. "Hope I didn't scare you or anything."

"You sure tried," Summer said. "You scared *me*."

"Someone had better explain this whole thing," Dash said. "Or I am going to blow a gasket."

"Juliette-Margot was not afraid," the little girl said to

Frankie, with a sniff. "She and Summer would dance *Swan Lake* for you now, Madame, but Summer must get ready."

With that, she took her father's hand and led him back down the hall. Dash looked back once or twice over his shoulder at Summer, but she just smiled and waved at him as she held on to Frankie again. "Enjoy the show," she called. "I'll explain everything later."

"All right, Summer," Dorothy said, as soon as Dash and Juliette-Margot were out of sight. "Why don't you fill *me* in on what happened before we got here?"

Frankie started to open her mouth, but Summer beat her to it. "Nothing, really," she said. "The Stick-'em-Up Queen here tried to pretend she had a gun, but it was just the end of a flashlight. I had to protect Juliette-Margot, so I shut her in the conference room after I grabbed Frankie and took her fake weapon away."

"Admit it," Frankie said. "I had you fooled for a minute there."

Dorothy frowned. Was this some kind of joke to her, or a result of her mental issues? Why had Angelica's mother done such a thing?

"I can't believe you tried to scare me and a little kid, too," Summer said. "Don't you understand how wrong that was?"

"I said I was sorry," Frankie said. "I didn't mean to scare the kid. And I didn't really have a gun. But I knew you'd seen me, and were trying to follow me. And I am not going back to Hibiscus Glen. I have important stuff to take care of."

Oh my. Dorothy exchanged a glance with Summer. What was it, exactly, that Frankie needed to accomplish? And what should they do with her now? The show was about to start.

"Summer, Juliette-Margot was right," she broke in. "You need to get to Ballroom A with the rest of the models. I'll take care of Frankie."

"Take care of me how?" Frankie said, frowning.

"Oh, I'll figure out something," Dorothy said. If that sounded like a vague threat, so be it. She couldn't trust Angelica's mother for a minute. They needed to talk with her again before handing her over to anyone, but this was not a good time. And the tiny woman would be a considerable flight risk.

"Can Frankie sit with you at the show?" Summer said. "We'll deal with her later."

"The heck you will, Goddaughter." Frankie crossed her arms and glared at them both.

"But we don't have a ticket for her," Dorothy said. "I'm afraid they won't let her in. They're being quite strict at the door."

"Oh, I have a ticket," Frankie said, reaching inside her blouse to bring out an engraved white card printed with a circle of holly leaves. "See?"

Dorothy peered closer. The ticket was made out to Margaret E. Donovan. "This isn't yours, Frankie," she said. "It belongs to Detective Donovan's grandmother."

Frankie shrugged. "Hey, it's legit, okay? I found it on our bedroom floor of that horror hole we were stuck in. She couldn't come here, anyway, with that giant boot on her foot."

"I wouldn't bet on that," Summer said. "Her grandson is bringing her."

That didn't surprise Dorothy. It was hard to imagine that Peggy would be easily discouraged from attending the fashion event of the season, injury or no injury. And if she did show up, the detective's grandmother was likely to throw quite a fit when she learned her room-mate had stolen her ticket.

But at the moment, she and Summer had no choice but to let Frankie get away with it.

"All right, Frankie," Dorothy said, taking the blue-haired woman firmly by the elbow. "You can sit right next to me."

And you'd better not twitch a muscle, Dorothy added silently. Sorry as she was for Frankie's loss, she couldn't help but worry that Angelica's mother was up to no good.

SUMMER SQUEEZED HER eyes shut and braced herself as Petra, her stylist, sprayed half a can of hair product into her chin-length bob. "Ew, that stuff burns my eyeballs," she said, as they watered up in spite of her efforts.

Ugh. She should have kept her mouth shut, because now it was full of chemicals, too.

"Tell me about it," Petra said. "I get to breathe it every day. You're getting off easy, though, because you have great hair. We don't have time to do a different style, anyway."

"Sorry," Summer said, her voice muffled behind her hands. "Something came up."

"Here," Petra said, handing her a clammy towel to hold over her face. "Your bangs keep falling all over your face. Maybe we should spike them up a little. And hey, quit crying, okay? You'll ruin your mascara."

She wasn't crying. That was the hairspray. But she'd already gotten a glimpse of her makeup in the mirror, and she'd hardly recognized herself. Maybe that was a good thing, because then Shane Donovan wouldn't re-alize it was her out there, looking stupid.

She had to admit, though, this show was a notch or two higher on the cool meter than the one at Waterman's. Most of the models were around her age this time—totally over the hill, she reminded herself—and some of the clothes were halfway decent, from what she'd seen everyone wearing so far around Ballroom A. Maybe she could take a few of the samples home.

"Is that what they're having you wear?" Petra asked, when she'd finished spraying and Summer had reluctantly ditched the towel. "I mean, it's a great outfit and all, but it's not really very holiday-ish."

"I have no idea," Summer said. "Nobody's said anything to me yet about clothes." At this point, maybe she'd end up modeling the dress she and Dash and Juliette-Margot had picked out from her closet.

The chair beside her spun around, and now that Summer's eyes weren't killing her anymore she recognized the occupant. It was the red-haired model from Waterman's, the one Esmé had told not to eat anything after pinning her dress. She was reading a trashy magazine with a bad photo of ZeeZee and Zoe arguing on the cover.

What was her name again? Brie, like the cheese? Diana? No. *Bryana*. A manicurist was just rolling a cart up next to the model's chair to do her nails to match her outfit. Summer quickly sat on her hands so no one would notice they were bitten down to the quick at the moment, thanks to Angelica being murdered and her almost losing Frankie and worrying about her pathetic love life.

"You were supposed to stop by Wardrobe so they could assign a rack of clothes to you," Bryana said, holding out her hands to the manicurist. Another woman zoomed up and rummaged through the colorful bottles to select a shade for the model's toes. "Didn't your booker give you the info?"

"Nope," Summer said. Actually, she hadn't checked her phone for a while. Maybe she should have. "I'm kind of a last minute sub."

"Monique came by looking for you earlier," Petra said, rubbing some kind of sticky goop between her hands and creating stiff little points out of Summer's bangs. "I told her you were in the ladies room, so it's lucky for me you finally showed up."

Phew. Well, that was nice of her, especially since the stylist hadn't even met her before. "Thanks, Petra," Summer said. "You're the best. So you know Monique, huh?"

"Unfortunately," Petra said. "I worked the Waterman's show on Wednesday."

Summer sat up straighter. "Really? Did you know Angelica Downs, too?"

Petra turned away to drop the comb she'd been using earlier into a glass container of Barbicide. "Yeah. Just from these shows, though. We worked together a lot. I almost backed out today, because I was so freaked out after what happened to her, but I really need the money. I'm a single mom and my kid and I live in a dump. The Milano Arms, ever hear of it?"

Esmé's place. "Um, yeah." Summer carefully suppressed a shudder. "Did Angelica ever say she thought she might be in any kind of danger or trouble? Or her mom was, maybe? My detective partner and I are trying to help solve the case."

Petra glanced around, suddenly looking nervous. "Are you some kind of undercover cop or something?"

"No, nothing like that," Summer said quickly. Was it possible the stylist really did have info about Angel-

ica's murder? Petra's English was great and all, but she
did have some kind of accent. Maybe she was worried
about being kicked out of the country because she'd
overstayed her visa or something.

"Dorothy and I are just, uh, really tight with the family," Summer said.

"Oh." Petra let out her breath. "Well, she did say
something kind of strange that day, but I didn't think
much about it until afterward. I mean, it may not be
important. But now that Angelica's dead, I guess I can
tell you."

"We'll take anything you've got," Summer said.

The stylist lowered her voice. "Angelica had confided
in me a few weeks ago that she'd gotten back together
with some guy who'd broken her heart once. She didn't
tell me his name but I got the idea they were keeping
things on the down low for some reason."

The not-new boyfriend had to be Monique's ex-
husband. Why else would they be keeping their relationship a secret? The last thing they'd want was to
tick her off.

So far, thank the fashion gods, it looked like the Majesty backstage operations were temporarily witch-free,
and a lot more efficient.

"Anyway, Angelica had seemed really happy lately,"
Petra went on. "But at Waterman's I could tell she was
jittery about something because I couldn't get her mascara on. She kept turning her head suddenly to look
around, and her eyelids were fluttering like crazy."

*Probably worried about her boss finding out she'd
been hooking up with the hubby again*, Summer
thought. Former *hubby*, she corrected herself quickly.

"I asked Angelica what was wrong, and she insisted

it was nothing. But then she said something about bad things in people's pasts coming back to haunt them. I thought that was kind of weird, so I asked her what she meant by that. All she said was, 'There's always payback, Petra. The truth always comes out.'"

"Huh," Summer said. So Angelica believed in karma, too. Was she the one who'd done something bad, or some other person? Either way, Petra's info didn't seem like it would help much for the case. Too bad.

"Well, *finally.*"

Summer peeked out between her hands, which she'd already put up to her face to defend herself from Petra's drippy spiking gel. Monique was standing next to the makeup chair, with an assistant hurriedly rolling up a dress rack behind her.

"I selected you for the honor of wearing my showstopper dress, but you were nowhere to be found, and now there's no time for a proper fitting. All of you models are alike, no sense of time. But anyway, *voilà.*" Monique stepped aside like a game show hostess, revealing the hideous red dress Summer had seen hanging in the dressing room at her boutique.

No no no no. NO. She was *not* stepping out in front of half the world—and one cute detective in particular—in that disaster. The raggedy fur trim alone made her want to puke, and the crisscross pull-ties in the back, with...

Wait. No way. Was that a bow hanging down from the butt, or a tail?

"Um, I don't think red is really my color," Summer said, weakly. "I had a palette profile done once and that shade was, like, a total fail on me. The dress is so awesome, though. One of the other models would be really lucky to get to wear it."

Behind her, Petra stifled a snort.

"Nonsense," Monique said, in a brisk voice. "Everyone looks gorgeous in Hothouse Tomato. It just screams 'holiday.' But we're saving this dress for the grand New Year's collection finale. In the meantime, we'll start you off with Christmas Casual." She clapped her hands toward a young woman trying to hide behind another rack overloaded with ho ho—horrible holiday clothes of every kind. "Bonita, the pink sweater dress—the one with the darling silver bells."

Summer squeezed her eyes shut, unable to look. But she couldn't avoid hearing all of those little bells jingling like crazy as the assistant removed the outfit from the rack and headed toward her.

"There's been a schedule change, Ms. Monique," someone else said, coming up behind them. "The Christmas Fantasy collection goes first now. Something about the music queue. The other models are already dressed."

"Well, this one will just have to wear whatever's left over," Monique said. "I certainly hope it fits."

I'm totally doomed, Summer thought. But hey, what was an hour or two of humiliation compared to what had happened to poor Angelica? She could do this to solve a murder.

But she and Dorothy needed a break in the case soon. Somewhere out there—maybe even right here at the twinkle-lit Majesty Golf and Tennis Club—a killer was planning his or her next move.

And at this point, they had no idea who might be Victim Number Two.

SEVENTEEN

THE MAJESTY FASHION show crowd was growing increasingly restless, waiting for the show to begin.

Dorothy sat on the edge of her velvet seat, fanning herself with the arty black-and-white program. She'd taken a quick glance through it first, but she hadn't recognized the names of any of the famous designers. Except Roland Cho, of course.

When had she become so out of touch with fashion? she wondered. Or had she ever cared that much about it?

She'd always tried to look nice, of course. It was important to appear well put together, and she had to admit she'd enjoyed Harlan's generous compliments over the years. Every now and then she'd splurged a bit on a fancy dress or shoes for extra-special occasions. She still did, thanks to Summer.

Some people were fascinated with clothes and accessories and such, though. Like Angelica Downs, for example. Perhaps it was in their genes. Dorothy stole a glance at a miserable-looking Frankie seated on the chair beside her, arms crossed.

Or perhaps not.

"When will the models come out, Madame Dorothy?" Juliette-Margot asked, from her perch on Dash's lap, on the other side of Frankie. "Juliette-Margot is tired of waiting."

"You and me both," Dash said, without looking up

from his phone. Fortunately, he'd been too polite to question why the grumpy older woman had squeezed in with them.

"I'm sure the show will start soon," Dorothy assured Juliette-Margot. Goodness, she hoped so. It was nearly nine o'clock, and the enormous stage curtain hadn't even rustled. "Just a little bit longer, I think."

At least she didn't have to worry about Frankie now. Well, not for the moment, at least. What were she and Summer going to do with her after the show? Turn her over to Hibiscus Glen?

After trying once again to get some answers from her for the case, of course. Dorothy had a feeling that might take a while.

"Yoo-hoo, Dorothy!" Gladys Rumway twisted around in her seat three rows up. "Isn't this exciting? And hey, nice dress. A little peekaboo action with the legs, huh?"

Oh my. Dorothy's face burned as several well-dressed and coiffed audience members turned to stare in her direction.

"The shorter hemline is on trend now for women *d'un certain âge*, Madame Gladys," Juliette-Margot said. "You need to read the fashion magazines."

Gladys's thick eyebrows shot toward the ceiling, and several people around them tittered.

"Okay, that's it." Dash finally glanced up from his phone. "I don't care what Grandmère says, she's canceling that *Vogue* subscription."

"So who's this, Dorothy?" Undeterred, Gladys jerked her large chin toward Frankie. "A new resident from the Pointe?"

"None of your beeswax," Frankie said, glaring.

Fortunately, the lights dimmed before Gladys had a chance to respond, and Martha Kirk, the Milano Women's League president, appeared in a blue spotlight to the side of the stage.

Tonight Martha was tightly enveloped in an all-gold version of the silver dress she'd worn for her emcee duties on Wednesday. The canned music tape slowly cut out, and a tuxedo-clad man seated at a baby grand piano played a few bars softly in the background as Martha bid everyone welcome to the Twenty-fourth Silver Belles Annual Holiday Fashion Show.

Feeling a bit of déjà vu, Dorothy hardly listened to Martha's rather drawn out speech, which entailed an overview of the Majesty Golf and Tennis Club's long, prestigious history, enthusiastic plugs for the various designers who had donated their time and creations, and the introduction of her very good friend, the founder of Silver Belles.

Ugh. Dorothy had finally managed to forget about the online dating service Summer had signed her up for as a cover to meet a lonely hearts suspect during their last investigation. She greatly preferred to think of the name "Silver Belles" in reference to the show's holiday theme.

Finally, Martha exited the stage on the arm of the dapper pianist. To the accompaniment of unusually loud, driving taped music, the curtain quickly rose on a line of models in every imaginable—and unimaginable—type of holiday garb.

"Where is Summer?" Juliette-Margot said, craning her neck.

Dorothy had been wondering the same thing. "There

she is," she told the little girl, pointing. "Near the back, in the black cape."

Summer, wearing high black boots, a considerable amount of black eyeliner and a startlingly hard expression, marched toward the audience with a group of tall, younger women modeling similar designs. They nearly ran over the models directly in front of them, who were rather unfortunately dressed in netted hoop skirts that gave them the appearance of floating cupcakes. Others were wrapped head-to-toe in red and white like human candy canes.

"A Christmas nightmare. Amazing." Dash seemed as fascinated now as Juliette-Margot, who had bounced off her father's knee to lean eagerly over the shoulders of the people in front of them.

"It's high fashion," Juliette-Margot said.

"It's garbage." Frankie's outlook had clearly not improved. "*My* daughter never wore anything like that."

Summer's line strutted to the front, dropping their capes to reveal red leather merry widows with black belts and rhinestone buckles as they twirled and struck a pose.

Goodness, Dorothy thought. If she hadn't known better, she would have sworn her friend was a professional model.

These particular outfits didn't exactly evoke warm, nostalgic holiday memories, but all of the young women had the figures and attitudes to pull them off.

"What did I tell you? Trash." Frankie stood up. "I'm going to the can."

"Right now?" Dorothy asked.

"Yep. When you gotta go, you gotta go." She started making her way toward the end of the row, loudly excusing herself to each and every person. Dorothy scrambled after her as fast as she could in the darkness.

Thankfully, Frankie headed straight into the nearest powder room. At least escape was not her primary game plan this time.

Dorothy positioned herself outside the stall, just in case.

"You don't have to wait for me or anything," Frankie said, blowing her nose.

Were those odd sounds coming from the stall actually muffled sobs? Dorothy's heart went out to the older woman. Poor Frankie. Watching all those models must have made her miss her daughter. No wonder she'd needed to leave the ballroom.

"Are you all right, Frankie?" Dorothy asked.

"Of course I am," Frankie said, in a wobbly voice.

"Well, I'm just going to wash my hands." Dorothy quickly moved toward the sink, busying herself with choosing between the pretty, star-shaped soaps. She wished she knew how to comfort Angelica's grieving mother.

The powder room door swung open, and a waft of heavy perfume with an odd undertone of cinnamon assaulted Dorothy's nostrils. "Why, Mrs. Westin," the petite blonde newcomer in the beige blazer said. "Imagine running in to you here."

The sobbing noises from the stall abruptly stopped.

Good heavens, how had Violet Downs gotten a ticket to the Majesty fashion show? Wasn't she from Vero Beach? And what an odd choice of activities for a woman who had just lost her only sister, and whose elderly mother, to the best of her knowledge, was wandering the streets and swamps and beaches of Southwest Florida.

"Yes, what a surprise," Dorothy murmured. Frankie's feet had disappeared from view, she noticed. Was the poor woman huddled up somehow on the commode?

Maybe the right thing to do was turn her over to her younger daughter. But Dorothy wasn't sure that was such a good idea, at least for now. Besides, she and Summer weren't done trying to get information out of Frankie for the case.

She needed to get rid of Violet as soon as possible.

"So is Mr. Westin—I mean, your attorney, Mr. Conlon—here at the show?" the real estate agent asked. "I'd love to talk to you both some more about that fabulous Flamingo Pass property we looked at together."

"Thank you, Violet, but I really don't think…" Dorothy began.

"I'm expecting multiple offers any minute," Violet said.

Dorothy sighed. She'd never get anywhere with her for the case at this rate. "Violet," she said gently, "Maybe this isn't such a good time for you. We heard about your sister Angelica back at Hibiscus Pointe. Ernie and I are so sorry."

For a moment, Violet stood completely still, her expression blank. "Oh," she said. "Well, thank you."

"And your dear mother," Dorothy added, ignoring a few slight rustling and clanging sounds from the stall behind her. "How is Frankie holding up?" She held her breath, waiting for the real estate agent's reaction.

To her surprise, Violet's expression didn't change. "I don't know," the woman said. "We don't talk much.

Mom can't stand me. Never has. The only one she ever cared about was her precious Angelica."

Oh, no.

Why did I ever bring Frankie up? Dorothy scolded herself. She'd gone too far. The family dynamics of the Downses were a bit beyond her understanding, but she should have been more sensitive.

"Work is all I have," Violet said. "It's good for me. You know, helps me deal with things. Always has. No one ever talks about it, but Angelica blew all her modeling money on spas and clothes and travel, until she married Mr. Moneybags. I supported my sister and mom for years, especially after Mom's business tanked. And did they ever appreciate it? Nope. Never."

Dorothy hoped Frankie wasn't hearing all of this, but of course she had to be. She was just a few feet away, no doubt twisted into some excruciating pretzel position.

And was all that Violet had just blurted actually true? she wondered. Angelica's condo had seemed quite modest, and it hadn't appeared that she'd owned many possessions, other than those few pieces of art and furniture and the lovely clothes hanging in her crowded closet.

Violet suddenly dabbed at her heavily mascaraed eye with a hand towel from the wicker basket on the counter, and the cinnamon notes of her perfume rose to overwhelm the air freshener in the powder room.

Oh dear. Maybe she wasn't as tough as she appeared. "There, there, Violet." Dorothy went over to pat her shoulder. "I'm very sorry, I'm afraid I've upset you."

"No you didn't," Violet said with a sniff. "I'm fine." She blew her nose and looked at Dorothy, her eyes glistening very slightly with what might have been tears.

Or maybe not. "So you'll look at the Flamingo Pass property again?"

What? Dorothy dropped her hand from the real estate agent's shoulder in dismay. She couldn't possibly be that uncaring and driven.

Should she mention that she knew Violet's mother was missing from Hibiscus Glen? Surely her concern for Frankie's welfare would outweigh the prospect of any lost business dealings.

Unless she was simply a cold-blooded fish. A jealous, money-hungry shark who had killed her only sister—and whose elderly mother might be her next prey.

"We'll see about the condo, Violet," Dorothy said. "Let me consult my attorney again, and we'll get back to you. If you don't mind, though, I'd like to return to the fashion show."

"All right, Mrs. Westin," Violet said, tossing a few business cards onto the marble counter and heading toward the door. "I'll expect to hear from you very soon, then."

You can count on that, Dorothy told her silently. As soon as the real estate agent was safely gone, she turned and knocked on Frankie's locked stall door. "You can come out now, Frankie," she said.

No answer. "Frankie?" Dorothy called, more loudly.

Still silence. She frowned in concern and put her eye up to the thin crack of open space near the door hinges.

To her dismay, an air-conditioning grate lay across the seat of the commode, and a gaping hole was visible in the wall behind it—just large enough for a very petite woman to squeeze through.

Frankie was gone.

EIGHTEEN

"QUICK, RAISE YOUR ARMS."

With a silent sigh, Summer did as she was told. It was pretty weird having two total strangers dress you. Not that she was super modest or anything, but it made her feel kind of stupid and helpless.

It was almost time for the big finale—yay—of the Majesty holiday show, and she'd hardly had a chance to breathe, let alone investigate for the case. Monique never let her out of her sight, especially now that Summer was wearing her trashy, tailed, tomato dress.

She had learned one thing, from a glance at the program credits: Monique's last name was Belleek. Too bad the boutique owner hadn't added it into her store name. Monique Belleek's Boutique. Ha. But if that was Monique's married name, maybe she could look up her ex-husband, and ask him about Angelica.

Did he even know she'd been murdered?

Roland Cho had been almost as much of a giant pain in the butt as Monique so far, too. He kept popping up to check on the models every two seconds, and changing out jewelry pieces just before they hit the stage. Right now she was wearing some ruby-and-onyx drop earrings that really weren't too bad. In fact, she might even wear them herself, for the right situation.

Speaking of which, she'd only spotted Detective Donovan and his grandma once or twice in the audience. One of them must have talked the fashion show security people into letting them in without Peggy's plus-one ticket. Summer's money was on Peggy.

The lights were too bright for her to see much, but she'd caught Shane smiling—just a little—during that merry widow number with the cupcakes and candy canes. Beside him, Peggy hadn't been smiling at her at all, but that wasn't exactly a huge shocker.

"Hey, Summer. You're really burning up the runway out there."

Summer turned, just as one of the assistants gave a yank on the side zipper of the monster tomato dress, catching her skin. "Ouch!" she yelped.

"Sorry if I scared you there." Mia Rivera-Jones, a good friend of Summer's since they'd met on her and Dorothy's first case, grinned and waggled her fingers with a blinding flash of bling.

"Yeah, guess I've been a little jumpy lately," Summer said, as the wardrobe assistants took off to torture another model who was totally stuck in her dress. These sample sizes were way too tight on all of them. "I thought you were on another cruise. Cozumel this time, right?"

"Well, I *was* on a cruise," Mia said. "For, like, a week. The whole crew and half the passengers came down with norovirus, can you believe it? Not me and the girls, though, thank the stars. But we had to return to port, anyway."

"Gee, too bad," Summer said. There was a really good reason she never did cruises. But Mia, who was what one of Summer's stepmoms used to call "filthy rich," always had a lot of time and extra cash on hand.

"It turned out to be a good thing, actually," Mia said.

"My mom is going totally crazy with all the prep work for her charity deal. It's the last show of Milano Fashion Week, at her and Daddy's place. Resort wear. So now that my holidays are ruined, anyway, I might as well help. Want another modeling gig?"

"Yeah. Maybe when Florida freezes over," Summer said, as she spotted Roland hurrying toward them. What did he want now? She was *not* giving up the red-and-black earrings.

"Mia!" Roland said, as he came up in his baggy black jumpsuit and little red scarf that matched his beret. The two of them exchanged air kisses, to Summer's disgust. "How is that little diamond-and-sapphire number of mine working out for you?"

"Oh, I've gotten tons of compliments on it," Mia said. "I just wore it to a friend's wedding, so you may be getting a few calls soon. Thanks again for such a generous gift."

Gift? Summer frowned. Ol' Roland probably wouldn't even give her a model's discount. Unless maybe she had Mia ask him for her.

"Let's go, let's go, let's go," Monique said, clapping her hands at Summer as she passed them at a fast clip. "No time for chit-chat. Everyone should be backstage at the ballroom by now and lining up for the finale. Roland, you'll be the last designer out at the credits."

"Guess I'll see you later," Summer told Mia.

The pretty socialite nodded. "Right. I'd better get back to my seat. Wouldn't want to miss a minute." She raised a perfectly shaped, dark eyebrow toward the tomato bag. "Nice dress there."

"Ha ha, very funny," Summer muttered, bending

down to adjust the back strap of her red satin shoes over her newly blistered heel.

Roland leaned his spiky head down close to hers. "Watch those earrings," he said. "I don't want anything happening to them, or it's on you. Those particular gems are irreplaceable, you know."

Summer stood up fast to get him out of her face. "They're attached to my ears," she said. "Super tight. Do you really think they're going to drop off or something?"

"No," Roland said. "I was pointing out the less than slim possibility that someone might want to steal them."

Summer frowned, and did a quick check around her. She had seen Zoe Z and her agent in the audience, right up front, during her second walk. As far as she knew, though, the sticky-fingered brat hadn't shown up backstage.

"Don't worry," she told Roland. "Your precious earrings are safe with me. They'd have to rip them out of my ears."

"It wasn't necessarily other people I was referring to." Roland gave her a pointed, condescending look.

What a jerk. Summer wanted to bop him on the head with her uncomfortable red shoe.

"Summer!" Monique was waving her arms around over her head, looking frantic. "Over here. NOW!"

Summer obeyed, almost tripping over Roland on her way. *How had Angelica put up with all these annoying people?* she wondered. Being a model, even a fill-in one for a night, was a lot harder work than she'd thought.

Plus, she was starving. They'd put out a service table backstage for the crew, but Monique wouldn't let any of the models eat anything, in case they spilled stuff on their clothes.

Martha Kirk and her Silver Belles bestie were announcing the finale as Summer arrived backstage and took her place in line behind Bryana.

"I can't wait 'til this is over," Bryana said. "Want to catch a drink with me afterward? Or a salad?"

"Sorry," Summer said. "I would, but my friends are here and I might have a date later." Hopefully, unless Shane was totally repulsed by this hot-mess dress. He might even change his mind about Saturday night.

How could she try to find him afterward with all those people out there, and his grandma to boot? She'd have to change and get out of here ASAP.

Except she still had to get paid. There was a PAGE rep around here somewhere who was supposed to hand out checks.

Maybe Detective Donovan would come backstage to find her. But if not, it didn't matter, because she'd see him tomorrow night.

Except…oh, no. She'd totally forgotten about Frankie. She couldn't go out and leave Dorothy to deal with her alone. Rats.

"Go." Monique gave her an impatient little push from behind and Summer suddenly realized that the music and clapping had gotten a lot louder and Bryana had already started her walk.

Here goes nothing, Summer told herself, stepping through the curtain. She had to remember not to smile, which wasn't too hard, as she walked to the edge of the stage floor and stood still for a couple of seconds, hand on one thrust-out hip.

The pounding semi-techno music gave way to the sound of sleigh bells as the spotlight turned to ice blue.

Fake snow began to fall over the stage and the long aisle through the grand ballroom.

Summer felt the flakes hitting her head and shoulders as she made her way the length of the room, stopped to pose, and headed back toward the stage again. This end part of the show was actually kind of cool.

Or it would be, if she didn't have to parade around in a stupid tail. Hopefully people wouldn't notice the ugly bow, but she was pretty sure it was a standout element. Dash and Mia were never going to let her hear the end of it.

As she approached the stage, she saw Juliette-Margot on Dash's shoulders, waving with one hand as she held onto her father's neck with the other. So cute. The kid was thrilled. This time Summer had to resist the temptation to smile.

Martha began calling names out over her microphone, and the clothing, jewelry, hat and handbag designers came out on stage, one by one, to take their bows. The crowd was applauding like crazy, and cell phone camera flashes went off everywhere in Summer's face.

"And last but not least, let's all give a Majestic round of appreciation for the world's latest jewelry design sensation, Roland Cho!" Martha practically screamed.

The world's? Summer thought. *Really?* That was probably pushing it just a tad. The guy wasn't *that* great.

She took her place beside Bryana and the rest of the clapping models, just before the spotlight, red this time, swung back to the curtains and a giant burst of snow dumped onto the stage.

Summer looked up into the darkness of the temporary catwalk above her head. Some guy up there must have gotten a little too enthusiastic with the white stuff. Or maybe they were just trying to get rid of the last of it quick.

"Roland Cho!" Martha called again, toward the empty spotlight.

Come on, get moving, dude, Summer thought. She had a life to get back to. And a murder investigation.

For a second she wondered how Dorothy had been managing with Frankie. Hopefully she wasn't going to get stuck putting her up for the night again.

The curtains finally parted, after a few false starts from someone bumbling around behind them, and Roland stepped out to more applause than anyone else had gotten so far.

Except he didn't step, exactly. He was kind of lurching around, as if he had no clue where he was.

Then Summer saw the bright red line running down the side of his head, and it had nothing to do with the color of the spotlight.

Blood, she realized in horror, just as the designer fell heavily forward, flat on his face.

NINETEEN

"OKAY, THAT'S IT," Dash said, shielding Juliette-Margot from the crowd of fashion show participants and audience members pressing toward Roland Cho's inert body on the stage. "We're going home. This is no place for kids. Or anyone else, for that matter."

"What about Summer?" Dorothy said, craning her neck in hopes of spotting her friend. All of the lights in the ballroom had come on by now, but her view was completely blocked by Gladys Rumway. The large woman was watching the action at the front of the room with rapt attention as she talked animatedly on her cell phone.

"Don't worry, Summer will be okay," Dash said, placing his wide-eyed and unusually speechless young daughter in front of him to guide her through the crowded row. "You're coming with us, aren't you, Dorothy?"

"Thanks, but I think I should stay," Dorothy said. "Summer and I need to try to find out what happened. It's very likely Roland was attacked by the same person who killed Angelica Downs."

"Even more reason to leave," Dash said. "Julian's home, so worst case I can come back again after we get Juliette-Margot to bed and pick you two up. And your friend Frankie if you find her, too."

"No, no," Dorothy insisted. "We'll find someone to bring us back to Hibiscus Pointe. I believe there's shuttle transportation, too. Go ahead now, so you can beat the crowd."

Most of the people were departing quickly, but quite a few were not, she noticed, after Dash and Juliette-Margot had left. Martha Kirk had called for a doctor over her microphone, and several physicians and nurses, retired or otherwise, were already assisting the injured designer. Fortunately, he seemed to have regained consciousness, and was sitting up.

She still didn't see Summer, but Detective Donovan was on the scene, directing bystanders away and fending off questions. To her surprise, she also spotted Detective Caputo, wearing a conservative-length plaid skirt, flat, thick-soled shoes and a black blazer. She must have been at the show the whole time.

Off-duty? Or undercover? The latter, Dorothy suspected. Detective Caputo didn't strike her as much of a fashion show aficionado. On the other hand, neither was she.

What had happened to all the security the Majesty Golf and Tennis Club had promised to provide for the models? Surely such protection had extended to the show's designers and crew members, as well.

Dorothy started to make her way toward the stage area, but then thought better of it and headed in the direction of the main hall. She had to meet up with Summer as soon as possible. They could look around for clues directly backstage first, and then head over to the models' staging area in Ballroom A.

Hopefully they would also manage to find Frankie Downs somewhere in the enormous Majesty Golf and Tennis Club. By this time, they both knew from experience, Angelica's mother could be just about anywhere.

Dorothy had searched for her, without success, before returning to the show from the ladies room. She'd half-expected to see Frankie back in her seat, waiting for her with a disgruntled expression, but that hadn't been the case. She'd told Dash that Frankie had had an unexpected family emergency, and had left.

That wasn't far from the truth, in fact.

How was she going to break the news to Summer that Frankie had managed to get away from them again? That woman made Harry Houdini look like an amateur—especially at her age, for heaven's sake. How Frankie had removed that grate and crawled her way through a narrow, stuffy duct was beyond her comprehension.

Perhaps she had also escaped from that Nevada prison. At this point, Dorothy wouldn't be surprised.

Fortunately, the Majesty powder room she and Frankie had used was located on the ground floor of the club. But who knew how far that awful tunnel led. Or to where? Hopefully not anywhere dangerous, like a laundry or steam room.

Right now, she reminded herself, her top priority was to find Summer so they could try to determine who had assaulted Roland Cho. Frankie, she felt quite sure, would be just fine on her own for now. The tiny woman had certainly demonstrated that she was perfectly capable of taking care of herself.

Unless… Dorothy stopped short. What if *Frankie* had attacked Roland? There had to be some connection between what had happened to him, and what had happened to Angelica.

Dorothy didn't even want to entertain the thought that Frankie might have harmed her own daughter. Of course it was possible, she supposed. But what motive could she have had for that?

Unless Frankie, a convicted criminal who'd done jail time, was so greedy that she'd murdered Angelica to rob her of that Roland Cho necklace.

Or maybe she'd killed Angelica by accident.

No. Suffocating a person with a plastic bag was hardly an accident. And the whole idea of Frankie doing such a terrible thing to a daughter she'd dearly loved— and who had taken such good care of her in her old age—was practically unthinkable.

Now Violet, on the other hand…

"Mrs. Westin?" Jennifer Margolis, the pretty young Resident Services director from Hibiscus Pointe, touched Dorothy's elbow. "Would you like Garrett and me to bring you home? We're taking Peggy Donovan with us, too."

"Thank you both so much," Dorothy said, as Garrett Reynolds, Majesty's head tennis pro and Jennifer's new boyfriend, waved from a short way down the hall. Peggy sat beside him in her portable wheelchair, a snowflake blanket thinly disguising her bulky black boot. "But I'm hoping to find Summer. Have you seen her?"

"Just during the show," Jennifer said. "She made a fantastic model, don't you think?" She lowered her voice. "But I'm so glad the whole thing is over. I mean, a murder and an almost-murder in the same week, at two different fashion shows—I can't believe it."

"I'm not sure I can, either," Dorothy said, with a sigh. "Tell me, has there been any news on Angelica's mother, Frankie Downs?"

That was pushing things, she knew. If Jennifer ever found out that Dorothy and Summer had actually had

a conversation with the missing woman this very evening, the Resident Services director would be sorely
disappointed. And probably more than a little irritated.

And she certainly couldn't blame her.

"No, not yet, unfortunately," Jennifer said. "We have
flyers up everywhere, and I've been going door-to-door
asking residents to keep an eye out for her. The Milano
PD put out an alert a few hours ago, too. But so far, no
luck. I really hope Mrs. Downs is somewhere safe."

"I'm sure she is," Dorothy said. "I just have a feeling about that."

"Her daughter Violet is very upset," Jennifer said.
"She's decided to delay any memorial service until after
Frankie is located and the medical examiner releases
the... I mean, Angelica...to the funeral home. She also
wanted to wait until after the holidays, so more people
could attend."

"Of course," Dorothy murmured. Well, Violet had
certainly fooled Jennifer. She couldn't help wondering
what information, if any, the police might have from
the ME's initial report. She and Summer knew from
experience, though, that Detective Donovan—and especially Detective Caputo—were unlikely to share anything with them in that regard.

After saying good-bye to Jennifer and waving to
Peggy and Garrett, Dorothy slipped through the door at
the furthest end of the ballroom, behind the stage area.
It was easy to slide herself in along the wall against traffic, as models and crew members were streaming out
in an ongoing flood of panic.

The entire space appeared to be in chaos. A few
young women were crying, and gowns and shoes and
accessories were strewn all over the room as other mod-

els tried to extricate themselves from overly tight, high-fashion outfits or bulky holiday-themed costumes.

Summer was still wearing the gaudy red finale dress from Monique's Boutique as she hovered behind the curtain, in prime position to observe the now much smaller group surrounding Roland Cho.

Detective Donovan and Detective Caputo were there, of course, along with a sole remaining doctor, a Majesty staff member who was literally biting her nails, and three paramedics who had just arrived on the scene. Gladys and the rest of the gawkers must have been dispersed.

"I have no idea what happened," Roland was saying, as Dorothy came up beside Summer. Her friend put a finger to her lips. "One minute I was there in the designer VIP section—starting to pack up my pieces during the finale—and the next thing I know, I'm waking up in a face plant on stage."

"Did you see anyone before you were assaulted? Did anyone say anything to you?" Detective Caputo said, scribbling on her tablet.

Roland shook his head, then winced as he touched it gingerly. His hand came back with a streak of dark red, and he quickly tried to hide it in a fold of his baggy jumpsuit. "Someone must have snuck up behind me and hit me on the head with something really heavy," he said. "I heard a crack—my head, I guess—but I don't remember anything else. I have no idea how I made it through that curtain."

"The poor man," Dorothy whispered to Summer. "He does look very woozy."

"He's refusing to let them take him to the hospital,"

Summer said. "But I think they're going to make him, anyway."

"Certainly a very good idea," Dorothy said. The already-large lump on Roland's head was rapidly rising.

Ignoring the designer's feeble protests, the paramedics began preparations to transfer him to their metal stretcher and a waiting ambulance. Just as they were about to secure the straps Roland jolted up, wild-eyed.

"*Tears of Atlantis*, my brand-new masterpiece!" he cried. "I just remembered, I was holding it before I blacked out. It's gone!"

"Don't worry, I'm sure it wasn't stolen," the Majesty staff person said quickly. "It's probably right around here—" she looked around the topsy-turvy room "—somewhere."

Dorothy and Summer exchanged glances as Roland spiraled into meltdown. "Why is this all happening to me?" he wailed, kicking and pounding his fists on the stretcher. "I'm ruined!" The paramedics quickly moved to restrain him.

"So I guess we know for sure now why Angelica ended up murdered," Summer said, turning away from the curtain. "Someone wanted that necklace she was wearing at Waterman's. And then they came back here to the Majesty show to steal more Roland Cho jewelry, and almost bumped *him* off, too."

"I'm afraid knowing the motive really doesn't help us much for the case," Dorothy said, with a sigh. "Any of our suspects so far could be a jewelry thief, and they've all been in the near vicinity at the times of both crimes. Or, at least, they could have been."

Dorothy saw Summer glance back at the scene out on the stage. Detective Donovan was trying to question the still-ranting designer as the paramedics began to roll the cart away.

Summer yanked a loose piece of red fur from her unfortunate gown in frustration. "Well, at least we can rule out Frankie, since she was with you the whole time."

Oh dear. How was she ever going to break the news to her that she'd lost the person who might now be their number one suspect? Dorothy cleared her throat. "About Frankie, dear…"

FOR ONCE, SUMMER was actually glad to get up early. She hadn't gotten any zzzs, anyway, tossing and turning all night while her mind spun with all the images that would have shown up in nightmares if she'd been asleep.

Beginning with the red dress she'd worn home last night, since her own clothes had gotten locked up by mistake in some room called Sand Trap. The whole key card system was down at the golf club, the girl at the desk had told her. She'd taken her name and address and promised her stuff would be delivered to Hibiscus Pointe ASAP, free of charge.

Now Monique's hideous creation lay in a heap on the floor next to her bed. *Next stop, the incinerator chute*, Summer thought, giving the furry dress a kick on her way to the bathroom. She wished. That's where it belonged.

Frankie was missing again. That was the worst thing, even worse than Roland getting attacked. And then Esmé had texted her at three AM that Zoe had gotten in a big scene with her manager outside some club after the Majesty show. Someone called the police and the paparazzi had gotten it all on tape—along with Zoe's claims that they couldn't arrest her because her BFF

Summer Smythe-Sloan was in tight with a cop from the Milano PD.

Zoe even had his picture to show them, and claimed Summer had sent it to her straight from her phone. Totally humiliating.

Summer grabbed her toothbrush from the medicine cabinet and slammed the door shut, rattling the mirror. Any second now, she'd probably hear from Shane Donovan that he was canceling their date tonight. She couldn't blame him, really. Maybe she should beat him to it and cancel first.

She had to be a hundred percent focused on solving the case now. No more messing around. She and Dorothy needed to find Angelica's crazy mom quick, before anyone figured out they'd let her get away.

She'd done a lot of online searches last night when she couldn't sleep, and she needed to talk to Dorothy.

First of all, she'd tracked down—well, sort of—Monique's former husband and Angelica's boyfriend, Patrick Belleek. He'd been out of the office the whole past week, according to his admin at the law offices of Hastings and Belleek, and wasn't expected back until after New Year's.

Summer did a quick check of his social media accounts. Yep, looked like he and his old law school buddies were trying to visit every pub in the West of Ireland. The pictures were plastered all over the place.

Patrick wasn't that bad-looking, for an older guy, but he should probably be a little more careful. Weren't lawyers supposed to be discreet? Apparently, he wasn't, because Monique had known exactly what he was up to with Angelica.

At least they knew now that Monique's ex hadn't

been hanging out with Angelica around the time of the Waterman's fashion show. That didn't mean Monique still couldn't have killed her in a jealous rage, but it was probably a little less likely.

But the big thing Summer had learned last night was that Frankie had been in "business," all right. The jewelry business. As in, the stealing kind.

Once Summer had started clicking, the articles and records came thick and fast. Frankie had even had a store in Fort Myers that went belly up after her insurance company refused to cover her losses for an unsolved robbery. Or so she'd claimed.

Apparently one of Frankie's employees hadn't locked up well enough one night while she was off at some jewelers' convention. And after her business tanked, she'd tried to rebuild her inventory by heisting a few major rocks from a Vegas casino safe.

Incredible. So now Frankie was running around Milano, stealing more jewelry. Maybe she was on a bus by now, headed back to Vegas to hit the blackjack tables. Summer wouldn't put it past her.

But could she have been so greedy she'd actually killed her own daughter?

Summer had had a few stepmoms who'd wanted to kill her, she suspected. Well, the feelings were mutual. But none of them had actually *acted* on those thoughts, luckily.

There was no doubt about it, though. Angelica's mom had to be her and Dorothy's number one suspect now. And both of them had let her slip right through their fingers. Twice.

Her cell buzzed beside her on the sink. She quickly spat out a mouthful of toothpaste and took a swig of water before answering it. Who would call her this early?

Dorothy, probably, wanting to meet up to talk about the case. Or Detective Donovan, just like she'd thought, to let her know he wouldn't be picking her up for pre-dinner cocktails at seven after all.

"Hey, Summer." Mia's voice sounded a little muffled. "Can you hear me okay? I'm getting my roots done, so I'm calling you from under the dryer."

"Yeah, I can hear you fine." Why hadn't her friend just texted? Mia never called. This had to be serious. Summer checked the time again. Seven AM. What salon was so desperate for business they'd be open this early? "You're downtown already?"

"No, I'm at Mummy's. Her hairdresser came to the house. But listen, I've got a major problem."

You and me both, Summer thought. She doubted she could help out her uber-wealthy friend much, other than being supportive. Mia didn't have regular-people problems.

On the other hand, neither did she, really. That came with the territory when you tried to solve murders.

"Remember I told you Mummy and a bunch of her friends were hosting that mega resort wear show?"

"Um, yeah." Summer headed into her bedroom with her cell, and began to hunt through her closet for something to wear. When was the last time she'd sent stuff out to the laundry? Everything in here was dry-clean-only, and the bills were piling up.

"Well, it looks like we're going to have to cancel it."

The last thing she wanted to hear about right now was another fashion show. But Mia sounded really upset. "How come?" Summer asked, even though she had a feeling she already knew the answer.

"Practically all of our models have quit, after what happened at Waterman's, and then at Majesty last night," Mia said.

Yep, that made sense.

"Someone from PAGE emailed me last night, after midnight, with a big apology. And now they aren't even returning my calls."

"It *is* a little early," Summer said.

"No, that's not it," Mia said. "They *always* return Mummy's calls, because she's a queen bee on the charity show circuit. I don't know what we'll do about the models. I'm hoping if we offer them double their usual rates, they'll be willing to take a little extra risk."

"Yeah, maybe," Summer said. "If you throw in a little extra security, too." No, a *lot* of security. Not that it had helped much at the Majesty show last night.

"It looks like most of the designers are still in, at least," Mia went on. "Even Roland. He checked himself out of the hospital already."

"That's good," Summer said. She was glad he was okay, even if she couldn't stand him.

"Listen, I can't really talk anymore, they have to take my foils out," Mia said. "But we're throwing together a casual brunch here at eleven for anyone involved with Mummy's show. You know, as kind of a psych-up deal. Even Roland said he'd try to make it, if his headache goes away. So what do you say? Can you drop by?"

"Sure," Summer said. "Okay if I bring Dorothy?"

She could definitely use some decent grub this morning. And her friend would be up for brunch at Mia's mom's estate, she was sure. She could tell Dorothy what she'd found out about Frankie's shady past on the way over.

If Frankie was still in town, and she somehow got wind of a new jewelry scouting opportunity, she might just show up.

Weirder things had happened. Especially when Frankie was around.

And if Angelica's mom was a no-show, she and Dorothy would get to hang out at the Rivera-Joneses' estate for an hour or two. With all those designers around, they could do a little more investigating for the case, and grab some food at the same time.

The best part was, they could question Roland— maybe even before any Milano PD detectives got to him again. Hopefully by now he'd remember Frankie sneaking up on him to bonk him over the head and steal his precious diamond choker.

"Oh, please do bring Dorothy," Mia said. "I'll put you guys on the list, but things are kind of crazy here with all the last minute prep. You might need to tell them you're a fashion blogger for *Milan-O!* online or something, just in case, and they'll give you a blue badge. Mummy and I are in tight with all the magazine editors, so if anyone questions it, just text me."

"Got it," Summer said. "This'll be awesome. Thanks."

"See you at eleven." Mia clicked off.

Things are already looking up, Summer thought, as she selected a sleeveless pink dress from her closet. After talking to Roland, she and Dorothy might be able to wrap up the Downs case pronto. All they had to do was track down Frankie and haul her in to the Milano PD after they'd finished their quiche and champagne. How hard could it be? The woman was, like, ninety.

She couldn't wait to see Caputo's face.

Plus, Mia's fancy brunch—nothing Mia did was ever casual—would be a great distraction from wondering whether Shane Donovan would back out of their date or not. Maybe she'd wait a while to cancel, just in case.

TWENTY

Ten-forty-three. Where on earth *was* that girl?

Dorothy sat on the uncomfortable black metal bench outside the main building at Hibiscus Pointe, clasping her red leather pocketbook as holiday music played from speakers hidden in the foliage behind her. *Summer will be here any minute*, she told herself for the sixth or seventh time.

It would never do to be late for brunch at the Rivera-Joneses', even after a last-minute invitation. One never knew whether a meal would be sit-down or buffet. But much worse, every lost second meant additional delay in gathering information for the case. This impromptu morning affair was an excellent opportunity for her and Summer to investigate, starting with a few questions for Roland Cho.

Hopefully he would be sufficiently recovered from his injuries last night—both the head wound and the trauma of his brush with a ruthless thief and possible killer—to speak with them.

They couldn't stay at the brunch for long, though, because they had to find Frankie.

Dorothy sighed and checked her wristwatch. Ten-fifty. Summer had better have a good reason for being late. Hopefully her friend would approve of the light wool red skirt she'd selected from her spare closet. The loose-knit holiday sweater with the pom-pom nosed reindeer, a present from Maddie before she and Harlan moved to Florida, may have been a mistake.

"Nice Rudolph there, Dotty." The bench creaked heavily as Gladys Rumway plunked down beside her. "Real festive."

Oh dear. If only she could run up to change—but Summer would be here any moment. She'd have to stomach Gladys for a minute or two, even after the woman had called her Dotty. How she hated that nickname. Ernie called her Dot, sometimes, but that was entirely different.

"Thank you," Dorothy said. "You look very nice also, Gladys. Are you headed somewhere?"

"Oh, just to brunch," Gladys said, with a wave. "At the Rivera-Joneses. A casual little Fashion Week party, no big deal."

Dorothy briefly wondered how Gladys had managed to wrangle an invitation, but she quickly dismissed that unkind thought. If it weren't for Summer's friendship with Mia, she certainly wouldn't be attending, either. "How wonderful," Dorothy said. "Summer and I are headed there, as well."

"Yeah, I heard that from Martha Kirk," Gladys said. "I figured you two could give me a ride, since there's no shuttle to that part of Swanky Town. And I hate taking taxis," she added. "Not enough room, you know? I can't scrunch up my outfit." She smoothed her extra-tight, geometric patterned Monique's Boutique pantsuit, which she had paired with a fuzzy, electric blue beret and matching scarf.

Dorothy refrained from pointing out that Summer's MINI was not exactly roomy. "The more the merrier," she said, forcing an extra cheerful tone.

"So that was something about Roland Cho getting bonked on the head last night," Gladys said. "Pretty scary, am I right?" She leaned closer, nearly stabbing Dorothy in the eye as she suddenly thrust out an oddly shaped object on a chain around her neck. "By the way, what do you think of my new glitz? I mean, I can't afford a Cho original or anything, but is this a great replica, or what?"

"Lovely," Dorothy said. "Very…colorful." That was entirely true. The heavy-looking, metal starfish pendant contained gems in every shade of the rainbow. Somehow, she'd missed it at first glance, no doubt due to the busy pattern of Gladys's jacket.

"Eye-catching accessories are the mark of a true fashion icon," Gladys said. "Even hard-boiled detectives can have a sense of style. Right, Dotty?"

Dorothy nodded politely, fervently praying that Summer would magically materialize. "So, Gladys, what have you heard from your cousin Merle?" she asked. "Do the police have any new leads on the Downs case?"

"Possibly, but nothing I can share with civilians," Gladys said. "Too bad you didn't decide to team up with me, huh? But the whole investigation is a mess on the cops' end, if you ask me. They're slower than road-killed turtles. Of course I have my own theories."

"Of course," Dorothy murmured.

"Yep. I can't divulge anything, even to the cops, until I have enough proof to build a watertight case for the prosecutors," Gladys said. "Besides," she added, dropping her voice, "things are kinda extra-delicate right now. On top of everything else, the dead woman's mother went and got herself kidnapped, can you believe it?"

"No," Dorothy murmured. "I can't."

"Personally, my money's on the other daughter, the real estate agent. The one with the flowery name."

So much for Gladys's top-secret theories. "Violet, perhaps?" Dorothy supplied, as Gladys crossed her arms with a smug expression.

"Yeah, that's the one. Here's how I'm thinking things went down. She loses big bucks in that housing bubble a while back and never recovers. She needs her inheritance fast, so she knocks off her better-looking sister first. Then she kidnaps her mother and drowns her in an irrigation ditch off I-85."

Well, *that* was certainly a disturbing image. Dorothy tried not to shudder. "I really don't think…" she began, but stopped short. Hadn't she also suspected Violet of killing Angelica out of jealousy—and possibly for potential financial gain? And what about that open safe she'd seen in Angelica's condo? She still hadn't figured out a way to get back there to take a closer look, without triggering Violet's ultrasensitive sales radar.

"Hey, speaking of real estate, sounds like you and Ernest are planning to blow Hibiscus Pointe, huh?"

Dorothy's jaw dropped, nearly as far as the reindeer's nose on her sweater. Everyone knew Gladys was a busybody, of course, but *that* was extreme, even for her.

"Well, don't worry, Dotty, your secret's safe with me," Gladys went on. "And no one's gonna put you down for a home wrecker or anything. You two are just looking for a place for after Grace kicks the bucket, right?"

Dorothy rose so quickly that she felt dizzy and nearly had to grab the back of the bench. "Gladys Rumway," she said sharply. "That is a perfectly outrageous idea,

and a terrible thing to say. How you could even dream
up such ridiculous…"

Luckily, her next words were drowned out by a
squeal of brakes as Summer zoomed up in her orange
MINI. "Hi, guys!" Summer called, bounding out of the
car. "Ready for mimosas and quiche, Dorothy?"

"Yes, I most certainly am," Dorothy said, marching
toward the passenger door her friend threw open for her
without a backward glance. "Let's go dear, we're late."

Gladys could find herself another ride to the Rivera-
Joneses' fancy brunch.

"SUMMER SLOAN AND Dorothy Westin," Summer told
the tall, muscle-bound guy in the black tee and tight
jacket at the gate of Mia's mom's massive brick estate.
"We're on the list."

He frowned at his tablet, and then down into the MINI,
his eyes taking in Dorothy's reindeer sweater. "Yeah?"

Summer rolled her eyes in what she hoped would
pass as extreme fashion blogger annoyance. "Check
again. We're with *Milan-O!* online, okay? It's bad
enough this event was such short notice. We have a lot
of other parties around town to cover today."

The guy still looked doubtful, and Dorothy leaned
forward. "Fashion Week, you know," she said.

He raised one bushy eyebrow, but rechecked his list.
"There's a Summer Smythe here from *Milan-O!* That
you?"

"Yes," Summer said, tapping the steering wheel.
"Look, sorry, but we're already late. And we've got
deadlines to meet."

Like anyone had a deadline on a Saturday morning. But it didn't matter, anyway, because the guy said

something into his headset and the ornate metal gates with the gold points on top slowly opened.

"Look at all these enormous white tents," Dorothy said, as they drove to the end of the long, crushed-shell driveway. "And so many people. I still can't believe Mia and her mother were able to pull off a party of this magnitude so quickly. Literally overnight, in fact."

"They had help," Summer said, trying to remove a spot of to-go coffee from her pink dress as a teenage kid in a white polo and navy shorts ran up to take the MINI. "It's amazing what some decent connections and a whole lot of money can do. Trust me on that."

"Well, we'll have to take full advantage of this opportunity," Dorothy said. "Remember, every minute here counts for the investigation. And if either of us spots Frankie…"

"We call Donovan," Summer said. "I mean, Caputo."

When she'd told Dorothy what she'd learned about Frankie's past, her friend had seemed even more upset than she'd expected. "I can't believe we let her get away," Dorothy kept muttering, over and over. "She had us completely hoodwinked."

"Don't feel bad, Dorothy," Summer said. "She's just slippery, that's all. She's a jewel thief."

"And a possible murderer," Dorothy reminded her.

"True," Summer said. "But we can't beat ourselves up over temporarily losing track of her, or we'll never get the case solved. Right?"

"Right." Dorothy sighed.

In almost no time, they got their blue badges and were ushered by a very tall young woman in a tiny white dress to an even more crowded area behind the house.

Roland Cho and a handful of other designers Summer

had seen at the Majesty show were circulating among the guests, Bloody Marys and mimosas in hand. Perfect.

"Oh, good, Roland made it," Dorothy said. "He must be feeling better."

Summer followed her friend's nod toward one of the smaller pools, where the designer, his hair spiked even higher than usual in a futile attempt to hide the ginormous bump on his head, was surrounded by a group of fawning older women. Whatever he was telling them—probably the story about him being clobbered and robbed last night—they were hanging on his every word.

"Yep," Summer said. "He seems perfectly fine."

Weirdly, the guy was wearing some kind of blue seersucker zoot suit deal. High waist, big-shouldered jacket, wide-leg trousers, suspenders, the whole thing. Ugh. That might work okay for him back in New York, but it looked pretty out of place here in Milano.

Roland suddenly looked in her direction and caught her staring at him. His nose twitched just a teensy bit before he turned his back on her.

Jeez. How had he fooled everyone into thinking he was so great? The guy made her skin crawl like it was covered with bugs. And even though he was a total jerk, she and Dorothy were trying to *help* him.

Not because they felt sorry for him, at least in her case. But if Roland could identify the person who had given him that lump on his head, they might figure out who'd murdered Angelica.

They'd probably get his ugly jewelry back for him at the same time, too, if it wasn't fenced already. Then he'd be groveling with gratitude, and there was a decent chance he might even offer them free jewelry like he'd given Mia. And then she'd get to say, super politely, "Oh, that's sooo nice of you, but no thanks."

On the other hand, his designs *were* worth some bucks. Maybe, if he happened to gift her any especially hideous pieces, she should accept them, anyway, and sell them to raise some super-quick cash.

Was that wrong? Yeah, probably.

"Why don't we get our food now and talk to Roland as soon as he's free?" Dorothy said. "The buffet tables look wonderful."

Summer was more than happy to grab a flowery plate at the first omelet station and load up on fresh berries and crispy bacon. Just a few feet away, a choc-olate fountain burbled, and the orange and grapefruit juice in the faux-crystal pitchers looked fresh-squeezed.

But ugh, there was Monique, having champagne added to her flute of OJ. Summer tried to stoop a little behind Dorothy so the woman wouldn't see her. The last thing she wanted was Monique asking her about that semi-trashed red dress. Hopefully she'd have a chance to drop it by the dry cleaner first. What a waste of money.

"Hey, Summer. I figured you might show up." Zoe, with her agent right behind her, reached across her to pluck the biggest strawberry from the pile with her freshly manicured French tips.

"Oh, uh, hi, Zoe," Summer said, trying not to sound surprised. How did she know Mia, and why would Mia want her anywhere around here? "What's up?"

She had to give the girl points on her outfit, though. The short lavender dress with the cutout shoulders was pretty cute.

"Aleesha got me on the list," Zoe said. "Because I'm one of Roland's best clients. We haven't officially announced it yet, or anything, but I'm co-designing an amazing new jewelry collection with him."

"Awesome." Summer concentrated on piling extra tater tots onto her plate. Zoe had been at Majesty last night. Could she have tried to bump Roland off to drum up a little pre-publicity for the jewelry premiere?

Nah. No publicity was bad publicity, everyone in the biz always said—but if Zoe got caught, even ZeeZee and Aleesha couldn't save her butt from cooling her heels for a long time in jail. Unless she got redirected to another extended vacay in rehab.

She still couldn't see the brat as an actual murderer, though. Killing people took a lot of effort.

On the other hand, jetting all the way to Florida and stalking her everywhere just to try and get a part in a stupid movie definitely took some effort.

"We're going to have a big launch party in LA," Zoe said. "Maybe I can snag you and your dad some invites."

The chef handed Summer her fluffy Western omelet, but her appetite was rapidly plummeting. "Great," she said. "Maybe we'll be able to make it."

Didn't Zoe get it? She was *not* going to beg her dad to put her in that movie. That was Aleesha's job, not hers. Syd would never do it, anyway, because he knew Zoe and all her crazy stunts could end up costing him big bucks.

He was no dummy.

"Well, just so you know, I'm going to have a re-ally big surprise for you real soon," Zoe said. "You're going to love it." She popped the giant strawberry into her mouth and walked away. Aleesha threw Summer a semi-apologetic smile and scurried after her client.

A surprise? Was it a good one or a bad one? Summer wondered. Hard to tell.

"Oh, hello," a well-dressed woman in a giant, Kentucky Derby–worthy hat greeted her as Summer placed her heaping plate down on the table next to Dorothy. "I see you two are both with *Milan-O!* magazine."

"What?" Summer said. Dorothy gave her a tiny nudge and she quickly remembered. "Oh, yeah, right. We're not with the magazine, actually. We're bloggers."

"How interesting," a second, older woman said. She smiled at Dorothy. "I think it's wonderful when seniors embrace the online world. I'd love to follow you on social media."

"Oh, yeah," Summer said. "She's all over it. Facebook, Twitter, Insta, Snapchat…take your pick." Beside her, Dorothy's forkful of Eggs Benedict froze in midair.

"It's Dorothy, right? How do you spell your last name?" the second woman said, bringing her phone out of her Chanel bag.

Dorothy's badge must have fallen off back in the pool, too. "E-A-S-T-O-N," Summer answered for her quickly, just as she spotted Roland moving away from his eager fans toward the pool house. "Sorry, but we have to go. There's someone over there we need to interview for our next blog post, and we can't let him get away. Come on, *Doris*."

Dorothy quickly gathered her plate. "So nice meeting you," she told the women. "Bye now." She hurried after Summer. "Thanks for rescuing me," she said. "That was a close one."

"Rats," Summer said, as they crossed the pool deck. "Roland was heading into the pool house, but now he's talking to Mia. Guess we'll have to wait."

"No, let's go over, anyway," Dorothy said. "I'm sure she'll just be a minute, since she'll need to keep circulating among her guests. We can just say hello and thank her for inviting us."

"Oh, hey," Mia said, as Summer and Dorothy came up. "So glad you ladies could make it. I was just telling Roland, I've got more major drama on my hands."

"What's wrong?" Summer asked quickly.

Her friend looked amazing in her simple white halter dress, accessorized with a gold pendant set with the huge diamond from a former engagement ring. But still, in spite of her perfect makeup job, she looked tired and upset.

Mia sighed heavily. "I think we're going to have to cancel Mummy's resort wear show for sure now. We have exactly one model left who's willing to do it. Bryana something."

"Hey, I know her," Summer said. "Sort of."

"Well, Mummy and I tried. But after what happened to Angelica Downs and then poor Roland last night—" she looked sympathetically at the designer beside her "—none of the others are willing to risk it, even with the massive bonuses we offered. Mummy's whole fundraising plan for the new Milano Palms Senior Center is up in smoke. And it's so late now, we can't get even partial refunds from any of the vendors. The show was set for Tuesday afternoon."

"A shame," Roland said. "A few of the more elite designers, including yours truly, were counting on auctioning off several major pieces."

"For the senior center?" Summer asked.

Roland smiled, sort of, but his eyes still looked mean. "A percentage of the proceeds would be donated, of course."

Probably not much, Summer thought.

"Daddy already spoke to someone at Roland's insurance company," Mia said. "They're going to expedite his claims on the pieces he lost, at least."

"I do hope I'll be able to recreate the designs, though," Roland said, with a sigh. "So horribly difficult to find just the right gems, you know. No stone is ever the same."

"I'm glad to see you've recovered from your injuries, Roland," Dorothy spoke up. "But Mia, that's terrible news about the models. Were they the same ones from the Waterman and Majesty shows?"

"Pretty much," Mia said. "We always book through PAGE, of course. Their senior division is key for resort wear shows." She twisted her diamond necklace between her magenta-lacquered nails in frustration. "I just don't know what we'll do now. Mummy has such a bad headache she couldn't even make it to brunch. She's up in her room with a pharmacy's worth of meds."

Summer looked at Dorothy, who was frowning thoughtfully in her nutty reindeer sweater. Was she thinking the same thing she was? Because she'd just come up with a crazy, but really awesome, idea.

"Can you guys excuse me and Dorothy for a sec?" Summer asked. "We'll be right back."

She pulled her friend aside to a café table set up near a pretty but noisy waterfall. "Didn't Monique say something like, 'the shows must go on' after Angelica got murdered? What if we got Mia and her mom some perfect new senior models? Not exactly professional ones, but…"

"Are you talking about the residents from Hibiscus Pointe?" Dorothy said. "Because that's exactly what *I* had in mind. It's a stretch, of course, but if we had enough security, some of them might be willing. Gladys, for sure. And maybe Helen Murphy, and all of her friends."

Summer nodded. "Exactly. It's a perfect PR angle. You know, seniors helping seniors. We could make a ton of money for the new center, help Mia out and…"

"…get another crack at bringing everyone together again—well, except for the models—for the investigation," Dorothy finished. "We'll need to convince Roland and the other designers to showcase their jewelry again, though. With all the recent events, they might not be too eager about that idea."

"Sure they will," Summer said. "Didn't you hear Roland back there? Last night he thought he was ruined, but everything turned out okay. They're all dying for the publicity, and to auction off their stuff."

"True," Dorothy said. "I think this is an excellent plan. Hopefully Mia will agree."

"Oh, she'll love it," Summer said. "A fancy charity fashion show for seniors, by seniors, like I said. The Rivera-Joneses don't lose any money—not that they need it—the Hibiscus Pointers will be thrilled, Roland and his designer buddies get to sell their jewelry, and *we* get to set the perfect trap for Angelica's killer."

"It would be even better if we find Frankie first," Dorothy said. "Hopefully, she'll turn up at the show, at the very least."

"Exactly," Summer said. "This is a win-win for everybody, right?"

"I certainly hope so," Dorothy said. "It's the only plan we've got."

TWENTY-ONE

"LADIES, YOU ARE BRILLIANT," Mia said, after Dorothy and Summer returned to the pool house area and told her and Roland their plan to save the charity resort wear show. "Using models from Hibiscus Pointe is an amazing idea, especially for the senior crowd. They'll be realistic and relatable. I'll have to run it by Mummy, but I'm sure she'll be all for it, too."

Dorothy gave a silent sigh of relief. Mia looked much less tired now. "We're so glad you think it might work."

"It's a fabulous idea," Roland said. "I can handle things from the designers' end. Maybe a few different choices in pieces here and there, since we'll be dealing with less glamorous models, but who's going to complain if we still have a show?"

Less glamorous? Dorothy gritted her teeth.

"Do you think you can get enough ladies who'd be willing to participate?" Mia said. "After the last two show fiascos, I mean?"

"Oh, sure." Summer gave a breezy wave. "Piece of cake."

Dorothy felt a stab of worry. Usually, whenever Summer said things would be a "piece of cake," they turned out entirely differently. *Don't borrow trouble*, she told herself. *All will be well.*

They'd make sure of that.

"Well, I guess we still have Bryana," Mia said. "And

Summer, since you were so great in the Majesty show last night…"

"No way," Summer said quickly. "I mean, I need to…uh, help handle things backstage," she added, with a glance at Dorothy. "I'm much better at that."

"Oh, I'm sure," Roland said, with an unpleasant smirk. "We'll all feel very safe with *you* in charge."

Dorothy frowned. Why was Roland always so unpleasant to everyone except Mia and his other wealthy fans? He was especially rude to Summer. From the start, the two of them had gotten off on the wrong foot.

"I'll talk to Jennifer at Hibiscus Pointe and see if we can arrange some kind of special transport here for the models," she said, trying to change the subject. "Most of them don't drive."

"You know, we could still change the venue," Mia said, slowly. "What if, instead of hauling everyone back and forth, we just set up the tents and stuff at Hibiscus Pointe? I went there once for a mother-daughter golf tournament. It's a nice enough place, with all the fountains and landscaping. There's plenty of room and parking, too."

"Well, a retirement community would certainly give a more mature feel, if that's what you're going for," Roland said. Not very enthusiastically, Dorothy noted.

"I'll run it by Jennifer," she said. "She might take a bit of convincing."

"Hey, it'll be great PR," Summer said. "And Mia already has a great security staff. Hibiscus Pointe will be featured in every paper and society column and social media platform, and it's all for a good cause. Think of the zillions of potential residents out there who'll hear about the place."

"Exactly," Mia said. "We'll still need some younger

models, though. Otherwise some of the resort and cruise clothes won't work. Like swimwear, for instance."

"Dorothy swims a lot," Summer said. "She's got a great figure."

"Thank you, dear," Dorothy murmured, ignoring the slight twitch of Roland's nose. "But no."

"Wait, I've got it!" Summer said, excitedly. "Mia, didn't you just say you were in some mother-daughter golf tournament? What if we made the resort wear show a mother-daughter deal?"

"That's a nice idea," Dorothy said. "But most of the residents don't have any family members nearby. And a number of the daughters would be seniors themselves, or close to it."

"That's okay, family is family," Summer said. "It could be mothers and daughters, or grandmas and granddaughters, or even great-granddaughters."

"We actually do have some kid clothes," Mia said. "And we'll need some guys, too."

Summer turned to Dorothy. "Oh, I think we could persuade a few around Hibiscus Pointe. But maybe you should ask Ernie, Dorothy. I'll work on Dash. I'm sure they'd do it for a good cause."

Dorothy bit back a smile, imagining Ernie twirling onstage in a pair of floral golf pants. "We'll see."

"Perfect." Mia looked positively perky now. "I'd better go work the crowd, and talk to Mummy, while she's still under her meds. But this is going to be fabulous, I just have a feeling. Let me know what Jennifer says, and I'll start working things on my end, okay? Talk to you soon," she added breathlessly, as she left.

"Well," Roland said. "Moving the Rivera-Joneses'

holiday resort wear show to a retirement community will make for an interesting event."

And hopefully a productive one for their case, too. "Yes," Dorothy said, ignoring the designer's sarcastic tone. "It certainly will."

"If it weren't for that sweet Mia, I would never have agreed to this," Roland added.

"Yeah, right," Summer said. Dorothy threw her a slight frown. They needed the designer to be in a co-operative mood.

"So tell me, Roland," she said. "Now that you're feeling better, are you able to remember anything at all about what happened last night at the Majesty show?"

"Absolutely nothing," he said, but Dorothy didn't believe him. Something in his tone sounded just a tiny bit evasive.

"Did you see anyone hanging around backstage before you got attacked?" Summer said. "Maybe someone said something to you, or to another person?"

The designer gave an exaggerated sigh. "You're worse than the cops," he said. "What part of 'amnesia' do you not understand? I've been through a highly trau-matic experience. The doctors in the ER said I need to avoid stress, and you're upsetting me."

"Roland," Dorothy said. "We are so sorry." Beside her, Summer nodded like a bobble head doll. "Please under-stand, we're hoping to help solve a murder here. We don't want anyone else to get hurt like you and Angelica did."

"Maybe you should both just butt out," Roland said. "Let the police take care of the crime stats. That's their job. You know, your tax dollars at work, and all that? You two are wasting your time, running around playing

Miss Marple and—" he looked disdainfully at Summer "—Charlie's clueless angel here."

Dorothy bristled. "That is very unkind," she said. "And entirely inappropriate."

"Jeez. What is your problem, dude?" Summer said. "Don't you want to see Angelica's killer—and who-ever tried to kill you—go to jail? You know, payback?"

"I don't believe in revenge," Roland said. "And now, if you'll excuse me, there are some Belgian waffles back at the party with my name branded on them."

He swept past Dorothy, knocking into her hard with his shoulder and sending her flying off the concrete. She frantically grabbed for him, landing hard on her back as a wall of cold water closed over her face.

"DOROTHY!" SUMMER DOVE into the pool and came up beside her friend. "Are you okay?"

Dorothy tried to reply, but coughed and sputtered as she swallowed more water. Summer quickly grabbed her under the arm and lifted her to the surface, then towed her swiftly toward the side of the pool.

"I-I'm okay," Dorothy gasped, her hands closing on the ledge. "Just give me a second to catch my breath. So em-barrassing. He caught me by surprise." She coughed again.

Summer patted her on the back and glanced over her shoulder at Roland, who was creating tons of splash as he doggy-paddled his way to the ladder at the other end of the pool. He'd get there eventually, but she sure wasn't going to help him. His hair was plastered down over his face now, making him look doubly pathetic. "He's the one who should be embarrassed, knocking into you like that. Serves him right you pulled him in with you."

Dorothy hoisted herself out of the pool. "Agreed."

"Let's get you out of here," Summer said. "You're shivering like crazy. And we don't want to ruin your reindeer sweater."

"Roland did that on purpose," Dorothy said, wringing out her sleeve. "I can't imagine why he would do such a thing."

"Because he's a no-good creep," Summer said. "I knew I didn't like that guy, from the first time I saw him. As soon as he shows up at the waffle table I swear I'm going to give him another lump on the other side of his spiky little head. Or…"

"No, dear," Dorothy said. "Neither of us is going to do anything."

"What do you mean?" Summer said. "He can't get away with pushing you into a pool like that. You could have drowned or something."

"Unlikely," Dorothy said, with a small smile. "I have to say, I'm glad I dragged him with me into the water. But we don't want to rock the boat any more with Roland right now, no matter how insufferable he is. We need him and his clunky jewelry at the Hibiscus Pointe resort wear show."

"I guess." Summer knew Dorothy was right, but it still ticked her off. And her friend was fine now, but she was standing there shivering, and sopping wet. And her own dress would dry fast, but it was sticking to her like crazy. "We should find some towels or something," she said. "They must have some in the pool house."

Fortunately, the building covered with leafy vines and tropical flowers—which was about ten times bigger than Grandma Sloan's condo—was open and well-stocked with fluffy, R-J-monogrammed towels. Summer grabbed a few and handed them to Dorothy. "Looks like they've got some spa robes in the closet, too," she said.

"Wonderful," Dorothy said. "I might even take a nice hot shower, and throw my clothes in the dryer over there. Except for the reindeer sweater. Too much heat might ruin it."

"Right," Summer said. Dorothy sure was attached to that sweater. It was kind of cute, though—the type of thing you wore to an ugly-sweater party, and made everyone want a selfie with you. "You go ahead," she said, wrapping her wet hair in a towel. "I'll wait and send my dress to the cleaners later."

"Well, I'll be quick," Dorothy said. "We have to track down Frankie, and now we have a fashion show to help plan, too."

And I have a date with Shane Donovan tonight, Summer added to herself. *So far, anyway.*

After Dorothy headed toward the luxurious marble showers, Summer checked out the main room. It was filled with boxes and rolling suitcases. Empty jewelry display stands and forms, covered in black or blue velvet, stood on the pink marble coffee table in the center, and there were more on the glass side tables.

Was this all Roland's stuff? She walked over to take a closer look at a stack of glossy promotional postcards set out beside a giant seashell. He had been heading here into the pool house earlier, she remembered. It looked like he was storing everything at Mia's mom's estate while he was in Milano, so maybe he'd wanted to do a quick check to make sure nothing had been stolen.

Or it could be he was so paranoid he carted his stupid jewelry around with him everywhere he went. That had to be pretty inconvenient, but he must have figured the

Rivera-Joneses had better security than whatever hotel he was staying at, no matter how fancy it was.

On the other hand, no one seemed to notice when Dorothy got pushed into the pool.

"Hands in the air, Miss," a gruff voice said.

"What?" Summer turned to see a guy about ten feet tall and at least half as wide looming in the doorway of the pool house. Behind him, another security guy watched her with narrowed eyes as he said something into his Bluetooth.

At least, she hoped they were security guys, and not jewelry thief thugs or something.

"I said, hands up," the giant said. "Now."

"Okay, okay." Summer did as she was told, and backed up slightly toward the kitchen area.

"Move again, and you'll be sorry," the guy said.

"I'm not stealing anything," Summer said. "I'm just…"

What should she tell them? With luck, if these *were* bad guys, maybe they wouldn't realize Dorothy was here in the pool house, too. They might not check the showers, and her friend could get away.

The two men started toward her, and Summer grabbed a cheese knife from the board beside the sink. "Back off," she said. "I'm a friend of Mia's. And, um, a fashion blogger."

"You don't have a badge," the giant said. "And we got a tip about a disturbance over here at the pool house. You got any other ID?"

Summer looked down at her still-wet, super-clingy dress. Great. The badge must have fallen off in the water. And she had no idea where her purse was. Probably back at the brunch table, with the food she never got to eat. "Come on, guys, give me a break," she said.

"My name is Summer Sloan. I'm on the guest list. You can check with your bosses."

"Sorry, you're out of luck," the shorter man said. "Ms. Mia asked that she and her mother not be disturbed right now."

"I was looking for a bathroom, for heaven's sake," Summer said.

"Over by Mr. Cho's jewelry?" the giant said, nodding toward the boxes and cases. "Check them out, and make sure nothing's busted open," he added to his companion.

Summer rolled her eyes. "Okay, fine, be like that. Ms. Mia isn't going to be very happy when she finds out how you harassed me." She frowned. "Hold on a sec. Did you say you got a *tip*?"

Just wait until she got her hands on that no-talent lowlife Roland now. He'd set her and Dorothy up.

"That's right," the giant said, twirling a pair of silver handcuffs out of his inside jacket pocket. "Too bad we caught you red-handed with someone else's very valuable property. But don't worry, you can explain all that to the police."

Hopefully not during dinner with Shane Donovan in the Milano PD lockup. Summer was about to try a different tack when Dorothy walked out of the shower room in her guest robe. "Look what I found just lying out on the counter. I'm pretty sure it's…oh dear." She stopped short when she noticed the hulking man in the kitchen.

Summer squeezed her eyes shut, trying to pretend she hadn't seen the sparkling emerald-and-ruby rope necklace in Dorothy's hands. Great. Now they were both cooked.

"Hey, Marty," the giant called over his shoulder. "We got another perp. Call the cops."

TWENTY-TWO

DOROTHY POURED THE remnants of her Fast and Frostee lemon shake down the disposal and tossed the plastic cup in the recycling bin beneath the sink. "What a mess," she said to Summer. "Just like our morning at the Rivera-Joneses' brunch. And pretty much the whole Downs investigation so far."

"Look on the bright side, Dorothy," Summer said. "Those security goons didn't call the cops on us."

"Well, they would have, if Mia hadn't seen your text," Dorothy said. "And at least that necklace I found in the shower room got locked up safe and sound. Imagine, she didn't even remember leaving it there."

"Guess that's what happens when you own a ton of bling," Summer said, cheerfully. "I misplace stuff all the time, and I don't have half the rocks she does."

"Mmm," Dorothy said. She herself had lost her engagement ring in the ocean once. Harlan had replaced it on their twenty-fifth anniversary.

"So what do you say, should we go back out and do some more hunting for Frankie?" Summer said. "Not that we had much luck this afternoon, and we spent *hours*. We must have covered half of Milano, including the fabulous bus station. Glad I can check that last one off my bucket list. Where else can we look?"

"Are you sure there were no direct buses to Vegas?" Dorothy asked.

"Positive," Summer said. "Just charters, no night departures, and I showed all the ticket people Frankie's picture from that Missing poster Jennifer made. No one recognized her, even with the blue hair." She reached across the counter to lift the lid on the cookie jar. "You never keep any cookies in here, Dorothy. Is it just for show, or what?"

"Only to fool the ants," Dorothy said. "There should be some pink-and-white MallowPuffs in the fridge."

Summer threw open the refrigerator door. "Mmm, yum, with coconut." She drew out the package and popped a cookie into her mouth. "How many do you want?"

"None, thanks," Dorothy said. "I think I'm sufficiently sugared up for the day. Possibly the entire week. But all that extra energy will come in handy, because I've decided I need to talk to Violet again, in person. I'm planning to tell her I want another tour of Angelica's condo before I can even think of making an offer."

"I'll go with you," Summer said, immediately.

"Thank you, dear," Dorothy said, "but I really think I should do this alone."

Summer's face fell. "Oh. You mean, you're just going to go with Ernie?"

"No," Dorothy said. "I want a chance to speak with Violet one-to-one. Don't worry, I'll be perfectly safe on my own. It will be broad daylight, so I can get another look into Angelica's closet for that safe, and there are plenty of people around Flamingo Pass if things take an unexpected turn. In the meantime, you can broach the Hibiscus Pointe fashion show idea to Jennifer. You're always good at persuading her to do things."

"Most of the time," Summer said.

"Good, that's settled, then. We can compare notes

tonight." Dorothy smiled. "Or maybe you should take the evening off and treat yourself to a nice dinner. With a handsome detective friend, perhaps."

Summer flushed. "How did you know about that?"

"I couldn't help noticing his text come across your phone when you ran into the ladies room at the Fast and Frostee."

"Oh. Right." Summer ducked her head to check her cell. "Looks like I have Juliette-Margot's makeup swim lesson at five, anyway," she said. "Gladys canceled, no surprise there. She's probably still recovering from all that booze she drank, between the Majesty show and Mia's brunch."

"I'm sure," Dorothy said. Or possibly she was hot on the trail for her own investigation, following some important clue she and Summer had missed. Come to think of it, Gladys might be the perfect person to enlist to find Frankie Downs. It was impossible for anyone to hide from her for long.

Summer was still absorbed in her phone. "I'm just checking out Violet again, in case any new info has shown up, before you meet with her," she said. "She seems pretty legit. So far I really haven't found anything at all about her personal life. It's a hundred percent Real Estate City here. A bunch of pretty lame ads, a few ribbon-cuttings and charity deals in the Vero Beach papers, and someone interviewed her last week for a local real estate board newsletter. She does a lot of promotional videos on her Facebook page, though. Want to see?" She held out her phone.

"No, thank you," Dorothy said. "I can imagine." She'd be hearing Violet's latest sales pitch soon enough.

"Her online reviews say she's the best real estate agent

in Florida," Summer went on. "Maybe even the whole country. Look, all these five stars out of five. Huh."

It was sad, in a way, that Violet appeared to have no personal life whatsoever. Or else she kept it extremely well hidden. Perhaps that idea was much more worrisome.

"Oh, wait, here we go," Summer said. "Here's a one-star. The person says she wished she could give zero stars, but the system wouldn't let her. Violet bugged her for months, even after she told her she'd changed her mind about buying anything."

"Not surprising," Dorothy murmured. She'd probably pester her and Ernie nonstop as well, once she found out they weren't really interested in Angelica's condo.

"Oooh, this is the best," Summer added. "Listen to how the review ends: *Whatever you do, avoid hiring Violet Downs to be your real estate agent. Otherwise you may have to change your phone number and move out of state like we did.'* Yikes."

"Good heavens," Dorothy said. "That's horrifying. Hopefully the person is exaggerating."

"From what we know of Violet, probably not," Summer said. "I bet she put up all those five-star reviews herself."

"How unethical," Dorothy said. "Which reminds me… I'll be right back."

She went into the bedroom and straight to the little metal cough drop box on her nightstand. She had almost forgotten she'd been holding on to the diamond earring she'd discovered on the floor in Angelica's condo.

She headed back to the kitchen and showed the earring to Summer. "I should have handed it over to Violet right away, or at least left it there in the condo somewhere," she said, after explaining how she happened to be in possession of a piece of jewelry that belonged to a dead woman. "I'm not sure why I didn't, but Violet did startle me at the time."

Summer turned the earring over in her hands, then held it up to the light. "Nice setting. Looks like real gold. Do you think the diamond is real?"

"I have no idea," Dorothy said, "but it doesn't matter. It belongs to Angelica's family now, or to whomever else she named in her will."

"*If* she had one," Summer said. "Maybe I can find that out from Detective Donovan tonight." She brought the earring close to her mouth, and blew on it.

"What are you doing?" Dorothy said, frowning in confusion.

"It's the fog test," Summer said. "If it's a real diamond, and you breathe on it, like you would in a mirror, it won't get cloudy. Not for long, anyway. See? I think this might be genuine. We'd really need a jeweler's loupe to tell for sure, but hand me that newspaper from the coffee table, would you?"

Puzzled, Dorothy retrieved yesterday's copy of the *Milano Sun* and brought it to her friend. Summer placed the earring down on a page and peered at it closely. "Yep, it's probably real. I can't read the print through it. If it was glass or something, you could."

"Ah," Dorothy said. "I've heard of scratching glass or some other surface with a diamond to see if it is genuine, but not those methods."

Summer shrugged. "Hey, if the gem isn't real, why wreck a perfectly good fake? And sometimes they put fillers and stuff in real diamonds, so the scratching thing is sort of risky."

"I'm impressed, dear," Dorothy said. "But valuable

or not, I need to return the earring to Violet today."
Or, at the very least, return it to the spot on the carpet
where she'd found it.

That way, Angelica's sister would never know she'd
taken it. And it was sad to admit, but deep in her heart
she felt less than eager to hand over anything of Angelica's to a woman who seemed so greedy and heartless—and may even have been her killer.

"SO WHAT DO you think?" Summer said, giving Jennifer a smile so wide her face almost split. "Is having a
cool resort wear show here an amazing idea, or what?"

"You've got to be kidding," the resident services director said. "It's the worst idea ever."

"What do you mean?" Summer said. "Everything
will be totally taken care of. You won't have to do a
thing. Well, maybe just a *few* things. The Rivera-Joneses
already have almost everything planned."

Jennifer glanced out her office doorway at the busy
four-thirty traffic streaming through the Hibiscus Pointe
lobby. Chattering groups of seniors, some with walkers
or an occasional wheelchair, were already headed to the
Canyons dining room for dinner. Most of the men wore
colorful sport coats and the women seemed to have
agreed ahead of time on silky floral dresses and color-
coordinated beads tonight. "We can't risk putting any
of our residents in that kind of danger."

Summer gave a dismissive wave. "No danger," she
said. "The Rivera-Joneses are hiring extra security
teams. And their people are tons better than—" she
dropped her voice as Bill Beusel, head of Hibiscus Pointe
Security, wandered aimlessly by in the opposite direction of the dining room "—uh, most other companies."

Jennifer was hesitating, she could tell. That was a good sign. "Some of them are ex-Secret Service," she added. "Mia's code name is Aruba."

She'd made that up on the spot, of course, but it sounded good. And it was possible that some of those goons at the Rivera-Jones estate *could* have protected the President, right? Or maybe a Congressperson, at least.

"Roger will never go for it," Jennifer said, nervously smoothing her shiny, dark hair. It was already perfectly in place.

The Hibiscus Pointe manager—Summer called him "Roger the Dodger"—spent most of his time on the golf course, so he left just about all of the day-to-day stuff up to Jennifer. True, he yelled at the poor girl whenever anything went wrong, which was a bummer, but mostly he was happy if the residents were happy.

"He'll love it," Summer said. "For one thing, think of the major publicity this place will get from hosting the last show of Fashion Week. I mean, there's a ton of turnover here on a fairly regular basis, so wouldn't it be a lot less pressure for you…"

"Shh!" Jennifer warned, frowning and looking back at the lobby again. "You don't need to bring up the turnover rate, okay? I get it."

Oops. Wrong tack. "Right, sorry," Summer said. "But you're short an Activities Director now, right?"

Jennifer sighed. "Yes, unfortunately. Mrs. Rumway drove Dolly crazy, and she quit. Again. I'm trying to get her back."

"Well, there you go." Summer leaned back in her chair. "You can tell Roger that you won't have to hire anyone for at least another week, because the residents will all be busy practicing or getting ready for the fashion show."

"I swear, Summer, if anything goes wrong…"

"It won't," she said. "You know why?" It was time for the trump card. "Because Dorothy's going to be helping run things on the Hibiscus Pointe end. Not me."

That wasn't exactly true, but it did the trick, just as she'd expected. Jennifer's forehead actually unwrinkled. "Well, gee, if you put it that way," her friend said, with a resigned grin. "I'll talk to Roger. No guarantees, though, okay?"

"Well, well, well." Gladys stuck her poodle-haired head into the office, making both of them jump. "Kudos to you, Jennifer. I hear we've got a major fashion event coming up here at the Pointe this week. Don't worry, I'm spreading the word. How'd you talk those hoity-toity Rivera-Joneses into it?"

And how did you *find out about it so fast?* Summer wanted to ask. Across from her, Jennifer was looking a little green behind her desk. But now at least she wouldn't have to bring up the subject with Roger. Gladys would beat her to it.

My job here is done, she told herself. "Hey, Jennifer, I'll talk to you later," she said, getting up from her chair. "I have a swim class to teach. Hope you're feeling better, Mrs. Rumway," she added over her shoulder, as she practically skipped past her through the door.

The Hibiscus Pointe resort wear show was a done deal—well, almost—for Tuesday, and the grand finale for Milano Fashion Week. Plus, she and Dorothy were almost equally guaranteed to find Angelica's killer—and whoever had attacked Roland Cho.

Piece of cake.

"YOU DID AN awesome job today," Summer told Juliette-Margot, wrapping her up like a tiny mummy in an over-sized beach towel. "I think we'll be ready to move to the deep end soon."

"Juliette-Margot would like that." She glanced over her shoulder at the darker-blue water, and shrugged. "Six feet, *pfft*."

"Spoken like a true Frenchwoman," Summer said. "You're not afraid of anything, are you, kiddo?"

"Absolutely not, Mademoiselle Summer."

"Well, *I'm* afraid of what your daddies will say if we don't get some more sunblock on you. There are still plenty of rays out here today."

"That is nonsense, don't you think?" Juliette-Margot said, but she hobbled across the concrete in her towel to the lounge chair where she'd left her pool bag and brought it back to Summer.

"Think of it as a special foaming moisture treatment," Summer said, shaking the can. "You'd have to pay big bucks at a spa for this. Close your eyes, okay?" No sense in torturing the kid like Petra with her hair-spray.

The little girl squeezed her eyes shut. "Juliette-Margot has thought some more about Santa Claus," she said.

Summer paused with her finger on top of the sun-screen nozzle. "You did?" Well, that was nice.

"Yes," Juliette-Margot said. "Papa explained that Maman could not come to visit us for Christmas, be-cause models are very, very busy. Every week is Fashion Week in Paris, even at the holidays. But I need Maman to get here in time for the mother-daughter fashion show on Tuesday."

Oh, *no.* How had the kid heard about that already? On the other hand, this wasn't the first time she'd underestimated Gladys Rumway, the Mouth-of-South-Florida.

"So maybe if Juliette-Margot believes in Santa Claus, and asks him very nicely, he will bring her here in his magic sleigh for just a few hours and take her back to Paris in time for her next show."

"Umm…" Summer replaced the top on the spray can and tossed it back into the pool bag. "You know what, I don't think we need that stinky sunblock stuff now. Why don't we sit down at a table and I'll get us some lemonade?"

"Okay," Juliette-Margot said, still huddled in her towel.

Luckily, there were enough bottles of sugar-free lemo in the unlocked pool bar fridge to float Hibiscus Pointe through the apocalypse. The staff kept them on hand to head off all those resident Arnie Palmer emergencies.

"So here's the thing, JM," Summer said, opening both of their drinks and sliding one across the glass-topped table. How was she going to explain how Santa Claus worked? And much worse, moms? Obviously, Dash had messed this up, but that wasn't surprising because his famous mystery writer mom was one for the books. And so was hers. "Santa Claus gets so many requests that every once in a while he has to…" Her voice trailed away. Has to *what*? Break kids' hearts?

"Juliette-Margot wrote him a letter," the little girl said, reaching into her pool bag again. "In her very best penmanship. And she sealed it with candle wax, so it would be extra special. And private. See?"

Summer felt a pang as Juliette-Margot held out the pale pink envelope with a blob of pressed-down white wax that she had tried to write her initials in with a

LISA Q. MATHEWS   243

toothpick or something. "Wow. Santa is really going
to be impressed."

"Juliette-Margot needs to mail it to the North Pole
quick. The show is only a couple of days away."

The kid seemed so worried, looking at her with those
big blue eyes. And hopeful, too. She'd have to figure
out some way to let her down easy, but now right now
just didn't seem like the right time. "I'll tell you what,"
Summer said. "I saw on the news that there's a special
box for Santa outside the post office downtown. How
about if we drive down there and mail it right now? It'll
be on its way to the North Pole, special Christmas de-
livery, first thing in the morning."

So maybe she wouldn't have much time left to get
ready for her date with Shane Donovan. But sometimes
a girl—especially if she was also a decent detective—
had to be flexible. And do the right thing.

TWENTY-THREE

DOROTHY FELT A rush of trepidation as she stepped into Angelica Downs's condo, but also a tiny bit of relief. She'd arrived at Flamingo Pass without being kidnapped or murdered, so maybe she hadn't made the wrong decision when she'd asked Violet to pick her up at the library and drive her across town.

But there was still the threat of danger ahead, of course. She hadn't informed the real estate agent yet that she wouldn't be signing any contracts.

"I'm so glad I was able to reschedule all my other important appointments this afternoon so I could bring you right over," Violet said, flipping a switch near the door.

The electricity must already be disconnected, Dorothy thought, when no lights came on. *Well, that was fast.*

"As you can see, we've made enormous progress in getting rid of all that horrible junk that was in here last time you visited."

Oh dear. Violet wasn't kidding. There was hardly a stick of Angelica's pricey furniture left in her once-pretty condo. One small moving carton marked "Kitchen" remained on the counter, but the rugs had been rolled up and there were a few sad holes in the plaster where the artwork had once hung. The drapes were still in place, but most of the light fixtures had been removed.

"The place does seem...larger," Dorothy murmured.

"I have a digital measuring device right here, in case you need to see how beautifully your own furniture will fit. So much better than those clunky, old-fashioned metal tapes." Violet reached into her Coach shoulder bag. "If the space isn't quite right, you and your attorney can just buy brand-new pieces. It's so much fun to shop and the Milano design stores are always on-trend."

"That won't be necessary," Dorothy said, her eyes sweeping the empty living room and dining area. Even the microwave was gone from the kitchen. "I'd especially like to get another look at the master bedroom closet."

"Oh, certainly," Violet said, leading the way. "I know you're going to be so pleased when you see what we've done with it."

Dorothy tried not to let her disappointment show when she saw the closet. All of Angelica's things had been removed, as she'd expected. So had the shelving and the doors. And...the safe.

"Is something wrong, Mrs. Westin?" Violet asked. "We could get Closet Cases in here and customize it for you in a jiffy, no problem."

Dorothy peered inside the space, taking care to sidestep the hovering real estate agent. No sense in setting herself up to be stuffed in a closet by a suspect. That had happened to Summer once. "I could have sworn there was a safe in here last time," she said, casting a glance in the corners and across the carpet for any hint of sparkle.

Angelica's diamond earring was burning a hole in the side pocket of her purse. But for some reason she couldn't bring herself to hand it over to Violet just yet.

"Oh, you need a safe? Well, you wouldn't have wanted that other one. So bulky and unattractive. But we can get another reinstalled for you by tomorrow."

"I suppose I could always rent a safety deposit box at the bank," Dorothy said. Good heavens, the last thing she needed was to give Violet the idea she was wealthy. "The safe the previous owner had was for larger items that might not fit one of those, perhaps?"

"No, in her case it was more an issue of excess," Violet said, as she checked something on her phone. "She could have opened her own jewelry store."

Ouch, Dorothy thought. Had she intended to make such a snide comment about her own dead sister? Whatever the answer, this little charade had to end. "This condo belonged to Angelica, didn't it?"

That certainly grabbed Violet's attention. "Why, yes, my sister did own the place," she said, dropping her cell into her suit pocket. "I was going to mention that, but I figured it would come up soon enough as a minor disclosure in the paperwork. I am—in a very technical sense—related to the seller."

"The seller is your mother, I take it?" Dorothy asked. Surely Violet remembered their discussion in the powder room at the Majesty fashion show.

"I'm not really at liberty to discuss anything about the seller," Violet said. "But she isn't around at the moment, anyway. I am handling her affairs."

"Will she be back soon, then?" Dorothy pressed. She was sorely tempted to add that everyone at Hibiscus Pointe, including her, knew Frankie had gone AWOL from the memory care facility. No need yet to also include the fact that she and Summer had had her in their custody—very briefly—and were doing their best to track her down.

"Oh, I'm sure," Violet said. "Not to worry, I can set everything up for a speedy closing." She gave a tinny chuckle. "I hope you didn't take that passing remark I made earlier about my sister's jewelry collection the wrong way, Mrs. Westin. I simply meant, none of us can take it with us in the end, can we?"

"No, we can't," Dorothy murmured. Violet's clarification had hardly made her comment more palatable.

The real estate agent pushed her tortoiseshell reading glasses up on her head and rummaged in her bag again, this time extracting a clipboard that held a thick ream of documents. "i've taken the liberty of filling out the initial paperwork," she added. "Just to save time. Your attorney can review it later, of course, but I can assure you everything is in order. We just need to fill in a few blanks."

Dorothy quickly closed her mouth, which she realized was hanging open. If she'd thought Violet couldn't be any more callous toward her sister's death, she'd been entirely mistaken.

"I'm afraid we don't have a table in here anymore," Violet went on. "But there are some chairs out on the balcony we could use."

Dorothy didn't recall any balcony off of Angelica's condo. All she remembered behind the drapes was the concrete wall Ernie had pointed out on their last visit. "I'm sure we can look at that paperwork somewhere else. The lobby, perhaps."

Flamingo Pass had to have some sort of security. From the way Violet was looking at her right now—her eyes were literally gleaming in the dim light—Dorothy wasn't sure she wanted to be alone with her any longer. Maybe she shouldn't have brought up the condo's connection to Angelica—or Frankie.

"How about right over here at the kitchen counter? You don't mind standing for just a few more minutes, do you? I can make this quick and painless, trust me."

Dorothy's heart began to beat faster. This solo meeting with Violet had been a mistake, after all. What exactly had she hoped to accomplish? Coming clean with a direct approach would be impossible now. Clearly, she should have taken Summer up on her offer to accompany her.

Violet began lining up the documents across the counter, pushing the small box of kitchen utensils aside to make more room. "Come on over here, Mrs. Westin, while we still have some light left." She patted one of the packets encouragingly. "Chop chop."

It was definitely growing dimmer by the minute in the condo. "You know, I believe I left my little pocket magnifier in the car," Dorothy said, her voice croaking slightly. She'd have to pass the kitchen on her way to the front door. If she made it past Violet, could she outrun her? Unlikely, but she could try. She walked quickly toward the door.

"You can use my reading glasses instead." Violet pulled the tortoiseshell glasses off her head and stepped out from behind the counter to block her way. "I'm blind as a bat without them, so I'm sure they'll work for you." She reached for Dorothy's arm, and guided her firmly toward the kitchen. "Oh, and there's one more thing we'll need. I'm just going to check this box..."

Dorothy took a step back, horrified, as the real estate agent rummaged inside and pulled out an enormous carving knife. "Put that down, Violet," she said. "Right now."

"Oh, of course, we don't want an accident, do we?" the real estate agent said, laying it carefully on the counter. "Let me see if there are any other sharp things in here."

That was quite enough. Dorothy turned and ran for the door, as fast as her AeroLite shoes could take her. She grabbed the knob, threw the door open and barreled straight into something bulky and solid.

Or, rather, *someone.*

"Where's the fire, Dot?" Ernie asked, as she collapsed against his shoulder in relief. "Everything okay in here? Just happened to be in the neighborhood." He peered inside Angelica's condo.

"Mr. Conlon! I had no idea you were joining us. You're just in time." Violet sounded delighted. "Mrs. Westin, are you okay? No need to panic, I found what I was looking for. I knew Angelica had to have some of these around somewhere." She held up a purple pen with "Violet Downs Realty" printed on the side in white letters. "So embarrassing that I didn't have one with me, can you believe that?"

No, she couldn't. Dorothy stepped away from Ernie and smoothed her blouse, frowning. She was grateful he'd shown up at the perfect time, of course, but also a bit annoyed. Summer must have told him she was here. And as for the odd and possibly dangerous scene that had just unfolded... Had her imagination gotten away with her? Or had Violet almost gotten away with another murder?

Either way, she wasn't about to stick around to find

out. She'd deal with the overly zealous Violet Downs—
and the overly protective Ernie Conlon—later.

Now THIS WAS a date, Summer told herself, as she used
her tiny silver fork to dip another chunk of lobster into
a bowl of melted butter. Perfect choice of restaurant,
perfect eats, perfect guy.

Well…okay, maybe Shane Donovan wasn't perfect,
exactly. Which was a good thing, because she sure
wasn't, either. But so far, they'd been having an amazing dinner on the twinkle-light strung patio at Go Fish!,
the latest four-star eatery on the bay.

For once, there was no canned holiday music playing
in the background. Just the murmured sounds of conversation from the tables around them, and the sound
of quiet waves below. And the couple at the next table
full-on making out.

"More champagne, miss?" Their waiter reached for
the bottle half-submerged in the silver ice bucket beside the table.

"Yes, please," Summer said, trying not to talk too
much with a mouthful of lobster. She loved champagne,
even though she hardly ever had it with dinner. One
of her stepmoms used to yell at her when she did that.
Or maybe it was because she was still in high school
at the time.

"I'm fine, thanks," Detective Donovan told the
waiter. So far, he'd stuck to one glass of beer.

"So how'd you get away from work?" Summer asked.
"I was afraid you'd have to cancel, after what happened
at the show last night."

He smiled. "I told them I was going off the grid for
something very important, and they could do without

me for the evening. Caputo seemed anxious to get rid of me for a while, anyway. She said to tell you she hoped we had a really good time, by the way. That was nice of her, huh?"

"Oh, yeah," Summer said. "Really sweet." Obviously, Detective Donovan didn't get that Caputo was being totally sarcastic. But it didn't matter, because she wasn't going to think about her right now.

She wasn't going to bring up the Downs case, either. Not yet, anyway. Maybe just for a minute, during dessert or something. But Shane seemed so chill right now, gazing out over the dark, quiet water under the stars. Even with the occasional Saturday night boat traffic, it was super peaceful.

She was glad she'd gone with the short black sundress with the cutouts at the back and neckline. She'd accessorized with white earrings, shoes and bag, just in case Juliette-Margot was right about guys liking contrasting colors. By the way Shane had complimented her earlier, and kept sneaking glances at her when he thought she wasn't paying attention, it seemed as if the kid hadn't steered her wrong.

"So that picture outside your grandma's room at Hibiscus Glen," she said. "Are those guys all related to you? They looked a lot alike."

Right away, she was sorry she'd asked, because he suddenly sat up straighter and she could tell his shoulders had tensed beneath his casual navy blazer. "My uncles, and a cousin or two," he said. "That was my dad's funeral. He was shot in the line of duty."

"Oh," Summer said, wanting to throw herself over the railing to the sharks. Way to ruin a perfect evening. That was the saddest thing ever. "I'm so sorry."

"That's okay," Shane said, looking away. "He was a great guy. I'm sorry I didn't get to know him that well. I was really young when he died."

"That must have been so hard on you," Summer said. She couldn't even imagine.

"It was," he said, turning his intense blue eyes back to her. "But I know my dad would have done it all over again. It was an honor for him to serve. All of us who commit to a career in law enforcement fully understand and accept the risks of the job."

Summer swallowed hard. She didn't even want to think about that. What if something happened to him? "So is everyone in your family a cop?" she asked.

"Pretty much," he said, with a small grin. "Except Nana. My mom is the chief now up in Steering, Mass. My uncles are all retired, but my brothers are Boston PD."

"How come you came down here?" Summer asked.

He shrugged. "I'm not exactly sure," he said. "Usually I'm more of a planner, but I just went with my gut on that one. And sometimes there's such a thing as a little too much family, you know?"

Summer did know. Really, really well. That was why she was in Milano, too. Well, part of the reason. Come to think of it, her sister Joy hadn't called to bug her about anything for at least a week. She made a mental note to check up on her later, because that never happened.

"Nana came down here to Milano on vacation and never went back. Someone needed to keep an eye on her, so I kind of volunteered. Plus, I can get out on my boat year-round. I have this crazy idea I'm going to sail around the world someday."

"Not on the boat you have now, right?" Summer said. She'd seen it, and no way would that thing make it as far as Fort Myers.

"No, that's just for fishing, really. It'll take a few more years before I can afford a more seaworthy vessel, I'm afraid."

"Would you go alone?" Summer asked. She loved the ocean, of course, but she couldn't think of anything more boring. Sure, stopping at all the amazing ports of call would be great, but when you factored in all those super long stretches of nothingness and being tossed around in hundred foot waves without a surfboard... no thanks.

"Maybe," Shane said. "Unless I found the right person to go with me, I guess." He smiled at her as the candle on their table flickered and that dimple she could never resist showed up again. Maybe she could fly to meet him in Greece or something, and then they could tour the islands in his boat.

By the time the waiter rolled over the fancy dessert cart, piled high with cakes, key lime pies, mixed berries and crystal glasses of chocolate mousse, Summer still hadn't brought up anything about the case. Why spoil the mood? The minute she said anything, he'd clam up on her, and the evening would be totally ruined.

She hoped things had gone okay for Dorothy, going over to question Violet like that. It was a good thing she'd tipped off Ernie to surreptitiously check on them, so she didn't have to worry about her friend's safety so much. Still, it made her feel kind of bad that Dorothy was working while she was here having fun with someone who might have some info for them.

What was she supposed to ask about? If he knew about the will, for starters.

Would Angelica have left the condo and all her money to Frankie, even if she and Violet weren't close? Frankie might gamble away every penny, if she managed to make it to Vegas. If she'd been in jail there once, though, would she want to go back? And if she really was mentally impaired now, and not just faking it, wouldn't Angelica have left her money in trust for her or something? Violet would probably be the trustee. On the other hand, she was so greedy that maybe her sister hadn't trusted her to take care of their mother.

Jeez. It couldn't have been easy for Angelica to deal with those two when she was alive—and it was probably just as much of a mess now that she was dead. At least neither Frankie not Violet had tried to kill each other yet, as far as they knew. But Angelica had seemed really worried about her mom's safety. Maybe it was just a matter of time.

"Do you need a bit more time to decide, miss?" The good-looking young waiter with the slicked-back hair was doing his best not to look impatient.

"Oh. Sorry." Summer snapped back to the immediate issue at hand. Dessert. Detective Donovan already had a ginormous slice of seven-layer chocolate and coconut mousse cake in front of him. "I'll take the banana crème torte with all the caramel on it. And some strawberries on the side, please, with a little extra whipped cream?"

"You want the fudge sauce, too?"

Was the waiter making fun of her? Well, if he was, who cared? It wasn't like she was dying to be a PAGE model or anything. "Sure, pour it on."

"So I heard there's a big event coming up at Hibiscus Pointe on Tuesday," Shane said, casually digging in to his black-and-white cake. "Another big fashion week show, maybe?"

Summer froze with a forkful of gooey bananas halfway to her face. "Um, yeah. The Rivera-Joneses' resort wear show got moved there."

"Was that your idea, or Dorothy's?"

He didn't look *too* mad. Actually, he looked as if he were trying to keep himself from laughing. "Um…it's kind of a long story," Summer said. "How did you find out about that so quick?"

He took a sip of iced water. "My grandma has decided that she's going to be a model. Mrs. Rumway was apparently rounding up the troops, and made the mistake of discounting her due to her broken leg and wheelchair."

"I can't believe it," Summer said, stabbing a strawberry from her plate. "I was talking to Jennifer in her office about the idea, like, a few hours ago and Gladys had already heard about it. I swear, I don't know how that battle-ax does it."

"Is Jennifer on board with this project?"

Detective Donovan always trusted Jennifer. "Oh, yeah, she loves it," Summer said. "We're going to have some pretty tight security, though. Much better than those other shows."

He didn't look that impressed. "So how did you and Dorothy happen to come up with this plan? Any particular, uh, reason that you two wanted to host a fashion show?"

Well, *this* was heading south fast. "Oh, we're just doing Mia and her mom a favor," she said. "You know, since all their models quit. And it will help Jennifer get some great PR for Hibiscus Pointe if everything goes well, and all the residents are excited like your grandma, and… Dorothy and I are, uh, really getting into this fashion world stuff."

"I see."

Jeez. He was staring at her again, but she couldn't tell if it was in a good way or a bad way. Then he suddenly started chuckling. What was so funny?

"I guess there's zero chance I can convince you two to back off this murder investigation for your own safety, is there?"

"No," Summer said, staring down at her gloppy plate of caramel, hot fudge and melted whipped cream. "I guess not." Oh, well. It was a great date while it lasted.

To her surprise, Detective Donovan reached across the table and took her hand in his. "You know what?" he said. "I give up. Maybe we'll just have to agree to disagree on this. But I want you to promise you'll be careful. And if anything—as in, *anything at all*—comes up that you think I should know about, you'll tell me. Deal?"

Summer let out her breath in relief and met his bright blue eyes with her own. "Deal."

As if on cue, the waiter reappeared to check the champagne bottle in the bucket of what was now completely melted ice. "Coffee, or digestifs?" he asked.

"We could do a nightcap at my place," Summer said to Shane. "I mean, if you want to."

He smiled, showing his dimple again, and turned to the waiter. "Just the check, please."

TWENTY-FOUR

"WELL, IT'S HARD to believe, but here we are." Detective Donovan reached over and tucked a stray strand of Summer's hair behind her ear.

"I know," Summer said. "Finally." This was turning out to be one of the best nights ever. Just her and Shane, together on the couch in her condo. They'd both left their phones on the counter, so there would be—hopefully—no texts from the Milano PD, no demanding calls from Nana, no Zoe emergency alerts from Esmé.

And she'd thought this date couldn't get any better, she told herself, as he poured her another glass of Pinot Grigio. It was a good thing she'd found that dusty, open bottle of bourbon for him in the back of Grandma Sloan's kitchen cupboard. So far he'd only had a sip or two, but apparently the stuff never went bad.

The only thing that wasn't perfect right now was the extreme tightness of her dress. Maybe she'd overdone it with that dessert. "I'll be right back, I promise," Summer said, getting up. "I'm just going to slip into something a little more comfortable, okay?"

Oh, wow. Had she really said that? It was the lamest movie seduction line ever, and it wasn't even what she'd meant. Or maybe it was, actually, but still. She didn't need to be super obvious or anything.

"Sure," he said, with a grin. "I'm not going anywhere." He leaned back against the cushions and loosened his tie. "Play *Bolero*," he instructed Summer's virtual assistant.

"Good luck with that," she called over her shoulder, as she headed into her bedroom and closed the door.

What to wear? she wondered, flipping on the light. She didn't own any cute nighties—or any nighties at all, actually. Just a few oversized tees she wouldn't even use as pool cover-ups and a bunch of camisoles with boxer briefs. Oh, and a few pairs of cutoff sweats and yoga pants. None of them were right for a late-night date. She should have just stuck it out in the dress.

She did have a cool, silky kimono, though. *That'll work,* she thought, heading toward her closet. It only took her a second to find, since it was almost always on the floor. The material was so slippery it never stayed on the hanger.

Oh, wait. Should she make the bed? It was still piled sky-high with all the clothes she'd tossed on it when she was trying on outfits for tonight's date. Well, *that* was embarrassing. She'd just hide those under the bed for now. The closet already looked super messy, and the doors didn't close.

She threw the whole jumble of dresses and skirts and blouses and bags and belts and shoes on the floor, and started kicking them under the box spring as fast as she could. Shane was going to wonder what was taking so long.

"Ow!" a raspy voice said. "Quit it."

Summer gave a muffled half-scream. *Someone was hiding in her bedroom.* She grabbed the nearest weapon she could find—a wire brush—from the carpet and peered under the bed.

Two pink, watery eyes stared back at her, under a messy mop of bright blue hair.

"Frankie!" she said, in a sharp whisper. "What the freaking freak are you doing here?"

"What do you think?" Frankie hissed. "Now shut up, or that detective guy will be in here asking a lotta questions."

"*I* have questions," Summer said. "And you are going to answer them. But not right this second."

"Hey, is everything okay?" Detective Donovan called from outside the door.

"Just fine," Summer called back. "I'll be right out." She leaned closer to Frankie's face, but immediately drew back in disgust. Her breath smelled suspiciously like Grandma Sloan's bourbon. "You stay right here," she said. "Don't you dare move, or we're both cooked. And don't even think of making another break for it, because he's got a gun."

She didn't know that, for sure, since he was off-duty, but it sounded good.

"I came here to talk to you," Frankie said. "I need your help, Goddaughter."

"Are you in any kind of danger? Is someone after you?" Summer asked.

"No," Frankie said. "Well, maybe."

Summer threw up her hands in frustration. "You're unbelievable." No wonder Angelica had stuck her in Hibiscus Glen. And why would Violet want to take her home to Vero Beach? "Remember, one peep and it's straight back to you-know-where."

No answer. She'd take that as a yes.

Sitting up, she crossed her arms and leaned against the mattress, fuming. Now what? She'd promised Shane she'd tell him the minute there were any developments in the case. And Angelica Downs's formerly-jailbird, currently-AWOL mother hiding under her bed probably fit the bill.

But she and Dorothy needed to grill Frankie before they handed her over to anyone. It wasn't like she was wanted for a crime or anything. It was only Hibiscus Glen that wanted her back, for legal reasons. And she might be the only person who could help them crack her daughter's murder. Unless *she* was somehow the murderer.

A long shot, but then they would really be in trouble.

Well, she couldn't stay in here forever. Might as well get this over with. Frankie Downs had ruined her life.

She tightened the belt of her kimono, did a quick check of her reflection in the mirror over the dresser, and flipped off the light on her way out.

Detective Donovan was waiting for her not far from the door. "Are you sure everything's okay?" he said, with a frown. "For a second I thought I heard something going on in there."

"Oh, I left my grandma's little TV on when I went out tonight," Summer said. "I do that a lot. To, uh, scare off burglars."

Well, that sounded totally paranoid. But he seemed to buy it. In fact, it looked as if he might even be impressed with her preventative crime skills. "Well, nothing to worry about tonight," he said, gathering her into his arms.

He felt so good. And smelled so good. Maybe just a few minutes...

No, Summer told herself firmly. Frankie was back there in her bedroom, listening. Ugh. And she doubted the blue-haired romance wrecker would stay put for long, anyway.

"I am so sorry," she said, pulling away. "But I can't do this right now. I feel super sick."

"What?" He looked concerned. "Hey, it's okay. I understand if you think we're moving too fast here. We haven't seen much of each other lately and…"

"It's not that at all," Summer broke in. "I swear. I think I have food poisoning or something." She clutched her stomach. "Or maybe I ate too much. But anyway, you should go. Really soon."

"Well, okay, sure." Shane headed over to pick up his blazer from the couch. Now she couldn't tell whether he was mad or hurt or didn't care at all. "I can stay here on the couch, if you want, in case you need me to drive you to Urgent Care or something later."

Summer felt a real pang in her gut now. That was so sweet of him. And she was such a jerk for lying to the poor guy. "No, no," she said. "I'll be fine. I just need a little quality time with the porcelain goddess, I think."

Oh, *no.* Why had she said that? She was sending him off with the worst image ever.

"We'll do this again sometime," he said as he left, giving her a tiny kiss on the top of her head.

"Definitely," Summer said, swallowing hard. She knew the drill, because she'd used that line herself in plenty of awkward situations.

She'd never hear from Detective Donovan again.

"SUMMER. AND… FRANKIE. Well, this is a surprise." Dorothy stepped aside to let them into her condo, feeling suddenly wide awake at eleven PM.

"Sorry if we woke you up," Summer said, heading straight to the breakfast bar with a bulging plastic bag from the twenty-four-hour SuperMart.

"I was just reading," Dorothy fibbed. She'd tried, but mostly she'd been turning today's incident with Violet over and over in her mind. Had she overreacted or had she actually been in danger? She still couldn't decide.

"Nice to see you, Dorothy," Frankie said. "Thanks for putting me up."

Dorothy raised an eyebrow at Summer. "I'm staying, too," Summer said. "It'll be a real fun sleepover party. Since I missed mine and all, thanks to our buddy here."

"I see," Dorothy said, raising an eyebrow before she could stop herself. "I'm sorry to hear that. Frankie, where on earth have you been?"

"Nowhere," Frankie said. "I've been lying low over at my daughter's place at Flamingo Pass. Or I was, anyway, 'til a cleaning crew came in and cleared out every last crumb and caboodle. I found an empty condo in another building, but now new people are moving in there, blast them. I saw you checking out Angelica's place with Violet. Is she trying to sell it to you?"

"I'm not interested," Dorothy said, trying to hide her annoyance. Good heavens, had Frankie been lurking somewhere in that condo, as well? "Would you two like something to eat?" she added, to change the subject. "Ernie and I stopped off at the Brooklyn Deli tonight and I have all kinds of leftovers. Everything's in the fridge."

Frankie zoomed straight over and threw open the door.

"So Ernie stopped by Flamingo Pass, huh?" Summer asked. "I thought he might, after I gave him a little hint."

"Mmm," Dorothy said. "I figured as much."

"Well, how did things go with you-know-who?"

"Let's discuss that later," Dorothy said. "Right now…" She nodded toward Frankie, who was busy opening and sniffing containers.

"Okay," Summer said. "We brought some snacks in the bag, just in case. And a nice box of hair dye."

"Hair dye?" Dorothy said, taken back. "For whom?"

Summer plopped down on a bar stool and reached into the bag. "Ta-da! You like red, don't you?" she called to Frankie, who was still investigating the food opportunities. "You'll look just like Peggy Donovan."

There was a muffled curse from the fridge, and Summer shrugged. "We picked all the stuff up on the way over here," she said. "I figured red would cover the blue better. And I got some hair-cutting scissors, too. Frankie here's going to have a whole new style."

"I don't want a new style," Frankie said, slapping a carton marked "Fried Clams" on the counter beside Summer and hoisting herself up onto a stool.

"Well, you have no choice," Summer said. "Because we're going to have to hide you in plain sight." She reached into the bag again. "And here's the perfect thing. A pair of those huge, dark glasses you wear after eye surgery. They'll cover most of your face and no one will question you wearing them in the daytime."

"I am not wearing those," Frankie said, popping open a container of tartar sauce.

"Yep, you are." Summer turned to Dorothy. "Maybe we should get her a wheelchair from the activities room, too. Then she won't look so tiny. And it'll be easier for us to keep track of her if we tie her in."

"Is anyone listening to me here?" Frankie said. "No. No. No."

"I don't think that's such a bad idea, actually," Dorothy said. Summer had clearly thought all of this out. She seemed completely re-energized for the investigation, at this late hour. Hopefully her date hadn't been entirely cut short by Frankie's unexpected appearance, but by the way her friend was violently tearing open the contents of the hair-coloring box, she suspected that was the case.

"I'll make some tea, and why don't we all move to the dining room table?" Dorothy said. "That way we can really talk. Frankie, we have some questions for you. We need your help," she corrected quickly, as Angelica's mother scowled. "And why is it, exactly, that you suddenly showed up at Summer's condo? Everyone has been searching for you, I'm sure you know."

"You're the most wanted woman in Hibiscus Pointe," Summer said, pulling back the lid on a plastic tube of chips. "Maybe even all of Milano."

Frankie looked pleased. "Not the first time I've had people looking for me. Been a while, though."

Was she proud of being caught heisting jewelry and put in jail? Dorothy wondered. Well, *that* was certainly a misguided point of view.

Once they were all settled at the table, she wasn't sure where to begin. "Okay, Frankie, so why did you run off like that at the Majesty fashion show? We're on the same team." She hoped so, anyway.

"You ditched me, too," Summer added. "I thought the three of us had a circle of trust thing going."

"I don't trust anyone," Frankie said, wiping her hands on the bottom edge of Dorothy's good tablecloth. "And you shouldn't either, Goddaughter. Look, here's the deal. You two are nice ladies and all, and I'm sure you're real good detectives, but I'm running out of time here. I know who killed my angel."

"Who?" Dorothy and Summer both said at once.

"A rotten piece of dung who screwed me over once. I'm not gonna tell you who or you might scare the person off."

"Frankie, Summer and I are very discreet. Aren't we, dear?" Dorothy turned to her friend, but she was already headed toward the bedroom, reading something on her phone.

"Sorry, I'll be right back," Summer called. "This is important," she added, before she closed the door.

Well. *That* was surprising, even if she had a good reason to excuse herself. *How unlike her*, Dorothy thought. Things must have gone very badly indeed with Detective Donovan.

Maybe she should try another tack with their guest. "Frankie," she said, clearing her throat. "Why did Angelica check you in to Hibiscus Glen? It seems to me that your memory is perfectly clear."

"Oh, it is," Frankie said. "Trust me on that." She leaned back in her chair and crossed her arms. "Angelica stuck me in that heck hole because she was afraid I might do something *she'd* regret. She told me it was for my own safety and that I wouldn't have to stay long. Just until the danger—well, that's what *she* called it, anyway—was past." She stopped, and looked expectantly at Dorothy.

What was Frankie talking about? "Go on," she said, encouragingly.

Frankie shrugged. "That's all there was to it, really. I may have played up the crazy a little for the staff, just for fun. I mean, that place was even more boring than the pen."

Dorothy found that hard to believe. "So this danger, then," she said slowly, "was about something Angelica thought you might do? Not something she was worried might be done to you by someone else?"

Frankie gave a dismissive wave. "Don't kid yourself. If the person found out I was after them, they'd try to get to me first."

"But the person had no idea you were interested in some kind of revenge?" Dorothy asked. What on earth had Frankie been planning? No wonder Angelica had been so worried about her.

"They should have," Frankie said. "They knew they had it coming. Do you have anything for dessert?"

Dorothy rose from the table to retrieve whatever was left of the marshmallow cookies. What were they going to do with this woman? Perhaps she should have Summer call Hibiscus Glen from the bedroom right now.

Where was she, anyway? Her conversation with the detective was lasting quite some time.

She placed a flowered plate with four cookies in front of Frankie and took one for herself. "These have coconut," Frankie said, wrinkling her nose. "I hate that stringy stuff."

Thankfully, Summer emerged from the bedroom and rejoined them at the table. "Sorry about that, guys," she said, reaching for a cookie. "So, Frankie, you said you needed help and you wouldn't tell me why on the way over here. What exactly do you want from us? Maybe we can make a deal."

"I heard you're having a fashion show here at Hibiscus Pointe," she said. "A big one. And I want in."

"Do you mean, a ticket?" Dorothy asked. "All residents—and you're technically living at the Glen, or *should* be, anyway—can participate or attend free of charge."

"I was thinking of being a model, see," Frankie said. "You know, to honor my late angel in the mother-daughter fashion show. She'll be there with me in spirit."

"You're kidding, right?" Summer said. "Modeling isn't fun, you know. It's harder than it looks."

Frankie shrugged. "Hey, if Peggy and that Gladys Rumway broad can twirl around out there, I can, too. I want the whole experience. The works. And don't worry, I'll do a great job."

My, Dorothy thought. This wasn't exactly the request she'd expected. Beside her, Summer seemed skeptical, gazing at Frankie with narrowed eyes. "Well, I'm sure that could be arranged, Frankie, but the show is on Tuesday," Dorothy said. "We'd need to get you back to the Glen right away…"

"No," Frankie said. "I'm going to get this new hairstyle and fancy glasses, right? No one will recognize me. I can be your visiting cousin from Reno or something."

"The Reno thing would be a dead giveaway," Summer said. "But it's a crazy plan, anyway. Forget it."

Frankie's lip suddenly trembled. "I miss my Angelica," she said, her eyes filling with fat tears.

Dorothy stood up again, and glanced at Summer. "All right, Frankie, we'll see what we can do. But in return, you must promise not to disappear again for the next seventy-two hours. It's for your own safety."

"Okay, okay," Frankie said.

"We'll be watching you every minute," Dorothy went

on, feeling as if she were addressing a child. "Much more closely than before. You'll need to be on your very best behavior, too. No wisecracks, no pick-up poker games."

"Better yet, just keep your mouth shut the whole time," Summer added. "The minute you open it, people will know it's you."

A bit harsh, Dorothy thought, *but undoubtedly true*. "And as soon as the show is over, we'll talk to Jennifer, our resident services director, and see how to best address your future living situation," she said. "She may recommend an attorney for you, or at least a mediator for your discussions with Violet."

"Okay, I got it. Whatever you ladies say. So when do we get the show on the road for my makeover?"

"Right now," Summer said. "Go on in the bathroom and get your hair damp under the sink. Not too wet, okay? Dorothy will get us some towels and I'll mix up the gunk here in the kitchen."

"I have a very bad feeling about this," Dorothy told Summer, as soon as Frankie had disappeared into the powder room.

"She's lying, you know," Summer said. "I know why she wants to be in the fashion show. She wants to get backstage so she can get even with Roland Cho."

"Roland?" Dorothy frowned.

Summer held up her phone. "Frankie said someone had screwed her over once. I did a little more research while I was in the bedroom, and made a call to a guy I knew back in Jersey. Remember that assistant who didn't lock Frankie's store while she was away and it got robbed? His name was Harold Koo. And here's his pic."

Dorothy peered at the photo on Summer's phone. No doubt about it.

Jeweler's assistant Harold Koo was celebrity jewelry design sensation Roland Cho.

TWENTY-FIVE

SUMMER SMOOTHED HER SHORT, tiger-print Lilly Pulitzer shift as she stepped out of the MINI right in front of Chameleon. Sunday mornings were the best time to find decent—make that any—parking in downtown Milano. Most of the population was either at church or sleeping off their hangovers from Saturday night club hopping.

Everybody else was at brunch. More specifically, at Chameleon.

"Summer!" Esmé motioned to her from the bar, where she was expertly lining up glasses for an endless stream of mimosas and Bloody Marys. "Want one?"

"No thanks," Summer said. "I'm working. Sort of on the case, but mostly helping Mia for the resort wear show. She wanted me to bring something down to the auction preview at some gallery on Fourth Street."

Esmé raised an eyebrow as she sabered a bottle of champagne with a knife. "Thought you'd be hanging out with the hot detective this morning."

"Nope." Summer sneaked an orange slice from behind the bar. "That's totally over. I don't want to think about it right now, though, okay?"

"Okay. But hey, really sorry to hear that." Esmé looked over her shoulder, then leaned closer to Summer. "Listen, I know this is probably the worst time to ask, but can I bribe you with free brunch at the bar to take my darling cousin to a sample show? I think the place is right next to where you're headed."

Summer groaned. "Seriously?" Esmé was right. It *was* a terrible time to ask. She'd planned to enjoy an hour or two of freedom from watching Frankie while she did the errand for Mia. It was going to be a long afternoon, with the organization meeting for the resort wear show.

"Well, I have to work until two and then I'm headed straight to Hibiscus Pointe for that show meeting with you guys. Monique actually asked me to help out, can you believe it? I think Mia forced her into it. So maybe you could bring Zoe back home with you and meet me there?" Esmé gave her an exaggerated pretty-please face.

Summer looked past the bar. Zoe had already spotted her and was already headed toward them from a crummy table for two near the kitchen. The kid was looking a little more demure than usual, in an all-white dress with a lacy bodice and a short chiffon skirt. And... flats? The outfit was sort of Juliette-Margot, but the smoothly pulled back hair, sparkly jumbo ring and Roland Cho diamond earrings screamed Mia.

"Where's Aleesha? Can't she babysit?"

"Aleesha quit," Esmé said. "Or Aunt ZeeZee fired her, one or the other. She flew back to LA about an hour ago."

"Oh." Well, that wasn't good. And her life was already ruined, so what was a couple of hours with the brat? No one could stand to be with the poor kid. Had she been like that when she was younger, always desperate for attention? She hoped not, but maybe. "Okay, I'll take her, I guess."

"You're the best," Esmé said, in obvious relief. "Two orders of Captain Crunch French toast with extra-crispy bacon and a side of fresh cantaloupe with ice cream, coming up."

An hour or so later, Summer walked up four flights of stairs behind Zoe to a dingy open space with a sign taped outside the door that said "Design Atelier."

"How did you find out about this sample sale, anyway?" Summer said.

"Oh, it's invite-only," Zoe said. "It sort of travels around to different cities. You know, New York, LA. It's pretty hush-hush and they contact you online, if you're on their list."

"Huh," Summer said. If the stuff was any good, she'd have to look into that.

Looking around, she didn't see any salespeople—they had to be hiding somewhere—but a guy in a black-and-white striped boatneck top came up to check Zoe's plus-one invite. "Remember, final sale," he said. "Can I offer you ladies champagne?"

"No thanks," Zoe told him, to Summer's relief. "I never drink while I'm shopping," she said. "I need to focus, you know?"

"Right," Summer said.

Due to the exclusive guest list, the large room wasn't exactly crowded, which was unusual for a sample sale, in her experience. The place was minimally decorated in what could probably be called a "rustic-industrial" style, with the exposed-brick walls, a few trendy hanging lightbulbs, wire chairs and long wooden tables spread with folded cashmere sweaters, scarves and coiled belts. Racks of dresses, blouses and pricey jeans were sorted by size, mostly zero through two.

That counted both her and Zoe out—she was too tall and Zoe was too curvy. Oh, well.

The shoes were cute, though, grouped together on top of oak wine barrels in strategic spots around the room, with boxes of available sizes piled neatly behind them. Minimalist jewelry hung from nails and what looked like sections of chicken wire at the far end of the room.

"Pretty cool," Summer said.

"I know, huh?" Zoe said. "Totally un-Florida."

And totally un-Monique's Boutique, Summer told herself. Not a tomato dress in sight—and definitely nothing with tails.

She and Zoe browsed around for a while. The kid picked out a pair of buttery-suede cowboy ankle boots and she chose a sheer-ish flowy blouse that could double as a dress and a splashy floral kimono so she could toss out the one she'd worn last night when Detective Donovan held her. She never wanted to see it again.

"That's three hundred even," the boatneck guy told Zoe as Summer waited behind her with her own purchases. "Do you have cash?"

"No, but the invite said credit cards were accepted," Zoe said, handing one over. Platinum, just like hers. "It's my emergency card," she explained to Summer. "Aleesha usually paid for stuff for me. She quit, can you believe it? She said I was too much work and she had other clients to take care of. Obviously, she hates me."

"She doesn't hate you," Summer said "No one does. It was a business decision."

"I'm sorry, Ms. Zee, but your card has been declined."

"What?" Zoe's head swiveled back to the boatneck guy. "It can't be. Try again."

Zoe looked devastated. Was the kid actually going to start bawling? "There's no limit," she said to Summer. "Aleesha must have canceled it."

Or Aunt ZeeZee got ticked off, Summer thought. "It could still be a mistake," she said.

"No," Zoe said, biting her lip to keep it from quivering. "Aleesha does hate me now. She was, like, my best friend. All those other people who hang around me just want to be seen with me because of that stupid TV show. That's why I want to be a real actress."

"Things don't change when you do movies," Summer said. "It gets worse, actually. And Aleesha wasn't supposed to be your BFF. Your mom hired her to help you make smart business decisions."

"I guess," Zoe said. The kid seemed totally sad and embarrassed. "Thanks, but I won't be taking these," she said to the sales guy.

"Yes, you will," Summer said, handing him her own platinum card. "My treat."

"Really?" Now Zoe was looking at her the way Juliette-Margot did when she bought her ice cream. "Wow, thanks."

"You're welcome," Summer said. "Pay it forward, okay?"

They had to check their bags at the entrance to Gallery 4 next door, where the jewelry preview for Tuesday's auction was being held. This place was super bright, all done in white, and nobody ran up to offer them free drinks.

"Good afternoon, ladies," an older woman with silver hair swept into a chic chignon said from behind a linen-draped table. Summer thought she recognized her from Mia's brunch. "Are you here to place a bid?"

"We're not sure," Summer said. "We'd like to take a look at the jewelry, though."

"Please sign in first." The woman pointed to an open black leather book next to a crystal bowl filled with Tiffany pens. "I think you'll find that we have quite a range of items on display, for casual and formal wear. A few spectacular pieces from some new designers to watch, as well. I'm sure you've heard of Roland Cho, and several others, as well."

"Yep," Summer said, as she turned toward the exhibit hall. "Oh, I almost forgot. I have an envelope from Mia Rivera-Jones that I'm supposed to give Michaela Johnson." Summer reached into her bag, which the security guys at the front had practically turned inside out.

"I am Michaela," their greeter said, holding out her hand. "I'll take that now, thank you, and provide you with a receipt."

"What is it?" Zoe whispered to Summer, as Michaela's heels clicked toward a back room marked "Staff Only."

"A check, I think," Summer said. "Probably a donation to help kick things off for the auction."

"Well, let's go look at the jewelry already," Zoe said. "She's taking forever."

Even though she was acting more like a normal kid today, Summer didn't want to let her anywhere near the jewelry exhibit by herself. That's all she'd need—another shoplifting incident for Zoe and another trip down to the PD for her. The last thing she wanted was to run into Detective Donovan.

Luckily, Michaela returned a few seconds later and Summer caught up with Zoe just as she entered the small exhibit space off the main hall.

They headed for the first display, a gorgeous, chocolate diamond teardrop necklace, but Summer stopped short and caught Zoe by the arm. "Hold on," she said.

Monique was hovering over a table at the far side of the room with a giant, black-and-white Roland Cho photo above it. It looked as if she was taking pictures with her cell phone—and making notes. What was she doing? And wait—was that a jeweler's loupe she was using?

"Oh, no, that's the mean lady from the Waterman's show," Zoe whispered. "The one who kept yelling at Esmé and that model who got murdered. I don't want her to see me. Let's go."

"Why don't you want her to see you?" Summer asked. If anybody didn't want to be seen right now, it was probably Monique. She sure was acting sneaky.

Actually, there were probably cameras all over this place, so it wasn't like she could get away with stealing jewelry, or anything. Besides, she carried Roland Cho designs in her own store. She could look at them all day long, if she felt like it.

"I dunno, she just gives me the creeps," Zoe said, shuddering. "Like when she told the model lady... Oh."

"What?" Summer pressed. "What did Monique say to Angelica?"

"I just remembered," Zoe said. "It was something like, 'Don't even think you'll get away with it. I'll make sure of that.' They were behind me, so when I heard that, I thought she was talking about me and the jewelry, so I guess I kinda blocked it out."

"Huh," Summer said. It sounded like Monique had made a pretty obvious threat, if what Zoe had said was true. Had she been referring to Angelica dating her ex-husband again?

"Come on," she said to Zoe. "We need to get back to the Pointe for the meeting. And we'll get another chance to see the jewelry at the show."

Just then, Monique turned around and spotted them. *Uh oh*, Summer thought, as the boutique owner quickly stuck her phone and the loupe in her purse and crossed the room.

"Lovely pieces, aren't they?" Monique said. "I was just updating a bit of inventory for Roland. I'm sure the entire collection will go for a pretty penny." She smiled at Zoe. "I see you're wearing some of his earrings." She leaned toward her, and Zoe drew away. "Very nice."

"We were just leaving," Summer said, pulling Zoe behind her. "I'm sure we'll see you at the resort wear show meeting."

"Oh, yes," Monique said. "Resort wear isn't my thing—not high fashion, really—but I'm happy to help. Don't forget to bring my red dress with you," she called after Summer as they hurried toward the door.

TWENTY-SIX

DOROTHY HAD TO hand it to Jennifer and the Rivera-Joneses. Between them, and Mia's highly efficient staff, they seemed to have everything well under control for the Hibiscus Pointe Resort Wear Fashion Show.

That meant it would probably be okay if she took a little break for the holiday sugar cookies and decaf iced tea the dining room had thoughtfully provided.

They'd already gone over the basics. The tents would arrive tomorrow, as well as the racks and clothes. Two stylists, as well as Esmé and the other interns from MIFD, plus Monique, of course, would be on hand to meet with the models in the morning. Right before dinner, Bryana, Summer's model friend from PAGE, would help block out the stage and give them tips for ways to show off their outfits to best advantage.

The caterers and music were all set, security was in place, the models' relatives had already begun arriving, and the Milano Women's League was handling the auction. Best of all, Frankie had been good as gold and not a single person had recognized her. She fit right into the crowd of additional guests. Really, what else could she and Summer ask for?

All she'd had to do was put out a sign-up sheet for models after Gladys had blasted the news and it was five pages long by lunchtime. Helen Martin and her friends were ecstatic, and even some of the men were game to be escorts. Ernie had gallantly offered to take a spin, but there were so many volunteer models already that she let him off the hook.

This was so much easier than organizing the Hibiscus Pointe Book Club. Dorothy bit into a cookie and surreptitiously put her feet her up on the chair in front of her.

"So, Dotty, why aren't you signed up to model?" Gladys plopped down heavily beside her and fanned herself with a Hibiscus Pointe napkin. "The ol' ticker not up for it?"

"No, Gladys," Dorothy said. "You may recall that I get plenty of exercise at the pool." *And swim a mile's worth of laps per day, as opposed to doggy paddling in the shallow end like you,* she refrained from adding. "I'm just making my small contribution for the show behind the scenes."

"Well, you should get yourself out there," Gladys said. "I've been really busy, too, with the case, but I make an extra effort, you know?"

Dorothy took a long sip of her iced tea. "And how *is* the case going for you, Gladys?"

"Fine and dandy." Gladys stood up again. "I'm just biding my time a little. You know, to sit back and let my prey come to me."

"That sounds like an excellent strategy," Dorothy said, tiredly.

"What about that weirdo friend of yours from Albuquerque?" Gladys jerked her thumb toward Frankie, who was sitting quietly beside Summer in her borrowed wheelchair, a pink chiffon bow tying up her newly titian-hued hair. No one would guess that she was seat-belted in. "She sure doesn't talk much. How come she's gonna model?"

Dorothy smiled. "Just a dream of hers, I guess. Now, if you'll excuse me, I should probably go over and see how she's doing. I'm afraid I've left her on her lonesome quite a bit this afternoon."

Frankie was frowning behind her dark glasses as Dorothy came up. "Everyone isn't here. Where are the designers?" she asked. "I wanted to ask them some questions about the jewelry they're auctioning off. Shop talk," she added. "I used to be a jeweler, you know."

"Yes, we do know," Dorothy murmured, exchanging a glance with Summer. Had Frankie planned to confront Roland here in public, she wondered. Or worse? That was ridiculous, of course. The tiny woman was well restrained in her motorized chair, although she did have a rather good-sized bag with her—the one that she'd kept her poker winnings in back at the Glen. Could she possibly have a *real* gun this time?

"They're not going to be here until the day of the show," Summer said. "And all the jewelry's downtown. I think Roland was here for a while, though. I saw him talking with Monique. She seemed really ticked off about something."

"Guess I'll have to settle for looking at *this* for now, then." Frankie reached into her bag and pulled out the diamond earring. "Found it on the counter next to the guest soaps in your bathroom, Dorothy, but it just happens to be mine. And it also happens I'm missing a lotta valuable loose rocks from my safe back in Angelica's condo. Someone cleaned me out after bumping off my daughter."

Oh dear. "I can explain," Dorothy said, quickly. "The safe was open in Angelica's closet when I visited there with Violet. I found the earring on the carpet. And I was going to return it when I went back the second time but Violet gave me a fright and I…" Her voice trailed away, as Frankie regarded her with a raised eyebrow.

"So the diamond *is* real, then," Summer said slowly, as if she were thinking aloud. "And a bunch of jewels were stolen from Frankie. Again." She knelt down beside the glowering woman's wheelchair. "We know about Harold Koo, Frankie. AKA Roland Cho. And that he stole the jewels from your store, years ago."

Frankie crossed her arms. "You're very smart, Goddaughter," she said. "But no one else ever bought that story."

"Where is Roland right now?" Dorothy said, looking around at the chattering crowd in the events room. "Did he definitely leave?"

"Doesn't matter," Summer said. "We can't prove anything yet. We'll have to wait 'til the show. Because we still have to find a way to tie him to…" She glanced at Frankie. "What happened to Angelica. But there's one thing we can tell for sure right now. Hold on a sec, I'll be right back."

Dorothy waited beside Frankie as Summer hurried over to say something to Mia and Zoe.

"What is she doing?" Frankie said. "She's not blabbing about Harold, is she? I don't want the cops involved. He's mine."

"Frankie," Dorothy said, "I understand you and Roland… Harold…have a history, but do you think Roland had anything against Angelica? Enough to want to kill her?"

"He wouldn't have the guts to take anyone out," Frankie said. "And he probably isn't strong enough, anyway."

"Hmmm," Dorothy said, trying to size up Frankie's

own physical prowess. She looked so vulnerable, almost frail, there in the wheelchair. But they both knew that wasn't the case. She still didn't believe that Frankie would have harmed her own daughter, and had no clear reason to do so, but she wasn't as sure whether the determined woman—and ex-con no less—would have any qualms about a man who'd betrayed and stolen from her years ago. And possibly again just this week.

They'd have to watch Frankie even closer now that she'd shown her cards. Revenge was always a powerful motive.

"Okay, I've got what we need," Summer said, sounding a bit out of breath as she returned. She opened her palm to show two pairs of Roland Cho custom-design earrings. Both had huge diamond centers, surrounded by his trademark moonstone, but one had ruby petals and the other, emerald.

"How on earth did you get those?" Dorothy asked in horror, glancing around them. "And what are you doing with them? If he's still here, Roland will have a fit."

"Nah," Summer said, with a wave. "They're Mia's and Zoe's. I told them we needed them as close-up features in a little Facebook promo video for the show. You know, since all Roland's stuff is downtown right now. Which is where I need to head right now, to find some jewelry place where they'll do a quick, on-the-spot gem eval and tell us for sure whether they're real or fake. My bet's on fake."

"Hand them over, and I'll tell you right now." Frankie motioned impatiently.

Dorothy frowned. Those earrings could be extremely valuable. Was it a good idea to give them to her like that, if she indeed had a gun in that bag? She doubted she could make much of a getaway in a motorized wheelchair, but she'd underestimated Frankie before.

Too late. Summer had already turned over the earrings. Frankie rummaged in her bag and brought out a jeweler's loupe.

"Wow, that one's a lot bigger than the one Monique had today at the gallery," Summer said.

Monique? Dorothy thought, confused. Clearly she needed an update from Summer on her trip downtown today, but there simply hadn't been time before the meeting.

"Fakes," Frankie pronounced. "Decent ones, but phony as that woman's face." She jerked her head toward Helen Martin, who was smiling her nonstop smile as she flirted with a silver-haired gentleman at the refreshments table.

"But wouldn't Mia and Zoe have had the pieces appraised for insurance purposes?" Dorothy said. "Surely they would have discovered that the jewels had little value."

"Unless there's a shady appraiser involved," Frankie said. "They switch stones all the time. That's why I always keep the plot diagrams." She patted the bag beside her. "All the gem's measurements and internal characteristics mapped. Can't argue with those."

"It's hard to believe, based on their usual thoroughness, that the Rivera-Joneses would work with unscrupulous professionals," Dorothy said.

"Except for Mia's ex-fiancé, the creepy cardiologist," Summer pointed out.

"True," Dorothy said, shuddering a bit as she recalled their first case together. "But what about Zoe? It would be quite the coincidence if she and her family also had a dishonest appraiser."

"Mia did tell me when she handed over her earrings that Roland always cleans her pieces for free when he's in town or she's in New York," Summer said.

"Bingo," Frankie said, and Dorothy was inclined to agree. It would have been very easy for the designer to switch the stones that way after the appraisal and get away with it."

"I told Mia and Zoe they'd get their earrings back by tomorrow all spiffed up, by the way," Summer added.

"Piece of cake," Frankie said. Dorothy hid a smile at one of Summer's favorite expressions.

"All right," she said. "Let's head back over to my condo. We can order in dinner and discuss our strategy for Tuesday." *While keeping Frankie safely hidden*, she added to herself. So far, so good.

With all the other residents and their guests moving in the opposite direction toward the Canyons dining room for dinner, the three of them headed for the doors to the front entrance. They had just made it onto the sidewalk when someone stepped out in front of them from the hibiscus bushes.

"Did you really think you'd get away with this, Mom?" Violet demanded. "The jig is up."

A GOOD FORTY minutes later, Violet Downs was still ranting in Dorothy's living room. "All of you lied to me! Why do people always lie to me?"

Oh dear, Dorothy thought. This was not going well. They'd tried to explain some of their decisions and actions over the last few days, and Angelica's more vocal sister wasn't having any of it.

"*I'm* the one trying to look out for my mother here, and everyone hates me for it. Why does everybody hate me?" Violet stopped pacing and threw up her hands.

"Because you're sneaky, loud, greedy and obnoxious, and no one trusts you," Frankie said.

Dorothy glanced at Summer. Frankie had just described herself to a T. No wonder she and Violet clashed so much.

"All you think about is real estate and money," Frankie added.

"And all you think about is gambling and money," Violet said. "And getting revenge on Harold Koo."

"Ladies, please," Dorothy broke in. "None of this unpleasantness is getting us anywhere."

"And *you*, Mrs. Westin." Violet turned on her. "You pretended you wanted to buy my sister's condo, and wasted my time. And then you and your junior detective sidekick hid my mother here at Hibiscus Pointe, after she broke out of a perfectly good assisted living facility."

"Well, we tried, but she kept getting away from us," Summer said.

"That wasn't living," Frankie said. "It was worse than prison, especially since I am of perfectly sound mind and body. Angelica only made me go there temporarily while Harold Koo was here in town, so I wouldn't do something sensible, like roundhouse his butt."

"You did hit him over the head, didn't you?" Summer pointed out. "He sure didn't do it himself, unless he was super desperate and stupid."

Frankie crossed her arms. "I did nothing of the kind, Goddaughter. I'm gonna get my payback when he least expects it. Besides, I spent most of that stupid fashion show crawling through steam tunnels. Lucky they had them turned off, or I coulda gotten scalded to death. I'm real grateful to whoever clobbered him for me, though."

Monique? Dorothy wondered. Zoe had been sitting in front of her with Aleesha. That left... She took a deep breath. "Violet, you were at Majesty the other night. We spoke in the powder room. Did *you* attack Roland backstage?"

Frankie and Summer both turned to stare at the angry blonde woman. She looked away, and shrugged. "Maybe. He needed to pay for all he did to our family. He may even have murdered my sister. But no one can prove I attacked him. I took that golf club I found in the men's locker room back to the hotel with me and threw it in the ocean."

"Wow," Summer said. "That's, um, terrible."

"Now *that's* my gutsy daughter," Frankie said, sounding proud. "Good girl, Violet."

Dorothy was horrified. Maybe Roland wasn't the most pleasant person in the world, but that was assault. On the other hand, so was pushing elderly women into swimming pools, she imagined.

"Frankie, why don't you and Violet go into the guest bedroom and discuss things privately?" she suggested. "Summer and I will order dinner. What'll it be—Chinese, Mexican or BBQ?"

TWENTY-SEVEN

So FAR THIS was the best fashion show Summer had ever
been to, at least in Milano. Everyone seemed so happy,
and it was totally relaxed and casual. The DJ was spin-
ning holiday tunes from the Beach Boys, instead of
weird songs about cats or the usual canned carols. All
she and Dorothy had to do was solve Angelica Downs's
murder for the grand finale.

True, it was a super-hot day for December in Florida,
as it had been all week, and she'd been busy handing out
endless cups of water to the senior models. It was a good
way to keep her eye on everything going on with the
show, though, and Dorothy was handling the perimeter.

Or, more to the point, the tent where the designers
were hanging out. They needed to keep Roland Cho
under constant surveillance, in case he tried to pull a
fast one with the jewelry right here at the show…or,
say, kill someone.

It was also for his own safety, in case Frankie snuck
away from the show somehow to finish him off by stuff-
ing his own jewelry down his throat or something. Right
now, though, she was about to strut her stuff in her
wheelchair alongside Violet—and Peggy Donovan es-
corted by her darling grandson.

She'd carefully avoided Detective Donovan all day,
even though she'd caught him stealing glances at her a
couple of times. She had no idea what he was thinking,

and she wasn't sure she wanted to know. Right now, her total focus had to be on the case.

She tried to check in with Dorothy on the walkie-talkies Mia had handed out to everyone involved with organizing the show. She couldn't really hear anything other than static, though, because the music was pretty loud.

She kept her attention on Frankie as she motored around the stage in a brightly colored beach dress, with Violet wearing an identical version. Peggy Donovan wore a lime-green tennis outfit, but she was *not* watching her and Shane, who looked extra-hot in white shorts and a Dash Hamel–worthy striped shirt.

It was almost time for Gladys and her daughter—who looked just like her, only a lot younger—to take the stage with her gaggle of friends. They'd volunteered for the swimwear collection. Maybe she could safely skip that, and check things out backstage. All the jewelry had been moved there to be ready for the auction during intermission. With luck she could get close enough to it with all the security there to try and see if Roland was going with real or fake jewels today.

Either way, even if she and Dorothy couldn't pin him for Angelica's murder today, they'd agreed to expose him for theft and fraud. Unfortunately, they still didn't have much of a motive for him to kill Angelica, unless he was trying to steal that bracelet off her arm and killed her by mistake while they were fighting over it.

She headed to the backstage tent, and found Juliette-Margot sitting by herself on a folding chair, while the other kids ran around playing tag among the tables of shoes and accessories. "Hey, kiddo, why so glum? You're about to make your big modeling debut out there."

"Maman did not come, and Juliette-Margot does not want to be a striped fish," she said, looking down at her zebra-patterned swim dress.

"Oh, come on now," Summer said, kneeling beside her in her hot-pink capris. "Santa said he couldn't interfere with your mom's job commitments, that's all. Those Paris holiday shows would have been ruined without her, right? And your black-and-white outfit is very chic. Way nicer than the stuff I got to wear at the Majesty show. Models don't get to choose. They just have to do their jobs."

Juliette-Margot sighed, and gave a little nod.

"I wasn't going to show this to you until later, and we have to be quick, but check this out. Santa sent it just for you." Summer took her phone from her canvas shoulder bag and pulled up YouTube.

Juliette-Margot watched in fascination as she played a short clip of a trendy Paris holiday show, complete with fireworks and pounding techno and the Arc du Triomphe in the background. At the end, a masked woman in velvet and feathers leaned into the camera and said in French. "See you in the New Year, *cherie*."

"Is she really coming?" Juliette-Margot squealed.

"Yep," Summer said, as the little girl jumped up to give her a hug. Dash's famous mystery mother mom, Georgiana Hamel, could be very persuasive. She would have shown up here today herself, if she hadn't been stuck touring the Galapagos Islands for the holidays.

"Excuse me," a familiar voice said, "but I need you to come with me, Summer. We have an issue."

Great. Monique had singled her out from all the volunteers at the show to do her bidding. "What's the problem?"

"Come with me," Monique said, pulling her away

with a disdainful look back at Juliette-Margot. "We need to talk somewhere private."

"We're fine right here," Summer said, as they reached the far end of the tent. She wasn't going anywhere with Monique.

"I'd handle this myself, but I can't leave the show. Some brash woman named ZeeZee has shown up—apparently she is some minor TV celebrity—and is insisting on being added to the show with her daughter. Mia told me that they must be squeezed in, against my advice."

"That doesn't seem like much of a problem," Summer said.

"No," Monique said. "But I must make sure they're both ready and the schedule is adjusted in the most efficient manner. My concern is with Roland Cho."

"Yeah? What about him?" Summer glanced out through a narrow gap in the tent. She should check on Dorothy.

Monique looked around. "I think he's up to no good," she said, dropping her voice. "In fact, he may even be fooling us all. He didn't come in with all the other designers, so I need you to go find him and bring him back. Last I knew, he was at the tent just over the hill where they were keeping the auction jewelry."

"Got it." Summer removed the boutique owner's talons from her arm and took off at a jog in her tennis shoes.

So Monique was on to Roland, too. That's why she'd been checking the auction pieces at Gallery Four with a jeweler's loupe. She knew he'd been switching the jewels and precious stones in his designs for fake ones, and claiming insurance on major pieces he claimed were stolen. Only he'd swiped them himself.

Maybe he'd killed Angelica because she'd found that out somehow. She was a jeweler's daughter and she'd gone to those trade conventions with Frankie in Vegas. She could have realized Roland was a fraud, and threatened to reveal him. Especially since he'd also ruined her mom's business years ago by stealing her entire store inventory.

Whoa, wait a second. Summer stopped short in the middle of the dry brown lawn. Roland and Monique had been doing business together. She sold his stuff in her store. Roland wouldn't have used real jewels for her pieces, because he couldn't have switched them by personally "cleaning" them for all her Milano customers. He wouldn't even have known who they were.

So as soon as anyone figured out they'd been paying top dollar for Roland Cho "originals" at Monique's Boutique, but they were actually fake, her business would be ruined. And she'd already sold plenty of faux jewelry.

Hadn't Zoe said Monique told Angelica she couldn't get away with something before she threatened her life? What if it wasn't starting to date her ex-husband again? What if it was…revealing Roland and Monique's jewelry fraud to the world?

They'd both be ruined. And probably spend a lot of time in jail.

She had no idea whether Roland was capable of murdering someone. But she was pretty sure Monique would stop at nothing.

She had to find Dorothy, quick. And Roland, too, while she was at it. Jerk that he was, he could be in serious danger. And so could Dorothy.

"SUMMER, DON'T COME in here!" Dorothy called, but it was too late.

"What the…?" Summer gazed around the jewelry

tent, empty now of everything except some boxes, a horseshoe of bare tables and two back-to-back chairs. With Dorothy and Roland duct-taped together in them.

"Here, let me undo you guys," Summer said, springing forward.

"No," Dorothy said. "It's a trap. Get out of here and call 911."

Too late. Monique had stepped noiselessly into the tent behind Summer, in her bright orange linen suit. She also wore blue rubber gloves and carried a stylish but effective-looking gun.

Dorothy could tell that Summer was mentally calculating what it would take to disarm her. But Monique had stepped to the other side of the tent near a pile of boxes, well out of range.

"Excuse me, I forgot to do this." She moved quickly around the tent, keeping her back to the flaps and her aim on Summer as she zippered the flaps one by one.

"What are you doing?" Summer asked.

"Just closing up some loose ends," Monique said. She motioned for her to move closer to Dorothy and Roland.

Could Summer reach her phone? Dorothy wondered. She'd seen her text on the sly that way before. A peculiar but potentially useful talent.

"Throw me your bag, Summer."

"No." Summer kept her eyes on Monique and reached inside it instead.

"You won't get away with this, Monique," Dorothy said, trying to distract her and stall for time. "Roland and I have been having a nice little chat. He's told me everything."

"I don't want to die," Roland whimpered.

"You won't," Summer told him. "I've already texted 911. There are tons of cops already on the grounds."

"I'll speed this up, then." Monique reached into her purse and took out a pack of cigarettes. She extracted one and lit it.

"I didn't know you smoked," Roland said.

"I don't," Monique said, throwing it on the ground and backing quickly toward the door with her gun. "This will look like such an unfortunate accident. You're not as smart as you thought you were, Roland. You're a lying, talentless wimp. And that goes for you two nosy ladies, too. Enjoy the fireworks now. *Au revoir.*"

"The boxes," Dorothy said in horror, as Monique turned and ran from the tent. "They're holding the fireworks for after dinner."

Before she finished speaking, Summer rushed toward the glowing cigarette and fell on it just as the dry grass began to ignite. She rolled to put out the flame, then jumped up and dashed out of the tent after Monique.

"Oh, no," Dorothy said. "Monique still has that gun." She struggled as she had earlier to free herself and Roland from the tape.

"I have a metal nail file in my back pocket," Roland said. "I think I can just about reach it. Do you think that would help?"

Monique was right. He wasn't very smart at all. Dorothy extended her fingers behind her to grab the file herself. She managed to cut through the tape just as there was a loud thud and commotion from outside.

Summer had caught up with Monique and wrestled her to the ground, pinning her wrists. She must have

FASHIONABLY LATE

kicked away the gun, because it was lying in the grass a short distance from them.

Thank goodness. And there was Detective Caputo with a whole slew of cops and security people behind her. Dorothy hurried toward her friend, just in time to hear her say, "Book 'em, Caputo."

TWENTY-EIGHT

DOROTHY COULDN'T REMEMBER the last time she'd had such a lovely and relaxing New Year's Eve.

She, Ernie and Grace had skipped the tiresome annual celebration in the Magnolia Events Room to join Summer, Detective Donovan and his grandma, and all three Hamel-LeBlancs in Summer's condo for Chinese food, champagne and cider.

None of them dressed up. No one seemed quite in the mood for fashion for a while, it seemed.

Zoe and her mother had returned to Los Angeles, and ZeeZee had declared herself Zoe's new manager. That way, she claimed, she could keep a sharp eye on her daughter—and it would make for highly compelling TV. Summer sympathized with Zoe, who wasn't very happy with that arrangement, and must have put in a word with her movie producer father. Zoe had landed her first film role in *Girl on the Edge*, and had sworn she'd invite them all to the premiere.

Frankie and Violet were out kicking the gong around somewhere in Vegas tonight. Frankie had moved back into Angelica's condo and Violet was heading home to Vero Beach after the memorial at the end of January. Apparently they were planning more mother-daughter trips together in the near future.

She wasn't sure exactly which incarceration facilities Monique and Roland were spending the holiday in, but wherever they were, they probably weren't celebrating much.

"Ready for some new cases in the New Year, Dorothy?" Summer asked, as the two of them got the instant fondue together in the kitchen.

"Absolutely," Dorothy said. She refilled both of their champagne glasses from the bottle on the counter. "To Angelica," she said, raising her glass.

"To Angelica," Summer said, joining her in the toast. "And a great detective team!"

* * * * *

ACKNOWLEDGMENTS

I WOULD LIKE to thank Alice Alfonsi and Marc Cerasini, who helped me banish the Red Fire Monkey for good (don't ask!), as well as the amazing staff at Carina Press; my ever-supportive agent, Stephany Evans at Ayesha Pande Literary; and my blog mates at Chicks on the Case: Ellen Byron, Kellye Garrett, Marla Cooper, Vickie Fee and Cynthia Kuhn. And once again, much love and many thanks to my undyingly patient family: Rich, Kimberly, Rory and my very chic daughter and fashion consultant, Stephanie.

ABOUT THE AUTHOR

LISA Q. MATHEWS prepped for her career as an author by studying ads in the back of her mom's magazines ("We're looking for people to write children's books!") and investing her hard-earned allowance in pristine spiral notebooks. She also devoured every Nancy Drew book in her summer-camp library, determined to outwit the perfect girl detective. She failed, of course, but years later she had another chance.

After graduating from college with a typing speed of twelve wpm, Lisa headed to New York to work as an assistant to four busy editors. Soon after, she became an editor herself—of new Nancy Drew books! She also wrote under a pen name for other kids' series, including Mary-Kate and Ashley and The Lizzie McGuire Mysteries, and was creative director at Random House Children's Books.

But Lisa had always dreamed of writing mysteries full-time—for grown-ups. During an extended stay at her parents' floral-themed retirement community in Southwest Florida—and a chance elevator meeting with a memorable senior—The Ladies Smythe & Westin series was born.

A former figure skater and lifeguard, and mom to three grown kids, Lisa now scribbles in her notebooks from New Hampshire, where she lives with her husband, a golden retriever named Farley and Lucy the

Lucky Black Cat. She is happy to report that her typing speed is much improved, and she and Nancy Drew are still fast chums.

To learn more about Lisa and her books, please visit her website and sign up for her newsletter at lisaqmathews.com. You can also follow her on Twitter, friend her on Facebook and share in her writing adventures at the group blog Chicks on the Case. Lisa hopes you'll enjoy The Ladies Smythe & Westin books as much as she enjoys writing them—and she looks forward to meeting you!